CW00456576

UNSOLVED

DS Hunter Kerr Thrillers
Book Seven

Michael Fowler

SAPERE
BOOKS

UNSOLVED

Published by Sapere Books.

20 Windermere Drive, Leeds, England, LS17 7UZ,
United Kingdom

saperebooks.com

ISBN: 978-1-80055-159-6

PROLOGUE

The Comfort Inn was a low-budget motel close to a small industrial estate. None of the views from the twenty bedrooms were spectacular, and the best anyone staying there could hope for was that they didn't get allocated any of the five rear ground-floor ones that faced the four rubbish bins and eight-foot security wall. The conditions were basic but clean, and at £39.99 per night breakfast wasn't provided, though a Wetherspoons next door opened up at 7.30 a.m. to sate the travellers' hunger. It was used mainly by visiting salespeople when it was too late or too far for them to drive home, and was especially popular with those embarking upon secret sexual liaisons, who only wanted to use a room for a few hours with no questions asked.

On almost a daily basis for two weeks, the killer had been watching and following the young woman to this place. Some days she had been there two or three times. Several times it had been with the same man. She had no pattern or routine to her visits, though lunchtime was by far her busiest time. Today was no exception. He had followed her in the taxi from the pub she frequented, keeping his distance and pulling into the car park just as she was climbing out. Her punter, a big overweight man in his forties, who he had seen her with before, was waiting for her by the front door.

The killer drove into a space, turned off the engine and kept sight of her in his rear-view mirror. She was just guiding her customer through the door. The killer checked his watch and slunk down in his seat for the wait.

It wasn't too long — fifty-two minutes. He saw the big man come out through the door, zipping up his coat before climbing into a dirty maroon Renault Clio and driving away. The killer knew she wouldn't be too long in leaving herself — a quick shower before heading back to the pub. He pulled on latex gloves and his baseball cap and climbed out of the car, sauntering casually across the car park, his chin tucked deep into his chest. As he approached the front, he concentrated his gaze on reception. There was no one there. He knew that was typical. Throughout the day, except for the two cleaners, who were usually gone by 12.30 a.m., there was only ever one person working reception, but they also had other tasks to perform and so were there only when a customer appeared.

He slipped in through the door, his head still hung low, and headed for the stairs. On the first-floor landing where double doors led into the corridor, he halted. He knew that beyond the doorway, up to his right, a security camera was mounted. He pushed open a door, took out a roll of pre-cut duct-tape, and peeled off a small strip. With one foot over the threshold, he reached up, feeling for the base of the camera. Finding it, he fastened the piece over its lens. *By the time they realise they have a problem, I'll be gone*, he said to himself.

Confident now, pulling off his cap, he replaced it with the mask he had in his coat pocket and began his stroll along the corridor. At the last door on his left before the cleaner's cupboard — the room she always booked — he came to a standstill. Pressing an ear to the door, he listened. He could hear her moving around inside. Breaking into a grin that no one could see, he rapped on the door. *This is going to be fun.*

CHAPTER ONE

It was Hunter's first day back at work since the dramatic happenings on Sark, and a lot of things were playing on his mind as he dressed. He had wanted to get in early, but he was running behind schedule. He hurriedly fastened the collar of his shirt and ran up the knot of his tie, quickly checking his appearance in the wardrobe mirror. *That'll do*, he told himself, taking his suit jacket off its hanger and draping it over his arm.

Stepping out of the bedroom he almost collided with Beth, who was anxiously chivvying their sons, Jonathan and Daniel. She threw him a scowl as she dodged past. It had been three days since their return from Sark, and things were still tense in the household following the events there. The past two evenings Hunter had tried to discuss the trauma the family had been through with Beth, but on each of those occasions she had broken down in tears the moment he began mentioning anything about their ordeal. He understood her anxiety. Things could have ended so differently. He might not be here. Worse still, Jonathan might not be either. And then there was his dad, Jock, who'd been wounded by a stray bullet. *Fucking Billy Wallace.*

Hunter was trying his best to support Beth, but the strain of not being able to resolve matters was showing. Yesterday he had suffered the most intense migraine, making him sick. This morning, thanks to another restless night, he still had the remnants of a headache. He really could have done with taking the day off, but he had so much to do.

'Everything okay?' Hunter asked, trying to catch Beth's eye. What he really meant was, *Is Jonathan okay?*

'Yeah. Seems okay,' she responded. Beth was on the same wavelength.

'I'll ring you later,' he said, descending the stairs.

'What about breakfast?'

'I'll grab some tea and toast at work.'

'Are you sure?'

'Yep, sure. I'll catch you tonight. We'll try and talk. Love you, you know.'

'Yes, I know. I might feel better tonight.'

Hunter sensed the tenseness in her reply. He picked up his briefcase and unlocked the front door, calling out 'Cheerio', and pulled the door behind him. He didn't want to leave things like this, but he had no choice; his boss, Detective Superintendent Dawn Leggate, had messaged him last night telling him she wanted to see him first thing in the morning and that she had also fixed up an appointment for him to see someone from HR. He knew that was just the start. Professional Standards — the rubber heel squad — would want to interview him about what went off on Sark, in spite of him giving a detailed account to detectives from Guernsey. As he climbed into his car, he let off a heavy sigh. He was stressed before he even got to work.

Hunter entered the car park of the new state-of-the-art complex which was now home to some of South Yorkshire's most highly trained police officers, including the major incident team of which he was the Detective Sergeant of Syndicate One. Hunter should have moved here with his team a fortnight ago, but the escape of serial-killer Billy Wallace from Barlinnie Prison — who was hell-bent on revenge after being imprisoned for the attempted murder of Hunter's father — changed all that. Instead, he and his family had been forced to flee, choosing to spend time with Beth's parents on Sark where they lived, believing the remote island would be a place where they could all relax until Billy had been caught. Unfortunately, it had proved to be anything but that, and he was now dealing with the aftermath.

Just before fleeing to the island, Hunter had managed to visit the new offices and source his desk, though he hadn't had time to unpack all his personal things from the old office. He'd already determined as he drove that unpacking them was his number one priority, even before he went to see the gaffer.

As he rode the lift to the first floor, he wondered what his reception would be. He had already spoken with Tony Bullars and Mike Sampson from his team, and held several lengthy telephone conversations with his working partner Grace Marshall as to what had happened on Sark, but he knew there still would be questions from other members of MIT he would have to face.

Hunter swiped his card through the electronic lock and made his way along the corridor. He could smell the newness of the carpet and fresh paint. Surprisingly, he found the office empty, and he cast his eyes around the spacious room that housed workstations for a dozen detectives. The entire left side was floor to ceiling reinforced UV protection glass that bathed the room in light without any glare and gave him a view across the Dearne Valley for miles. The desk he'd earmarked for himself was next to the window, and he saw that no one had hijacked it while he had been away — his box still lay on top.

Looking at all the other desks, Hunter could see everyone had settled in. Until his eyes settled on Barry Newstead's space. Seeing his desk triggered an explosion of grief that overcame him without warning. Except for a computer and phone, Barry's was bare. Hunter gulped hard, tears welling up in his eyes. Barry's death — murder — just over a month ago had slipped to the back of his thoughts given recent events, and seeing his empty desk suddenly ignited the memory of that fateful evening when Barry had lost his life — the flashback as clear as if it had happened yesterday. They had been celebrating the capture of 'The Beast', and a few of them had just left the pub and were walking across the car park when a speeding car had come tearing towards them, bearing down on Detective Superintendent Dawn Leggate. Barry had been the first to react, throwing himself at the boss, saving her life. But in doing so, he had taken the full impact. The vision of him being tossed in the air like a rag doll followed by the sickening crunch as Barry smashed into the ground had visited Hunter many times since then. Together with the incident on Sark, he knew it was something that was going to haunt him forever.

As Hunter took a last watery glimpse of Barry's empty desk, he felt his spirits drop even lower as his thoughts drifted back to times they had spent together. Barry had been a seasoned detective with an exemplary reputation when Hunter had started the job back in 1991, and he had mentored him when he had joined CID three years later. They had instantly hit it off, forming a formidable partnership that many detectives were envious of. Barry not only became a loyal and trusted colleague but also a friend, and when he retired in bitter circumstances Hunter managed to persuade him to return to policing as a Civilian Investigator in MIT. Although Hunter had a new partner in Grace, he and Barry had still managed to work together, picking up where they'd left off, dabbling with their own form of justice from time to time. In that moment, some of those instances whirled inside Hunter's head, causing him to smile. *I'll miss you, big man.*

Hunter knuckle-dabbed his eyes, trudged across the room and dumped his briefcase on the floor beside his desk. Pulling out his chair, he began unpacking. First things out of the box were his handcuffs and parva spray. He confined those to his top drawer. Then he pulled out a handful of his case files — duplicate copies of cases he had recently worked on. He always kept copies of his most interesting jobs, telling himself that when he retired he would write a book about his exploits. He looked at a couple of the titles, fanned through the pages and then placed them in his bottom drawer. He was halfway down the box when his desk phone rang.

'Detective Sergeant Hunter Kerr,' he announced, snatching up the handset.

'I thought I heard you mooching around.' It was Dawn Leggate.

'I'm just sorting my desk, and then I was going to pop down and see you.' Hunter paused and added, 'Where is everyone, by the way? No one's come in yet.'

'An incident came in late last night. Vulnerable missing person who's disappeared without reason, and we believe something might have happened to her. There's a briefing at ten, so no one will be in until nine. I need to speak with you before the others come in.'

Hunter sensed an edge to her voice. She didn't sound her usual buoyant self. 'That sounds ominous, boss.'

'Just nip down to my office, will you?'

'Two minutes, boss.' Hunter put down the phone, his stomach flipping over. This didn't sound good. He wondered if he was going to be suspended for the Sark incident. He had already been suspended once this year for operating outside the rules, which had got an informant of his killed, and this was the last thing he needed right now. With a heavy sigh, he glimpsed his still half-full box. His day wasn't getting any better.

Detective Superintendent Dawn Leggate's office lay at the far end of the corridor. The front of it was constructed entirely of green smoked glass panels and as Hunter approached, he could just make out his boss's silhouette behind her desk. He rapped on the toughened glass door and pushed it open without waiting to be told to enter. He was taken aback to see her desk and bookshelves bare, and spotting a box of her stuff on the floor and two cardboard boxes brimming with her personal things on her desk, he wondered what was happening. Stepping inside, he dipped his head towards the boxes. 'Going somewhere, boss? You got promoted while I've been away?'

'I wish,' she answered, pointing Hunter towards the chair in front of her desk. Her soft Scottish brogue lacked its usual chirpy notes.

'Something to do with me?'

Dawn's lips pursed. 'No, nothing to do with you. Let's just say things have been going on behind my back that I only found out about late yesterday. It had been my intention to welcome you back this morning, Hunter, but instead I'm afraid I'm saying my cheerios.'

Hunter gazed across the desk. His boss looked as though she had the weight of the world on her shoulders. 'Gosh, boss, I'm so sorry to hear this.' Pausing momentarily, he asked, 'Is it something you can talk about?'

'To be honest, Hunter, I had intended just saying a quick goodbye to everyone and then going, but I thought that knowing you lot, you'd come up with a whole raft of rumours that would bear no resemblance to the truth whatsoever.' She gave a quick burst of laughter and continued, 'And so I thought if I shared it with you, you could break the news when I'm gone.' Pausing, she took a deep breath and said, 'The bottom line is that the Chief thinks I need some time out with what's going on with my ex — the trial coming up and everything.' She took another deep breath. 'That's the official response, but between you and me they've never been happy with a wee Scottish lassie in charge of MIT, and they're using what's gone off with my ex as an excuse to side-line me. The rumours are that I'm not up to it. That it's too big a job for me.'

'But you've done a great job here, boss. What about all the recent investigations? The capture of The Beast for one? It made huge headlines.'

Dawn flipped her hand dismissively. 'Counts for nothing, Hunter.' She sucked in a gulp of air. 'I'm going to be bad press when the court case starts, with my ex-husband killing one of my own detectives and seriously injuring the Force Crime Manager.'

Hunter knew she was talking about Michael Robshaw, his former boss. Michael and she had got together eighteen months ago — following her separation from her husband Jack — during their involvement in a joint operation. Unbeknown to her, Jack had followed her to Yorkshire, begun stalking her and upon discovering her relationship with Michael had tried to kill him by mowing him down with his car. Michael had been left with serious leg and hip injuries and was still off work. Following that, Jack had tried to do the same thing to Dawn, and that's when Barry had been killed. Jack's trial was due to start in one month's time.

'That's unfair, boss.'

'Tell me about it. Shit happens even at Detective Superintendent level.'

'Can't you do anything? Can't Michael pull any strings?'

Dawn sighed. 'He probably could have done if he'd been around. Sadly, that isn't the case. Michael can officially retire in eighteen months, and they've offered him a medical pension with immediate effect because it's going to take him that long to be fit again. They've already lined up someone to take over as Force Crime Manager.' She paused and added, 'By the way, that's for your ears only. What I've just told you is not official until next week. Please keep that to yourself.'

Hunter nodded.

She continued, 'The die is cast, as they say.'

'So, where are you going?'

'They're giving me a desk job in headquarters, heading up the policy unit to give me time to prepare for the case against Jack. At least that's what they're saying. What happens after the trial, I have no idea. If it wasn't for Michael, I'd hand in my notice and go back to Scotland.'

'I'm so sorry for you, boss. We'll really miss you.'

'You'll miss Miss Jean Brodie?'

Hunter looked at her, his lips parting.

She let out a sharp laugh. 'Oh, I know what you all call me. I find it quite fetching, actually.'

Hunter smiled with her. 'It was said with affection, boss.'

'I'd be very disappointed if I hadn't got a nickname. At least it means I've made my mark.'

Hunter gave a nod. There was silence between them for a short while, and then Hunter said, 'Why are you telling me all this?'

'Because this is going to affect you as well.'

'Oh!' Hunter sat up sharply.

'The person replacing me is DCI St. John-Stevens. He's starting this morning. He'll be taking briefing on the new case that came in last night.'

The manner in which she pronounced his name — Sinjin-Stevens — grated on Hunter as much as the man himself. A grim shadow suddenly moved through his mind, and his thoughts went into tail-spin.

'Something else I need to make you aware of.'

Her comment brought back his attention. 'You mean there's more bad news?'

Dawn gave him a light-hearted smile, and then her mouth set tight. 'Guernsey Police are conducting an extra investigation into what happened on Sark.'

'But they know what happened. I've given them a detailed statement,' Hunter interjected. 'What do you mean an extra investigation?'

'Because it's a UK detective involved, and someone was killed in extraordinary circumstances, they want to dot all the i's and cross all the t's, so to speak. That's the official line they're saying. Specifically, they're also looking into my role in this. Why I agreed for you to go there in the first place instead of putting you in a safe-house. It's me they're after, Hunter, not you. But you could get caught in the cross-fire, I'm afraid. That's also why we're having this conversation.'

Hunter's feet felt leaden as he trudged back to the office. *St. John-Stevens. That's all I fucking need.*

Entering the office, his thoughts were interrupted by the sight of his partner Grace just setting down her bag on her desk. Her face lit up when she saw him and she hurried across, embracing him.

'It's so good to see you. I was really worried about you.' Grace let him go and took a step back, eyeing him up and down. 'You look well. None the worse for wear at any rate. Are you feeling okay?'

Hunter felt a jolt of emotion that made him gulp. Swallowing hard, catching himself, he latched on to her gaze. Her smile as ever was radiant and welcoming. He noticed her dark hair was braided again, like it used to be when she was a rookie cop. It suited her. She was wearing a dark blue fitted jacket and matching slacks with an orange blouse. Designer fashion, as always.

She slipped off her jacket and draped it over the back of her chair. 'How's Beth and your family? How's Jonathan bearing up?' She was rattling off the questions without giving Hunter time to respond. She stopped and held up a finger. 'I'll make us a drink, and you can tell me everything.'

Dropping into his chair, Hunter watched Grace making her way across the room to the filing cabinets where the kettle and cups were.

'I bet it was a nightmare for you, wasn't it?' she called back, checking the kettle had enough water. She clicked it on and picked out two mugs.

'I've certainly had better holidays.'

Grace laughed. 'Have they found Billy's body yet?'

'Not that I know of.'

'Well, good riddance to him, that's what I say. Nobody will miss him. How are Beth and Jonathan bearing up?'

'Beth's full of anger at the moment. She's still blaming Dad for all of this, and she's giving me the cold shoulder because I won't agree with her.'

'She cares about you, that's all. It could have ended so badly, don't forget.'

'I'll never forget. I've hardly slept since we got back.'

'What about Jonathan?'

'He seems to be fine. A little quiet, but he appears to be coping with it better than us.'

'That's kids for you. What about counselling? Have you thought about it?'

'That's something we have talked about. Beth's going to have a word with someone she used to work with who's now with mental health services. See if she can pull any strings and get an early appointment.'

'Good. It helped Robyn no end.'

The mention of Grace's eldest daughter's name triggered memories from two years ago, when fifteen-year-old Robyn had been snatched outside her school by serial-killer Gabriel Wild — The Demon — who held her hostage, threatening to take her life. It ended with Robyn being rescued and the Demon killed. A similar scenario had played out to that on Sark, with Hunter's son Jonathan. It prompted him to say, 'I've never really asked you about this, but how did Robyn cope after what happened to her?'

Grace cocked her head. 'I thought she was fine at first. She showed no signs of anything until about six weeks after her ordeal. Then she started having the most awful nightmares, and there were times in the day she would just break down and cry. She would also fly off the handle at the most minor thing. We had an awful time with her. Her schooling especially suffered. The Force helped me out. They put me in touch with a counsellor called Simon. He was brilliant. We started off with weekly sessions, and she had six of those and then she went monthly. Within a year, she was back to her old self. She's now doing well at college and the nightmares have stopped.' Grace crossed her fingers. 'I have to confess it affected me longer than her. And there were times when I'd take things out on David for no reason. When I look back, he must have wondered at times why he married me. I still think about it from time to time, how differently it could have ended, even two years down the line.'

'I didn't know that, Grace.'

She shrugged her shoulders and then poured boiling water into the mugs. 'They're my problems, not anyone else's. I cope.' Stirring a teabag, she added, 'I'm sure Jonathan will be fine. He's like his dad, made of strong stuff.' She threw Hunter a smile. 'I can speak with Beth if it will help?'

'As you can imagine, it's been a bit manic since we've been back. Things have not stopped. I've been having to deal with daily phone calls from Guernsey, and I've been worrying about the press getting wind of the incident, which hasn't helped. Me and Beth haven't really had time to sit down and talk. When we do, I'll let you know. Thank you.'

Grace ambled back and set down his mug of tea. She touched his shoulder. 'That's what buddies are for. You supported me when I needed it.'

Hunter felt himself getting emotional again. He lowered his gaze, his eyes filling up.

'What's the gaffer say to you this morning? Has she been supportive?'

Hunter squeezed his eyes and then looked across the desks. 'She's got her own problems. She's just dropped me a right bombshell.' Pausing, he added, 'Three, actually.'

Grace threw him a puzzled look. 'Oh!'

'She's told me that Guernsey are conducting a more thorough investigation into the incident.'

'Well, that's not going to bother you, is it? It's straight up self-defence from what you've told me. Billy Wallace threatened to kill Jonathan, took a shot at your dad and went over the edge of the cliff and into the sea when you tackled him. That, in my book, is a cut and dried case.'

Hunter nodded. It wasn't strictly the truth, but it was what he had told the Guernsey Police, and it was close enough to the truth. At this moment in time, his only thoughts were on protecting Jonathan. He replied, 'You'd think so, but they might be thinking it wasn't self-defence and that I deliberately pushed him over the cliff and into the sea.'

Grace's face took on a phoney stunned look. 'You didn't, did you?'

Hunter burst into laughter. 'No, of course not! But you can bet your bottom dollar that's what they'll be checking. And that's worrying me for Jonathan's sake. I don't want him questioned again. He's been through enough.'

'They won't, Hunter. They'll see this for what exactly it is.'

'I hope so. I just want this putting to bed.' Pausing, he said, 'The boss is also thinking this might not be just about me. That there might be some underlying factor, someone scrutinising her capability. She also thinks they'll be looking at the role she played in it all.'

'Her role?' Grace questioned, frowning.

'Why she allowed me to go there instead of putting us all in a safe-house here.'

'Because Beth's mum and dad live there and it was the easiest solution, for Christ's sake. And it was Beth's idea anyway, wasn't it? That's all she has to tell them, surely.'

'I think it's a little bit more complex than that.'

'It's not complex. It's someone just trying to cover their backs. It does make me sick sometimes.'

Hunter smiled. It would normally be him talking like this.

'What are the other two bombshells?'

'She's being moved.'

'What?' Grace locked eyes with him. 'Because of Sark?'

Hunter shrugged his shoulders. 'She's not sure. She thinks someone's got it in for her. She says that the top brass are using what went off with her ex, Jack, and his forthcoming trial as an excuse for giving her a less high-profile role. They're giving her a desk job in headquarters. Policy.'

'Policy! God, she'll hate that. What an absolute waste of her skills. Can't she refuse?'

'Apparently, it's a done deal. I've just come from her office. She's already boxed up. It's happening today.'

'Crikey.' Grace inhaled deeply. 'Who's replacing her?'

'That's the third bombshell.'

CHAPTER TWO

Temporary Detective Superintendent Dominic St. John-Steven's entrance into MIT brought about a hushed response from the two syndicates of detectives in the room. He was only five feet nine inches but carried himself a lot taller. Dressed immaculately in a Harris tweed three-piece suit, everyone's eyes followed him to the front of the podium, where he stopped in front of the blank incident boards.

Hunter eyed him up and down. His brown hair was shorter than when he'd last seen him, and he now sported a closely cropped beard. Hunter zoned in on his gaze, waiting for the SIO to make eye contact, wondering if it would stir a reaction from him. The last time they had locked eyes was six months ago across an interview table, when St. John-Stevens had been a DI with Professional Standards. The DI had grilled him about the killing of an informant from Hunter's drug squad days. Hunter had been conducting his own enquiries into who had mown down his former boss Michael Robshaw, and believing it was linked to a drug gang, he had contacted a past informant and fixed up a meet. The meeting place was a back-street derelict engineering office they had used many times to trade information. Hunter, believing he had taken all precautions, had headed over there with Barry — without telling anyone and without a trained handler — not knowing that two gang members were following his informant. He was shot dead before the meet happened. Hunter and Barry had violated informant handling policy big-style, and off-record, after their interview, St. John-Stevens had accused them of being to blame for the informant's death and told Hunter he was going to make sure he was put back in uniform. Hunter had told him to 'fuck off' and Barry had responded by calling him a 'jumped-up little wanker.' It had not ended well. He and Barry had been suspended.

Afterwards, Dawn Leggate had given him the biggest dressing-down in his career, but she had also supported his decision-making and within a week had got the judgement overturned. He and Barry were both re-instated. Hunter had later learned that St. John-Stevens had been furious that *his* recommendation to suspend them had been usurped by Dawn and had tried to get the ruling reversed but failed. It had left a very bitter taste with all parties, and Hunter suddenly wondered if St. John-Stevens was responsible for Dawn's enforced move; he had a lot of high-level backing, including the Police and Crime Commissioner, who was his uncle. In that moment, as Hunter's gaze lingered on his new boss, he felt extremely vulnerable.

St. John-Stevens made an attempt at adjusting the knot of his tie, dusted invisible flecks from the front of his tweed jacket and loudly cleared his throat. 'Good morning, everyone, I am sure you will all know by now that from today I am replacing Detective Superintendent Leggate, and I am sure from the jungle-drums you will have already heard things about me. All I ask is that for the next week or so you put to one side the rumours you've heard until you've got to know me better.' He paused, slowly roaming his eyes around the room. For a moment they fastened on Hunter, and he could have sworn he caught the faint hint of a mischievous smirk creasing St. John-Stevens' mouth, but in a split-second it was gone.

The Temporary Detective Superintendent snatched away his gaze, picked up a marker pen, wrote OPERATION HYDRA up on the incident board, stabbed at the sentence and turned to face the team. 'Ladies and gents, this is your new investigation of which I have the pleasure of being the SIO.' Below the title he scribed, VICTIM: RASA KATILIENE and then continued his address. 'Rasa Katiliene is twenty years old and we believe she is from Lithuania. Exactly seven days ago today, at just after eleven in the morning, she left thirty-one Angel Court, where she had been staying with her friend, a Miss Janina Budriene, telling her she was going to The Junction pub here in Barnwell and that she would see her later that evening in the pub and buy her a drink. Miss Budriene was working a late shift that day at the care home where she was employed, finishing at eight p.m., and she went to the pub, arriving around eight-thirty, to find Rasa wasn't there as promised. She hung around until ten and when she didn't show, went home. She has not seen her or heard from her since.'

Taking a deep breath, pursing his lips, he drifted his gaze around the room again. 'Our witness, Miss Budriene, has only known Rasa for seven months. She met her at The Junction, going to her aid when she saw her being beaten up by a man outside the pub, scaring him away by threatening to call the police. She offered to take Rasa to the hospital, which she refused, and so she took her home, cleaned her up and let her stay the night after Rasa told her that the man who beat her up was her pimp and that if she went home that night she feared another beating from him. The story Rasa told her that night was that she had been tricked into coming to this country on the promise of work in the hotel industry but instead had been forced to work as a sex-worker by a Lithuanian man and woman who she only knows as Matis and Ugne, and they had taken away her passport. Rasa told her that it was Matis who had beaten her because she hadn't earned enough money that day.

'Miss Budriene has told officers that Rasa stayed for two days, after which Rasa told her she must go back to the couple because she was afraid of bringing trouble to her. Miss Budriene tried to persuade her to go to the police, but Rasa told her she was afraid of being locked up for being an illegal and that they wouldn't believe her anyway because of what she did. Miss Budriene said she felt sorry for her and so told Rasa that she could come and stay anytime she was in trouble. Since making that offer, she says Rasa has stayed at her flat on the occasional night and together they have gone around Rotherham drinking a few times with Miss Budriene's work colleagues.

'Miss Budriene reported Rasa missing three days ago after not hearing from her for four days. She says this is very unusual because even if she doesn't see her, they speak to each other almost daily on the phone, she mainly checking on Rasa's welfare and what she's up to. When Rasa didn't turn up at the pub seven nights ago, Miss Budriene rang her mobile several times but it went to voicemail and so she left her a message to contact her. She did that for four consecutive days and then her phone went dead. Three days ago, she went to The Junction to see if she could see Rasa and ask if anyone had seen her, but no one had. Convinced that something had happened to her, she rang 101 and reported her missing. Officers taking that report have made their own enquiries, and the bottom line is that Rasa has not been seen for one whole week and her phone is offline, and given what we know about Rasa Katiliene, the belief is that she is either being held against her will or has come to some harm.'

St. John-Stevens scanned the room for several seconds, a studious look on his face. Then with his marker pen he wrote on the board 'POI', the abbreviation for Person(s) of Interest, adding beneath it the names MATIS and UGNE. 'Rasa told our witness that these are the two people who brought her to this country from Lithuania. Given what she told Miss Budriene, we have to consider the likelihood that Rasa has been trafficked here for the purpose of sexual exploitation. And given that Rasa has told our witness that she lives with them, it is imperative that we discover who this man and woman are and where they live.

'Officers have spoken with the manager of The Junction pub and he has confirmed that he knows Rasa, that she is an almost daily visitor to the pub, and that the last time he saw her she was talking with a heavy-set man in his late forties, early fifties, who he doesn't know but has seen in the pub previously. He didn't see if Rasa left with the man, but he hasn't seen either of them since. He was asked if he knew anyone called Matis, but he says not, and so we can't confirm whether the man was Matis or not. He has also been asked about Rasa being assaulted, and although he has confirmed he is aware of it, he did not witness it. He has told officers that the information came to him from our witness Miss Budriene.'

St. John-Stevens let out a heavy breath. 'So where are we at?' He paused. 'Well, according to the manager of The Junction pub, we know Rasa Katiliene was in there after she left our witness's home a week ago and that she was last seen in the pub talking with a heavy-set man in his late forties or early fifties. After that we have no other sightings of her. We also know from Miss Budriene's phone record that the mobile number Rasa used to contact her was a pay-as-you-go and that the phone is now offline. At present, we have no idea what

Rasa looks like other than the description given to us by Miss Budriene. Indeed, we do not know if that is her real name, though there seems to be no reason why she should give our witness a false one.'

He gave another pause. 'Your tasks are to confirm the identity of the woman we know as Rasa and trace her last movements. Where did she go after she left The Junction pub? Who is the man she was last seen talking to? As far as we know, she has no vehicle. Did she use public transport? Who are the Lithuanian couple, Matis and Ugne, and where do they live? We need to determine if there is CCTV at the pub and also on buildings and shops nearby.'

He bullet-pointed the tasks up on the board and then set aside the marker, returning to his audience. 'It would be fair to say that we are in catch up. Rasa Katiliene leads a chaotic lifestyle, but she is also vulnerable if what she has told Miss Budriene is true; given the fact that she hasn't been seen or spoken to for the last seven days, we have to assume that something sinister has happened to her. She may have been abducted — she could even be dead — so it is imperative we move quickly on this. Are there any questions?'

'Is our witness, Miss B, a sex-worker, Guv?' It was Mike Sampson asking the question.

'Miss Budriene is not a sex-worker as far as we know. She is Polish, has been living in this country for two and a half years and is a care assistant in a nursing home in town.' He paused and added, 'And I would prefer to be addressed as 'sir' in the future.'

Hunter saw everyone's heads whipping sideways, seeking out their nearest colleague, sharing surprised looks. His reaction was the same as he exchanged looks with his partner Grace before returning his gaze to St. John-Stevens. *Supercilious prick*, thought Hunter.

'And before anyone asks if there is any intimate relationship between the pair, there is none that we are aware of. It appears Miss Budriene and Rasa have struck up a friendship following her rescue of Rasa. You could say it is an unusual friendship given their different circumstances, but there it is.' Casting his eyes around the room again, he said, 'And if there are no more questions, the DI will allocate you your tasks. We will reconvene here at eight o'clock this evening for debrief, unless something urgent crops up. Thank you, everyone.'

He set off towards the door but after half a dozen steps came to a halt, turning to Hunter. 'DS Kerr, can I see you in my office?'

Hunter had the condemned man feeling as he made his way down the corridor to the Detective Superintendent's office. The reinforced glass door was open, and he could see St. John-Stevens sat behind Dawn Leggate's desk, his chin resting on clasped hands, eyes locked on him as he approached. As Hunter entered the office, he noticed that St. John-Stevens had already made himself at home; a good number of personal effects were laid out across the desk and a couple of framed photographs sat on top of the wall units.

Dawn's seat hasn't even gone cold before he's claimed it as his, Hunter thought as he studied his features. Dominic St. John-Stevens had heavy eyelids, a wide nose and protruding ears that gave him the look of a prop-forward, though Hunter could never see him in any ruck. He knew that the man before him was someone who had entered the force on the fast-track system, spending a brief spell in different departments to grasp just enough of an understanding of how things operate — though not enough to gain experience — before moving on. A Butterfly Man.

Hunter pulled back a chair to sit down.

'No need for that, Detective Sergeant Kerr. This is not going to take long.'

Hunter stiffened, feeling the back of his neck reddening. *He's addressing me like a fucking child.*

'I'm guessing Detective Superintendent Leggate's already told you that Guernsey police are conducting a thorough investigation into the death of Billy Wallace.'

Hunter nodded.

'Did she also tell you that the case has been referred to the IPCC?'

Hunter knew he was referring to the Independent Police Complaints Commission, an independent body who investigate serious deaths following police contact. Hunter held eye contact with St. John-Stevens, opening out his hands and throwing him an 'I've nothing to hide' look.

'They are also looking at Detective Superintendent Leggate's role in all this as well. Are you aware of that?'

Hunter responded with a shrug. He had no intention of disclosing the earlier conversation he'd had with the boss he'd worked with for the last eighteen months.

'They will be looking at not only your contribution to his death but whether either of you failed in your duty to protect his life.'

Hunter could feel himself getting het up. The blood was starting to rush between his ears. 'Excuse me, but am I missing something here? Billy Wallace was a serial-killer. A fucking psycho. He had my eldest son as a hostage with a gun at his head and was threatening to shoot us all. Was I supposed to just stand there and let it happen?'

28

St. John-Stevens unclasped his hand and pushed himself back in his chair. 'That will be for the Guernsey police and the IPCC to determine. In the meantime, while that is going on, I think it would be best for all concerned if you were removed from your current duties.'

'What!'

'This is a delicate situation, DS Kerr, and I am concerned about your welfare.'

'My welfare is fine.'

'It's my belief that this could affect your thinking. And I also think that you might need more flexibility to be with your family at these troubled times, and for that reason I am posting you to the cold case unit.'

Hunter felt his heart rate pick up. 'The cold case unit. You are joking, aren't you?'

'This is no joke, DS Kerr. This is for your own welfare.'

'The cold case unit is for those who want to put their feet up. Who are ready to retire. Not for a front-line detective like me. And I've already told you my welfare is fine. I am well capable of juggling my present job with the care of my family.'

'Well, it's my belief that you need a less stressful job whilst you are being investigated over these serious matters. I wouldn't be doing my job properly if I didn't put your welfare first, so from tomorrow you will be in charge of the cold case unit.'

Hunter had held on to St. John-Stevens' gaze for the entirety of their conversation, and as he finished his sentence he thought he caught the flash of a spiteful sneer as he delivered the fateful decision. In a flash of anger, Hunter responded, 'You're loving this, aren't you? Giving me all this HR bullshit, but I know what this is all about. This is about my snout getting killed and you trying to get me suspended. You threatened you were going to get me put back into uniform. This is your way of getting back at me, isn't it?'

St. John-Stevens' face turned beetroot. It looked like he was about to explode. 'I'm going to put this insubordination down to the stress you're under, DS Kerr, but if you speak to me like this again, I will put you on a disciplinary. Do you understand?'

Hunter balled his hands into tight fists. He didn't respond.

St. John-Stevens pushed himself forward. 'Do you understand, DS Kerr?'

'Yes,' he spat back. 'Are we done here? I've got work to do.'

St. John-Stevens' face grew even redder. 'Are we done here what, DS Kerr?'

Hunter stared at him for a second, then said, 'Are we done here, SIR?'

'That's better, DS Kerr. You may well have had Detective Superintendent Leggate wrapped around your little finger, but not me. You're a liability, Detective Sergeant. You take risks. Go against procedure. The cold case unit will hopefully give you time to reflect and mend your ways. This conversation is over. There's the door.' St. John-Stevens swept his hand dismissively.

In that instant, a desire for vengeance coursed through Hunter. He wanted to punch the living daylights out of the jumped-up boss but knew that would be the end of his career and would be playing right into his hands. Instead, he threw him a granite stare, turned sharply on his heel and stormed out of the room, leaving the door wide open. If he'd have closed it, it would have shattered against its frame.

Returning to the office, Hunter saw that most of his colleagues were huddled around the DI, collecting their tasks for the day. He couldn't see his partner Grace among them and wondered where she was. He thought about hanging around and giving her the news, but decided the last thing he needed was to enter into a conversation with anyone about his fall from grace. He snatched up his briefcase and car keys and made a quick exit.

He drove home, his head in a whirl. He was fuming. All he thought about were ways of hurting St. John-Stevens while also knowing there was no way he could carry them out if he still wanted a career. By the time he pulled on to his drive his stress levels were through the roof, a tight clamp gripping his chest.

He was surprised to find the front door unlocked, and opening it he suddenly remembered it was Beth's day off. Hunter entered the hallway, setting down his briefcase and taking off his shoes.

'Hello.' Beth's voice came from the kitchen.

'It's only me,' Hunter called back, walking through to the lounge.

Beth poked her head around the door. 'You're home early.'

'Lost my job.'

She released a snort of laughter, and when Hunter didn't respond she met his gaze. Spotting his wounded look, she said, 'What's happened?'

'I need a beer,' he replied, brushing past her. He went to the fridge, pulled out a can of beer, flipped the top and took a long swallow.

'This must be bad, you drinking beer at ten in the morning.'

He took another slug, wiped residue from the side of his mouth with the back of his hand and squeezing the can, imagining he had hold of St. John-Stevens' neck, he blurted out what had gone off.

'God, Hunter. They can't treat you like that. This is not your fault.'

'Try telling that to St. John-Stevens.' He spat out his name with venom.

'Cold Case Unit!'

'Cold Case Unit,' Hunter repeated.

After a short pause, Beth said, 'That's not too bad.'

'It's where those seeing out their time go. It's a steady nine-to-five job.'

'I'm sure that's not the case.'

'Believe me, it is.'

'But isn't that where they look at all those historical cases?'

'The unsolved ones, yes. The cases that have, for one reason or another, come to an end.'

'But then that's the precise reason why they should put someone like you in there.'

He stared at her. 'What do you mean?'

'You've seen all those programmes on telly. All those families who for years have no idea what's happened to their loved ones, or know what's happened but not who's done it. Every day is a nightmare for them, and it's dedicated officers like you who they need to ease their pain.'

Hunter let out a loud laugh, shaking his head. He set down his can. 'Has anyone ever told you you should be a salesperson or a diplomat? You're already making my new job sound interesting.'

'It is, Hunter. And it's important, especially for all those people who need closure. You may think this is punishment, but I'm a firm believer in everything happening for a reason. You're exactly the right person for that job. And right now, after all that's gone off with this family, it's couldn't have come at a better time.'

'It's a pity that St. John-Stevens couldn't say it like this to me. I might have had some respect for him.'

'Hunter, right now it's important Jonathan has more time with you. He needs you for support. I need you.'

Beth's words were so soothing, he could feel his anxiety lessening, the tightness in his chest easing. He no longer needed the beer.

'This has worked out just right for all of us,' Beth continued. 'Your day will be less manic and your hours regular. This is just what we all need.'

Hunter studied Beth's face, re-running her words through in his mind. Even though he hated what had just happened to him, he knew she was right. He said, 'Talking about Jonathan, has he said anything to you about Sark? I've had a few bits of conversation with him since we got back, asking him how he's feeling, and all I get is, "Stop fussing, I'm fine." Though I know he can't be. Has he said much to you?'

Beth shook her head. 'I get the same. I've spoken with Dr Raj this morning about him, and he's told me not to worry. He's also going to try and pull a few strings to get me an early appointment with a child psychologist he knows.'

Hunter knew she was talking about her colleague at the practice. He nodded. 'Good. Even if it's just a couple of sessions, it will help. I've spoken with Grace this morning about Robyn, and she says counselling helped her no end. She told me that Robyn bottled it up at first, but after twelve months of counselling she was back to her old self, with no ill effects.' He held back the mention of the nightmares Robyn had endured and the impact on her school work. He hoped that wasn't going to happen with Jonathan.

Beth's face lifted. 'That makes me feel better.' Suddenly, she spurred into action, vigorously rubbing her hands. 'Do you know what, seeing as we'll all be home for tea, I'm going to cook us a roast dinner. What are you going to do for the rest of the day? Do you have to go back into work?'

Hunter picked up the half full can of beer and emptied it down the sink. 'No chance. I'm owed enough time. I'm going to get changed and go for a run down to Dad's gym and have a session with him, if that's okay.'

'Well, give him a few extra whacks from me.'

'Are you still furious with him?'

Beth pursed her lips momentarily, and then she gave him a weak smile. 'I was until this morning, and then your mum phoned me and told me how bad he was feeling about everything, and I realised it wasn't his fault. I guess I just needed to take it out on somebody, like you with this St. John-Stevens.'

Hunter pulled Beth close and gave a kiss. 'Have I told you I love you lately?'

Hunter quickly changed out of his work clothes and into his gym gear and hit the street at a quicker pace than normal. Within ten minutes, his thoughts had gone from wanting to beat the shit out of St. John-Stevens to looking forward to sitting round the table with his family — something he hadn't done in his own home for ages. As he pounded the last half mile to his dad's gym, looking forward to putting in some pad and ring-time with him, he found himself thinking about his new challenge tomorrow. He was determined to make a good fist of his new job and let St. John-Stevens see he hadn't ground him down.

CHAPTER THREE

Hunter slept restlessly that night, his thoughts wrestling with the images going around inside his head. It started with the memory of Billy Wallace with an arm wrapped around Jonathan's neck, pressing a gun to his head, threatening to kill him. That was replaced quickly by the apparition of Jonathan kicking backwards, sending Billy over the edge of the cliff, falling 150 feet into the raging sea, his cries of shock and terror quickly silenced by the maelstrom of foaming water that engulfed him. These visions weren't confined to Hunter's dreams, they visited him when he was awake, and he just wanted them to end. He would like to be able to say the incident hadn't affected him, but it had. Deeply. Since they had returned from Sark, he had double-checked the doors each night before going to bed and lain awake longer — listening to the sounds outside. And whenever he was with Jonathan, he watched him like a hawk.

Hunter's thoughts were also taken up by his conversation with St. John-Stevens, resulting in anger once more gnawing away inside him. And although he tried his best to beat away the frustration, he failed miserably, and just before 6 a.m. he stopped tossing and turning, realising it was pointless trying to get to sleep. He snuck out of bed, showered, dressed and tiptoed downstairs to the kitchen, where he made himself tea and toast.

When he stepped outside to get in his car, he was greeted by a fine but regular drizzle of rain that shrouded the sky in a grey mist. As he drove to work his concentration was all over the place, his spirits as damp as the weather.

Upon his arrival, the only people in the new complex were the cleaners, and in spite of feeling low he pasted on a big smile and bid them a hearty 'good morning' as he made his way to the MIT office. The place was empty; it was far too early for any of his colleagues to be around, and that suited him because all he wanted to do was remove the items from his desk as quickly as possible and hide himself away in his new department. Emptying the drawers, refilling the box that he'd started to empty yesterday, he hoisted it up into his arms and made his way out of the office and across reception to the opposite corridor where the Cold Case Unit was situated. It was the second room along and the door was open.

Stepping inside, Hunter saw it was a good space with six new desks all fitted with low screens that gave the occupants their own pod, and he looked around them to see which one he could take. He was surprised to see that only one looked as if it was in use. He set down his box on the nearest desk to it and ran his eyes around the room. Four whiteboards occupied two of the walls, one of them full of contact emails and telephone and fax numbers, while the other three contained newspaper cuttings of the team's triumphs. He recognised two of the cases — The Rotherham Shoe Rapist and the Barnsley Rapist. They brought back memories from two years earlier, when he had called upon this team to help him out with a murder case from 1983, where no body had been found and there had been a miscarriage of justice. Help from the Unit had been invaluable and had assisted in the MIT finding missing witnesses, discovering the whereabouts of the murdered victim and tracking down the real killer. Back then they had been based in a tiny office at Maltby, and the unit had been six strong. Looking around at the spare desks, Hunter hoped that was still the case and that the empty desks were because not everyone had moved across yet.

He re-scanned the room. To his left was a bank of filing cabinets, and sitting on top of one of them was tea-making facilities. That lifted his mood. Stepping across the room, he decided to make himself a drink while waiting for his new team to arrive.

At 9.30 a.m. Hunter was still the only person in the office. In the two-and-a-bit hours he had been in he had made three drinks, discovered that the five desks void of items were definitely empty by checking their drawers, chosen the desk next to the one that looked to be occupied and transferred all the stuff from his box to the drawers and desktop. For the last half hour, he had spent the time reading the newspaper cuttings on the boards.

Returning to his desk he checked his watch again, huffing loudly. He wondered where everyone was, and running his eyes across the desk next to his, he searched to see if there was a note that would indicate their whereabouts. There was none. He could feel himself getting grouchy. This was not a good start to his first day. He wondered what his colleagues in MIT were up to with the new investigation. At lunchtime, he would track down Grace and catch up with her out of interest. On that thought, he could feel anger against St. John-Stevens creeping up inside him again and he closed his eyes, pinched the bridge of his nose and took a deep breath, willing it away.

'Sorry, Sarge.'

The woman's voice made Hunter jump, and he sprang open his eyes. Coming towards him was a slender female in her mid-thirties dressed in a dark blue pullover and fitted slacks. She had auburn-tinted dark brown hair tied back in a ponytail, revealing a red, flustered face. At first glance, she reminded him of local actress Katherine Kelly.

'My daughter had a dental appointment. I didn't know you were starting this morning until I got a phone call last night from the new Detective Superintendent, so I couldn't let you know I'd be in later.'

'St. John-Stevens?'

She nodded, setting down her bag on the desk next to his. 'That's him. He's replaced Superintendent Dawn Leggate, so he told me. Pity, I like her.'

'Yeah, so did I,' Hunter returned with a sigh. Then he asked, 'Where is everyone else?'

With a burst of laughter, she replied, 'I'll stick the kettle on, put on my face and fill you in.'

Twenty minutes later, make-up on and looking refreshed, Detective Madeline Scott, — Maddie, as she preferred to be called — sat at her desk, a steaming mug of tea clasped in her hands, facing Hunter. She said, 'I'm afraid, it's only me, Sarge.'

'You and I are the Cold Case Unit? That's what you're saying?'

She nodded. 'And I'm only here because of what happened to my daughter.' Maddie Scott went on to explain that she had transferred to the Cold Case Unit following a serious accident involving her ten-year-old daughter, Libbie, six months previous, who had been thrown from her horse, landing face-down on hard-standing at the stables. It had caused multiple fractures to her face which required reconstructive surgery, and now she was undergoing dental surgery to replace the teeth she lost. Maddie told Hunter that before the accident she had been a front-line detective in Rotherham, and she had been offered the place in the Cold Case Unit because there were less operational constraints and it therefore gave her the flexibility to handle all the hospital appointments without impact on the department. 'That's why I was late coming in this morning. Libbie had to have some impressions made for her new implants.'

'Gosh, I'm sorry to hear that, Maddie. That must be really hard on you.'

'It has been. It was a real worry at first. She had to be airlifted to hospital, and seeing the state of her face after all that surgery freaked me out, I can tell you, but she's getting there now. There's still some considerable work to do with her teeth, but the consultant said that by the time she's a teenager no one will be able to tell anything at all.'

'That's good to hear.'

'It's been six months of worry, that's for sure.'

'I bet it has.' Hunter studied her face a moment. She wore a look of quiet contemplation. He said, 'So what happened to everyone else?'

'Police cuts. The Cold Case Unit was the first to be wound up when they needed to back-fill detective posts. Because the work wasn't seen as being front-line, it wasn't as important and so the department was culled. I only survived because of my daughter. I've been working alone since the move to this place six weeks ago.'

Hunter pursed his lips, shaking his head. It suddenly hit home how underhandedly St. John-Stevens had operated. He had totally fucked him over. He was a detective sergeant in charge of one person. He could feel the heat rising to his face, his anger boiling to the surface again, and he fought to restrain it, taking a drink of tea to hide his emotion and steady his agitation. Swallowing slowly and setting down his mug, he said,

'So Maddie, now all that's clear, do we actually have cases to investigate?' He found his voice wavering.

'Oh yes,' she blurted out, then quickly followed up by adding, 'of sorts.'

'That sounds ominous. What do you mean "of sorts?"'

'The force has seven outstanding murders, the longest going back to nineteen-sixty-two, but all of them were reviewed a year ago and there are no further lines of enquiry or fresh evidence, or so it's been determined. To be honest, I haven't looked at any of the murder cases. I've looked at the outstanding sex crimes, and while some have lines of enquiry, none of them present themselves as a series. The cases I've been focussing on, because there's only been me, are missing persons, to see if there is the likelihood that any of them have come to harm.'

'And how many of those do we have, Maddie?'

'To be honest, Sarge, I've not counted them. Quite a few. I've looked at dozens these past six weeks, and I've got three on my desk that I feel have lines of enquiry that can be followed up.'

'Okay, thanks for that.' Hunter took a deep breath and let it out slowly. This wasn't the type of work he was used to. It sounded laborious, almost mind-numbing. St. John-Stevens had well and truly done a number on him. He gave Maddie an earnest look and said, 'I hope you don't mind me asking this, Maddie, but don't you find the work boring, going through old missing cases that many people have already done work on and come to a dead end?'

'I thought so at first, until I started the enquiries, and then I found some of them really got under my skin because of the element of mystery to them. Why did they disappear like that? I just kept telling myself I could be looking at a case of someone who's been murdered by a serial-killer, and that'd be a real Brucie Bonus for my career if I identified that. Thinking like that spurred me on when it started getting tedious. And because I've been on my own for the last six weeks, that positive thinking has kept me going.'

Maddie's sermon suddenly made Hunter think of his conversation with Beth the previous day, when she'd talked about victims' families getting closure and about everything happening for a reason. Both women's words pricked his conscience. He said, 'Do you mind if I have a look at them?'

'Not at all. I'd be glad of a new pair of eyes. Besides, it's you who now makes the decision as to the cases we investigate.' Maddie set down her mug and lifted out three blue folders from her tray.

As she handed them to him, Hunter could see the top folder was crammed with paperwork, an elastic band securing the contents. He clasped a firm hand around it, plonking it down on his desk. He would look at that one last — he guessed there was at least three hours of reading material in there. Taking the two thinner folders from her, he said, 'And no need to call me Sarge whilst there's only us two in the office. Hunter will do just fine.'

Later that morning, Maddie went out to grab lunch for them both. With the office to himself, Hunter separated the two slimmer files and picked the one bearing the name Alison Chambers. The first document in the file was the missing report. As Hunter cast his eyes over it, he was surprised at the age of Alison — seventy-nine years old. He knew from experience that the majority of people that went missing were young, mainly teenagers. Someone of Alison's age who went missing tended to have dementia, Alzheimer's or depression of some kind and simply wandered off, only to be found in a confused state, hours, or at the most a couple of days, later. He saw that Alison had been missing since 1991, disappearing on Friday the 12th May, after telling a neighbour she was heading to Rotherham shopping centre. Alison had suffered a minor stroke six weeks earlier and was making her first trip out to buy some meat, salad and fruit from the market, she had told her neighbour. She was last seen at a bus stop a quarter of a mile from her home.

Hunter speed-read through the information detailing everything that had been done to try and locate her, saw that there was no suggestion Alison had been acting out of character or was mentally ill and that there was no reason to believe she was likely to commit suicide. All this information had been provided by her fifty-two-year-old son, who was in regular contact with his mother and had spent a few weeks at her home, looking after her following her stroke. As Hunter finished reading the missing report, he saw that all avenues to trace Alison back in 1991 had borne no fruit and an attachment to the report showed that media appeals had been made to locate her for three consecutive years, none of them resulting in anything positive.

There were three witness statements in the file, one from Alison's son, one from the witness who had seen her at the bus stop and one from the female neighbour who had seen Alison on the morning of her disappearance, when she had told her she was going shopping. That last statement detailed what Alison was wearing. Hunter made a note of the witnesses' names and wondered if any of them were still alive. He worked out that Alison's son would now be seventy-one. Flipping back to the missing report, he made a note of the name of the constable who compiled the report and the officers involved in conducting enquiries to trace Alison. He recognised a couple of the names, none of them still working at Barnwell station, and knowing that they would be now in their early fifties he reckoned they had retired. The last thing Hunter looked at were three photographs in Alison's file. He noted on the back of one that someone had pencilled the age of sixty-eight, eleven years younger than her seventy-nine years, but had added 'good likeness.' He put the photos back in the folder, gathered together all the paperwork, clipped a sheet of plain paper to the cover and compiled a list of enquiries to do and slipped it across onto Maddie's desk. As he turned to the next folder, Maddie appeared, holding a supermarket carrier bag which she dumped on her desk.

'I've bought us some biscuits as well,' she said with a smile, slipping off her jacket. She pulled out a bottle of milk and made her way over to the kettle. 'Been up to much?' she asked, turning to Hunter.

'Read one file and listed a number of enquiries that can be done. I've put it back on your desk if you can oblige?'

'Sure, no problem. It would be good to be able to do some detective work for a change.'

'It's nothing earth-shattering, I'm afraid, but at least it will show we've done a review.'

Maddie nodded, lining up two mugs, dropping a teabag into each one. 'I'll crack on with them when I've made us a brew.'

Hunter gave her the thumbs-up and picked up the second folder. This one bore the name Catherine Dewhurst and he flipped it open. The first thing he noted was her age: seventy-five. Another elderly lady. He immediately skipped past the descriptive details of Catherine to the vulnerability section to see if there was anything recorded. There was nothing. Like Alison Chambers, there was nothing to suggest Catherine had any mental illness or was deemed to be a suicide risk. Hunter quickly read on, taking in that Catherine had disappeared almost eleven months before Alison, on the morning of Sunday the 23rd April 1990 after leaving her home to walk to church half a mile away, where she'd been an active member of the congregation. She'd never made it to church, which was completely out of character.

There were some old newspaper cuttings in this folder and he could see that her disappearance had generated a lot of publicity; nevertheless, it had not produced one shred of evidence as to what had happened to her. Like Alison Chambers, she had disappeared without a trace. There were witness statements enclosed and photographs of Catherine, but before looking them over Hunter raised his head and said, 'Maddie, the first two files I've just read through relate to two missing elderly ladies, one seventy-nine and the other seventy-five. Although they are eleven months apart and the circumstances of the two disappearances are different, I'm curious because of the age of the pair. It just seems so unusual.'

Maddie looked his way.

He continued, 'You said you've already gone through and reviewed a number of missing files. Are any of those of elderly women?'

Maddie processed the question for several seconds and returning a studious frown answered, 'Not that old. The oldest was a mid-thirties male from what I recall. Most of the others were teenagers and a few were in their early twenties. Why? Do you think there could be a link with their disappearances?'

Hunter shrugged his shoulders. 'Not sure. It might be just a coincidence. These two women have no reason to disappear and they don't fit the profile of people who go missing for no apparent reason, but I also might be reading too much into what's in the files. I'm going to write down some lines of enquiry for both of them. Can you do some digging and give me your opinion?'

Maddie nodded sharply. 'Sure. Love to. See what I said about some cases getting under your skin? You've caught the bug already.' She winked at him.

Hunter returned a smirk and revisited the file, picking out the witness statements.

At lunchtime Hunter changed into his running gear and went for a jog, taking the mile-long route to nearby Manvers Lake, completing its full circuit of three miles before heading back to the office. He pushed himself hard to combat the urge he still had to throttle the life out of St. John-Stevens and by the time he'd got back, he felt a lot less stressed. He showered, changed and made his way back up to his new office where he saw Maddie busy at her computer with one of the missing person files open.

She glanced up as he entered and said, 'I'm just going through the missing persons archives to see if there are any others that are in the same age group as these.'

Hunter acknowledged Maddie's comment with a nod, made them both a cuppa and took up the seat at his new desk to go through the last folder while he ate his sandwich. The bulging folder showed all the signs of being well-handled, and its contents were secured by an elastic band. The moment he started to slip off the band, it snapped and some of the paperwork spilled across his desk. He could immediately see that there was no semblance of order to any of the documentation, and so the first thing he looked for was the missing person report. He was surprised when he found three of them mixed among a number of witness statements, all handwritten and showing the patina of ageing. He was about to pick them out when he spotted a quantity of typed sheets that appeared to be a summary of the file. Knowing these were his best starting point, he picked out the first page.

The title instantly grabbed him — *A summary of facts relating to the missing Banister family*. The second thing that caught his eye and piqued his interest further was the date — 16th July 1991 — and it instantly triggered a vague recollection of seeing something about this case on the news at the time. It flashed into his thoughts because it was the year he'd joined the Force, and he'd been at training school when this had happened. He pulled out the remaining pages of the summary — it stretched to six pages — and began reading.

The first thing he noted was that twenty-six-year-old David Bannister, his wife, twenty-five-year-old Tina and their daughter, two-year-old Amy, had all been reported missing by David's mum the next day, Wednesday, 17th July, 1991. She'd reported them missing at just after ten in the morning when she'd visited their house and found the doors unlocked, and in the lounge signs of a disturbance. Those signs were a small side table overturned, the phone ripped from its socket, a photograph that normally sat atop the fireplace smashed on the floor and a few droplets of blood on the tiled hearth. She'd immediately called the police.

The house had instantly become a crime scene, and following examination by SOCO a further smear of blood had been found low down on the door jamb that led into the back kitchen, which tests had later revealed was the same blood-group as Tina's. Further staining had been found on the kitchen floor, and although it had proved to be blood, there was evidence that someone had used bleach to clean it up, resulting in the blood being corrupted and disabling tests to determine who it belonged to. Numerous fingerprints had been uncovered, but all had been eliminated as people who'd had access to the house.

During enquiries into the family's disappearance, it had been reported that police attended the Bannister home three weeks earlier following a report of a domestic disturbance, and Hunter noted that no action had been taken after Tina Bannister had refused to make a complaint — standard police response in those days. On the day police had taken the initial report of the family going missing from David Bannister's mother, it had been discovered that David's car had also disappeared. An extensive search had been carried out, but it had never been found.

After several days of intensive investigation, interviewing family members, neighbours and friends, it had been uncovered that although Tina had been a doting mum to her daughter Amy, she'd had a reputation as a woman who'd regularly flirted with men in the pub where she'd worked as a barmaid. David's mum had revealed that the domestic incident followed David's discovery that she'd had a sexual fling with one of his work colleagues.

Two-thirds of the way through the report, Hunter read that another work colleague, George Evers, had tipped off David that he had seen Tina having lunch with a man in a local pub and had seen that same man leaving the Bannister home one afternoon the week before the family's disappearance. On the day the family disappeared, David had told George Evers that he was going home at lunchtime to hopefully catch his wife with the man in question. That was the last time David had been seen. Whilst extensive searches had been carried out locally, together with a number of media appeals, no concrete information had come forward that determined the whereabouts of the family.

The conclusion of the investigation findings was that David Bannister had gone home that lunchtime, that there had been an altercation of sorts at the family home, and that David had more than likely killed Tina and his daughter and then driven away with their bodies and committed suicide by driving into a river or lake. Several local waterways had been searched during the six-month long enquiry, but neither David's car nor any of the bodies had ever been found.

Finishing the report, Hunter lifted his head and stared at the ceiling as he considered the contents. He found it very difficult to understand how a complete family could just disappear like that and instantly came to the conclusion that the circumstances warranted further investigation, if only to satisfy himself that every avenue had been considered. His first port of call would be to talk with the officer who'd headed up the investigation and the officer who'd conducted most of the enquiries. Dropping his gaze to the typed report, he turned to the back page to see who had compiled the summary. As his eyes danced across the name, he grimaced. *Detective Constable St. John-Stevens. That's all I fucking need!*

On his way home, Hunter decided to swing by the house that once belonged to the Bannister family to fix the sense of place before he began his enquiries. He knew the locality fairly well because he'd once lived only a few streets away as a child, and that was another reason why the event triggered a memory: having once resided in the same neighbourhood, the sudden disappearance of the Bannisters in 1991 had been something his parents had frequently asked him about on the weekends he had come home from police training school. All he'd been able to tell them back then was that it was something he wasn't involved in and wouldn't be involved in until he actually started on the beat. When he had finished his training and got his posting to Barnwell, the enquiry had been 'closed pending further information — believed murdered by David Bannister, followed by his suicide', and that was why his recollection of the event was so fleeting. Speaking with his mum and dad about their memory of the family's disappearance was on his list of priorities over the next couple of days.

Wath Road was made up of two rows of identical Victorian terracing, all in private hands. It was a street of houses with no driveways, and so the occupants' cars lined the road either side, leaving only a narrow passing. Hunter eased off the accelerator but kept going, allowing himself enough time to read the house numbers that he passed. As he approached the junction, he saw that the old Bannister home was the end terrace on the right-hand side. It had an alleyway to the side giving easy access to the rear, making it different from the other properties, and as he stopped at the give-way markings he gave the house the once over, fixing an impression of it. As he turned left out of the street, he took a last glance in his rear-view mirror. He remembered these streets and some of the occupants well from when he was a child. Tomorrow, he would begin finding out who was still here from 1991 when David, Tina and their daughter Amy had gone missing.

The moment Hunter entered his home, the wonderful smells of cooking greeted him. Setting down his briefcase, he shouted, 'It's me,' slipped off his coat, draping it over the stair rail, and flipped off his shoes.

Beth called back, 'I'm through here,' and he made his way to the kitchen.

'Something smells good,' said Hunter, eyeing several pans on the large stove.

Beth wore an apron over a T-shirt and jeans and her hands were in oven-gloves. 'There's a beer in the fridge,' she said, pulling open the oven door. A waft of steam poured through the gap, and Beth pulled back her face.

'You're home early,' she said. 'I can't remember the last time you were home at a civilised time and we ate together as a family. If this is what your new job means, then you can stay in it until your retirement.'

Hunter pulled two half-pint glasses out from a cupboard and split the bottle of beer. He handed one glass to Beth. 'Cheeky mare,' he returned and took the head off his Theakston's. It hit the spot. He took another, longer drink, almost draining the glass.

'I've put another in the fridge for you. I thought you might need it.' Beth took a sip of her own beer, then asked, 'How did your first day go?'

Hunter finished his beer. 'Okay. Not what I'm used to, but it looks as though it could be interesting.' He told her about Maddie being his only supervision.

'Is she nice?'

'Seems it.' He told Beth about her circumstances. Then before Beth could respond, he said, 'Where are the boys?'

'In their rooms. Jonathan said he has some homework, and I think Daniel's on his X-Box.'

'I'll grab a shower, and then have ten minutes with them both before we eat.'

While Hunter ate, he chatted with the boys about what they had done at school and discussed getting tickets for Sheffield United's next home game with Jonathan, and suggested taking

Daniel to rugby on Sunday — family things he hadn't been able to do for the best part of a year. And whilst St. John-Stevens entered his thoughts during the odd moment, he couldn't help but think it had been a long time since he had felt this chilled; work was constantly in his thoughts, especially when a big case was running.

After the meal, he helped clear away the dishes, and while the boys disappeared back to their rooms he switched on the TV to grab the remainder of the local news. There was a piece on about Rasa Katiliene. They were showing a screenshot from CCTV footage of her in the company of a big-built overweight man, believed to be in his late forties, leaving The Junction pub. It wasn't of good quality, and Hunter was of the opinion it had been captured by a camera a good distance from the pub and had been blown up. St. John-Stevens was telling the reporter that it was the last sighting of Rasa, and that if anyone knew who the man was, they should contact the Incident Room. The news-clip only lasted thirty seconds, and Hunter mumbled the word 'wanker,' as it switched to another news item. Operation Hydra had slipped from his thoughts, and he reminded himself to speak with Grace about the case purely out of curiosity.

As the weather report started, Hunter turned off the TV and switched his thoughts to the Bannister family. He had brought the missing file home with him in his briefcase, and he decided that he would go through the remainder of it before Jonathan and Daniel's shower and bedtime.

CHAPTER FOUR

What a difference a day makes, Hunter thought as he exited the lift on the first floor of the training complex and made his way to his new office. He had slept well, only waking when his alarm went off at 6.45 a.m., and he felt the most refreshed he had done for days. Although he was his own timekeeper now, he had already decided he was going to continue to aim for 8 a.m. starts, even though it was only himself and Maddie.

The office was empty — Hunter wasn't surprised given Maddie and her daughter's circumstances — and dumping his briefcase on his desk he made his way across the room and switched on the kettle. As it boiled, he booted up his computer and took out the Bannister file. He had noted last night while flipping through it that among the witness statements there was also a set of crime scene photographs of the Bannister home, which had immediately pleased him — a photograph was better than any written evidence — and after giving them a cursory look through, he'd decided upon a more thorough scrutiny of them this morning. His aim was to read through the file and establish if there were any lines of enquiry.

One of the things that already concerned him was knowing that St. John-Stevens had been the investigating officer in this case. Notwithstanding his issues with him, Hunter had doubts about his experience as a detective back in 1991. He had done his homework on him since their run-in and discovered that St. John-Stevens had joined the job in 1988 as a twenty-one-year-old graduate, with a degree in law. Three years later he was a Detective Constable at Barnwell, and while he undoubtedly had knowledge of the law and procedures, Hunter knew that it took more than that to be a detective. It takes years of honing skills from hard-earned experience, and the only experience St. John-Stevens would have had in 1991 was three years of policing, two of those as a probationer constable.

A vision of Hunter's mentor, Barry Newstead, suddenly leaped into his head. He remembered Barry telling him of several run-ins he'd had with a uniform chief inspector of similar character to St. John-Stevens. What had Barry said about him? 'He couldn't detect shit on his shoes.' That thought made Hunter chuckle, and as he gazed again at St. John-Stevens' name on the last page of the summary, he told himself, *This case definitely warrants a thorough going-through before being filed away again.*

There were a dozen photographs of the Bannister home, the first three of which showed the outside of the house, front, side and rear. The only difference Hunter could see from his visit yesterday was that PVC doors and windows had replaced the wooden ones in the photos.

In the fourth photograph, Hunter saw that the front door opened straight into the lounge. The room was very well furnished and decorated. The walls were covered in wallpaper of two different designs separated by white dado rail. The bottom section was green and white stripes and the top paper a series of green designs on a white background. It was furnished with a green Dralon three-seater sofa and matching chair, a wooden coffee table, and a glass cabinet that contained a mix of wood and pottery ornaments together with a brown glazed coffee service that Hunter recognised as Hornsea ware. A TV was on a stand in the right-hand alcove next to a tiled fireplace. He remembered that the summary mentioned a side table being overturned and a photograph smashed, and he could see in the photo that there was a small wooden table on its side next to the fireplace and a shattered picture frame beside it.

The fifth and sixth photographs were closeup shots of the tiled hearth and fireplace, and Hunter could see a number of dried blood splashes. There were only half a dozen splodges, the biggest of which looked to be about the size of fifty-pence pieces. He remembered that it had been identified as belonging to Tina. While she had obviously been injured, looking at these two photographs, it couldn't have been a bad injury, he told himself.

The seventh photo was a wide shot of the daughter's bedroom. It contained a cot, the bedding of which had been made, a cream coloured bedside cabinet and a double wardrobe that matched. By the absence of other photos of Amy's room, Hunter guessed that nothing untoward had happened there.

The remaining five photographs were all of the kitchen, three of them of the floor area which looked as if it was covered in light brown vinyl with a tile design. One of the photos had crime-scene markers set out over the floor, but it appeared clean. Two others of the kitchen had been shot from the same angle, but in these Hunter saw sizeable tracks of something smeared across it. He guessed he was seeing this because Luminol had been sprayed across the vinyl floor, which picks up blood and other stains when subjected to a certain type of ultra-violet light, and he recalled mention of significant amounts of bloodstaining being found in the kitchen that someone had attempted to clean with bleach. Hunter could clearly see the signs that someone had been badly injured in this room.

The last shot was of the door jamb that led from the lounge into the kitchen. Low down, very close to the floor was a bloodstain smear. The first thought that jumped into Hunter's head was that this was where Tina had made a last-gasp effort to stop herself being dragged into the kitchen after being assaulted in the lounge. He tried to remember if that had been accounted for in St. John-Stevens' summary. He scribbled a note to check and then lingered over the last three photographs before setting them aside and reading the witness statements.

The first he picked out was from David Bannister's mum, Alice. It began with background information relating to when her son was born, when he met Tina, when they married and the date when Amy, her granddaughter, was born. All standard preamble for a statement of this type. It led on to when David moved into the house on Wath Road, his occupation — a warehouseman at a local building firm — and when he started work there. It was short and to the point.

From there, it jumped to 3 p.m. on the 16th July 1991, the time and day when Alice visited her son and daughter-in-law's house. The initial detail of her visit mirrored the summary — that she first found the front door unlocked — thereafter it was expanded, describing how she opened the door and shouted into the house, and after not getting a response as expected, she stepped inside and found the disturbance in the lounge and from there made a cursory search of the kitchen, and seeing the back door was also unlocked, and no one around, made her way upstairs expecting to find her daughter-in-law and granddaughter up there. Not finding them, she returned to the lounge and this time noticed the blood droplets on the hearth. She became immediately concerned that something had happened to either Tina or Amy and finding the house phone ripped from its socket, nipped next door to the neighbour and made a telephone call to her son's workplace.

She learned that David had left at lunchtime and hadn't returned back to work, and at that point Hunter recalled that the summary had made mention of a work colleague tipping him off about a man he had seen drinking with Tina in the pub and leaving their address a week earlier, and that David had said he was going home to try and catch them. Hunter held on to the page while he skim-read back over the summary to find the details of the man tipping David off. He found him. George Evers. He made another note and returned to Alice's statement, picking up where he had left off.

He read that she then rang Barnwell General Hospital, asking if any of them were there. When she was told they weren't, she rang the police and reported them missing. Finishing Alice's statement, Hunter realised that with the exception of Alice's more detailed account of her actions following her entrance into her son and daughter-in-law's home, the phone calls to her son's place of work and the hospital enquiry, he hadn't learned anything different to what he'd read in the summary, and he put it to one side and picked up the next document.

This witness statement was from thirty-two-year-old Denise Harris, who lived directly opposite the Bannisters. He read that was she was a married mother of two boys aged eight and six and worked part-time as a cashier at a local supermarket. On the day of the Bannister's disappearance it was her day off, and after taking her sons to school, she walked into Barnwell town centre to do some shopping and then returned home, arriving back about 10.30 a.m. when she put on her washing machine and started to clean her house.

At around noon of that day, Denise Harris was in her lounge, hoovering, when she noticed a man at the front door of the Bannister home. She described him as white, of medium height and medium build, with dark hair and wearing a dark-coloured long coat with the collar up so that she couldn't see his face, and was therefore unable to give an estimate as to age. She stated that she only gave him a few seconds' attention, because she continued hoovering. When she looked through her window again, about a minute later, he had gone.

A little under an hour later, she was again in her lounge when she saw David Bannister let himself in by the front door. After she saw David go into the house, Denise then went into the backyard of her house to hang out the washing and saw no more activity at the Bannister home. The following evening, she became aware of police activity in the street, especially around the Bannister home and learned that they had all been reported missing.

Hunter finished Denise Harris's statements, tightening his grip on the pages. None of this was in the summary, and he knew that it should have been. The presence of a stranger at the front door of the Bannister house a day before their reported disappearance — albeit for a few seconds and with a poor description that wouldn't enable identification — was still worthy of investigation. It also tied in with the information from David's work colleague, George Evers, who had seen Tina drinking with a man in a pub and had seen the same man leaving the address one week prior to them all disappearing.

Hunter set down Mrs Harris's statement and searched through the paperwork for George's statement. Whilst there were other statements in the folder, there wasn't one from George. For a moment he was puzzled, until he remembered how the file had only been held together by a flimsy elastic band and guessed that it had fallen out at some stage over the years of handling and filing. He noted down George Evers' name as someone to trace. There were clear lines of enquiry here that warranted following up. Putting his list to one side, Hunter was just thinking it was time for another cuppa when the office door opened and in stepped a flushed Maddie. He looked at his watch. 9.30 a.m.

Maddie hurried past him, unbuttoning her coat. She dropped her bag onto her desk. 'Nightmare of a morning! I'm so sorry, Sarge. Libbie was in loads of pain again last night, and I didn't get her down until three this morning. We slept in.' She shook herself out of her coat. 'I'll work later and make up for it.'

Hunter could see she was flustered. He answered, 'Okay, don't worry about it, Maddie.'

'Thank you.' She let out a deep sigh. 'And I'm sorry about this, but I also need to sort out something that's urgent before I start.'

Hunter eyed her anxious expression. 'What's that, then?'

She let out another heavy sigh. 'I forgot to set my handbrake, and my car's rolled back into another car in the car park.'

'Oh, crikey, Maddie! Do you know whose it is?'

Tightening her mouth, she shook her head. 'I'm just going to do a check.'

Her face gave away how overwhelmed she was feeling, and Hunter saw her eyes starting to well up. He said, 'Don't get upset, Maddie. There'll not be much damage if you've only rolled into it. Take me down and show me the car you've hit before you do anything.'

Maddie picked her bag back up and followed Hunter out of the office. They took the lift down to the car park and Hunter let Maddie show him where she had parked her VW Golf.

As he approached Maddie's VW, Hunter thought that it looked to be perfectly parked.

As if reading his thoughts, she said, 'I pulled it back after I'd hit it.' She pointed to the shiny silver Mercedes parked behind her car.

Hunter took a deep breath. It was a brand new E class model. Not cheap. Hunter couldn't help but think this had 'gaffer's car' written all over it, and sneaking a quick look around and seeing they were the only people in the car park he bent down to examine the Mercedes' front bumper. Below the number plate was a foot-long black scuff mark from Maddie's bumper. Without commenting on the damage, Hunter said, 'Do you have a wipe?'

Ferreting around in her handbag, Maddie produced a wet-wipe which she handed to Hunter.

Scrubbing the mark, he managed to rub away most of the black, but beneath the scuff were several small scratches which he couldn't remove. He gazed up, and seeing her face still wearing a troubled look, he said, 'It's nothing, Maddie. T-cut or one of those scratch-pens will easy get rid of those.' He added, 'Give me another wipe.'

Maddie handed him another wet-wipe and with it he scrubbed her bumper. It took him less than a minute to make it look good as new. Casting his gaze over it, he knew it would take more than a close-eye inspection to detect she had been the culprit. Pushing himself up and holding her gaze, from the pained look she returned he knew that the last thing she needed right now was one of the bosses giving her a dressing-down for a simple error of judgment. Making a snap decision, he said, 'Look, I'll sort this, don't worry. You've got enough on your plate. I'll park in your place and say it was me. Okay?'

Maddie held Hunter's gaze. She blinked back a tear. 'I don't mind owning up.'

'As I say, this can easily be sorted without it costing a penny. Leave it with me. You've got enough problems right now.'

'Are you sure?'

'I'm sure.' Hunter reached out and reassuringly patted her shoulder. 'Now, let's get our cars switched around, we'll grab a cuppa and then I'll sort it.'

Back in the office, after freshening up her face, Maddie put the kettle on and made two teas. Hunter picked up his steaming mug and glanced across at Maddie, who was just turning on her computer. She was still wearing a worried look.

He said, 'I'll sup this and then find out who the Merc belongs to.'

'Thanks, Sarge, and if it's going to cost anything, I'll pay.'

'It's Hunter when it's just you and me, and it's not going to cost anything, believe me.'

'Thank you again.'

'You're welcome.' He took a slurp of tea and said, 'And then do you fancy doing a bit of detective work for a change, Maddie?'

'Certainly would. What have you got?'

'Remember the Bannister file you handed me?'

'Them all going missing?'

Hunter nodded. 'That's them. Well, I've found a couple of things that need following up. It might be something and it might be nothing, but it wants checking. I've also made a list of things that I want you to make a start on. We'll finish our cuppas, you sort out what you need to and I'll make a couple of phone calls. I've got two witnesses I need to speak with and if they're still living on Wath Road, or near there, I'm going to fix up an appointment for you and I to go and see them. Is that okay?'

Maddie rubbed her hands together, breaking into a grin for the first time. 'Sure is. Detective work at last.'

Steadily drinking his tea, Hunter ran the registered number of the Mercedes through the computer. It was registered to a dealership in Sheffield, and he guessed the DVLA hadn't yet logged the new owner. Hunter made a note of the dealer's name to call later and then returned to the Bannister file, picking out the remaining witness statements. There were three. One from the crime-scene photographer, another from the scenes of crime officer who'd examined the house and found the attempted clean-up of bloodstains in the kitchen, and the last one from the first police officer who'd attended the Bannister home, recorded the signs of disturbance in the lounge and taken Alice Bannister's statement.

Hunter saw that the officer undertaking those roles had been Roger Mills. *What a surprise.* Roger had been the constable who had tutored him at the beginning of his probationary period in 1991. He was retired now. He glanced at Roger's signature on Alice's statement. This was one officer Hunter knew he could trust to have done a thorough job.

His thoughts suddenly swung back to his first few weeks on patrol with Roger. It had been with Roger that he had dealt with his first sudden death, that later turned out to be a rape and murder committed by a man called Dylan Wolfe. The victim had been called June Waring, and coincidently had lived only four streets away from the Bannister house, on Mexborough Row. They had found the sixty-four-year-old dead in bed and Roger had led him through the process of what to do as first officer at the scene of a death; initially it hadn't been suspicious until the post-mortem revealed her sexual assault and suffocation, and that had led to a major

61

enquiry in which Hunter had played a key part, including Wolfe's capture. For several seconds Hunter's thoughts lingered on that case; in 1991, Dylan Wolfe had attacked four women in Barnwell and had been given a life sentence for his atrocious crimes.

Hunter's reflections triggered a lightbulb moment. This was something he couldn't ignore. The Bannister family's disappearance had occurred only four months before the rape and killing of June Waring, and whilst there were differing anomalies to that case, the victim, Tina Bannister, was a young woman of similar age to Dylan Wolfe, who more than likely would have known him. And Denise Harris's witness statement put a stranger at the house only an hour prior to David Bannister coming home, and George Evers mentioned that he'd seen a man coming out of the house a week before they all disappeared. The fact that Dylan Wolfe's first victim only lived four streets away certainly put his name up there as a Person of Interest.

Hunter scribbled down Dylan's name and doodled a star beside it. He also added Roger's name on his list of people to see; even if he couldn't add anything to his follow-up review, it would be nice to catch up with him again, he thought.

Hunter found that Alice Bannister still lived in the same house as in 1991, and except for a one-digit addition to the area code she still had the same telephone number. Hunter rang and she answered on the fourth ring. The first thing she asked, after Hunter introduced himself, was, 'Have you found them?' He told Alice he hadn't, that they were reviewing the family's disappearance and that he'd like to talk to her about the case. Whilst she responded somewhat downheartedly, she welcomed their visit.

Alice's house was a three-bedroom 1960s semi on an estate only half a mile from Wath Road. As he and Maddie walked down the short driveway, Hunter cast his eye over the front of the house. It was of a typical design from that era: flat-fronted and characterless with a constructed stone lower half and red-brick upper floor, an exact replica of each of the forty or so houses that filled the street.

The front door was encased by a glass and wood porch, and Alice appeared before Hunter had time to knock. He and Maddie showed their ID and she let them in to a carpeted hall, taking them through to the lounge.

Alice guided them into a lounge that was clean and tidy but cluttered with framed photographs of all sizes, all of which, at a quick glance, appeared to be a down-the-ages collection of family portraits of mum, dad and son. They filled the shelves of a bookcase in one alcove and lined the mantelpiece of a faux Adams fireplace. In the frames atop the mantelpiece Hunter saw photographs of David, whom he recognised from his photo in the case-file. In a couple of them he was holding a baby, which he guessed was Amy. There were none of Tina. Hunter made a mental note as he sat down on the sofa with Maddie.

'You said on the phone that you were reviewing their disappearance. Does that mean you've got some new information as to what's happened to them?' Alice asked, eyes probing.

'No, we haven't, I'm afraid. I work in the Cold Case Unit with my colleague Maddie here,' Hunter returned, settling back in the sofa. 'Our job is to go through all the old cases and see if we've missed anything from the past. Your family's case is one we're currently reviewing to see if there is anything that could give us a lead as to what happened to them back in nineteen-ninety-one. The beauty about doing this, aside from refreshing people's minds, is that forensic capabilities have advanced so much this past decade that we also look at any forensic evidence we recovered at the time and see if it's worthy of being examined to give us a fresh clue. What we're here for this morning, Alice, is to go over the statement you made to officers back in nineteen-ninety-one and to see if you can add anything to it that may give us something extra to focus on. I don't want to build your hopes up. This is us having a look with a fresh pair of eyes at the investigation into your son's, daughter-in-law's and granddaughter's disappearance to see if there is any avenue of enquiry we can make that might indicate what happened to them. Is that clear?'

Alice let out a heavy sigh. 'That's all I've ever asked for. I've been waiting for this for years.'

Hunter sensed frustration in her reply. He said, 'What do you mean, Alice?'

'All those letters I've written that you've ignored.'

'Letters?'

'Yes, letters! I've written to your lot every year asking for you to re-look at what happened to them, and all I've had back is two letters telling me that you've done everything you could and that you'll update me if there are any changes. Since nineteen-ninety-three, I've heard nothing.'

Hunter sensed rising tension in her voice. He thought about the case file he'd gone through. He hadn't seen any letters from Alice in it. He responded, 'I'm sorry to hear that, Alice...'

Mrs Bannister interjected, 'Can you imagine how I felt being told that David had killed them and then committed suicide and seeing it spread all over the papers and on the news? I told that detective, St. John-Stevens, that he'd got it wrong, but all he kept saying was that the evidence pointed to that. I got so angry with him that I told him not to come back until he apologised and had something different to tell me. In the end I went to see my MP, and he wrote on my behalf asking for the case to be re-opened, but he was told the same thing: that my David killed them.'

'And you don't think that at all?' Hunter said, taking back his lost ground with a compassionate tone.

'No! My David would never do anything like that. He doted on Amy. She was the light of his life. He would never have harmed her.'

Hunter studied her face, giving her a few seconds of breathing space, making sure she had got things off her chest. He continued, 'I can't promise you a different outcome, Alice, but I can promise you we will be doing a thorough review of all the evidence. We will be speaking not only to yourself but other witnesses as well to see if any new light can be cast on their disappearance. We will be coming back here once we've visited everyone to update you, and if there is anything that's a lead, I can assure you we will follow it up. Okay?'

Alice let out a sigh, nodding slowly. 'Thank you. As I say, that's all I've ever wanted.'

Hunter let his words sink in for a few seconds, then he said, 'What I want to do now is slowly go through that day you discovered them missing. My colleague, Maddie, is going to make some notes. Are you able to do that?'

Alice nodded sharply. 'I've lived that day for the past nineteen years. It's as fresh in my mind as it was back then.'

'Good. So, in your own words, can you tell me what happened?'

She briefly glanced upwards before returning her gaze to Hunter. 'Well, just to fill you in first, after Amy was born, I'd taken to going around more to their house. It was mostly to see Amy, but I occasionally dropped by when I had some shopping to do to see if they needed anything. I also helped out with the washing and ironing. Before then, it was usually David who came to see us, usually on his way home from work. And when Tina got a job, I started having Amy. It wasn't every day, just when I was needed.' Alice let out a quick sigh, adding, 'Tina's mum wasn't much help. The only person she was interested in was herself. Fawning herself around with whichever fancy-man she was with at the time.' Then with continued disdain she said, 'You can see where Tina got it from.' Following a quick shake of the head, she continued, 'Tina got a part-time job at the sewing factory to help with the bills, but she hated it and then she was offered work behind the bar of The Tavern. But she wasn't there for long. David put a stop to it because of the rumours, and so she got a job at the bingo hall a couple of days a week…'

Alice's opening sentence instantly jarred with Hunter's thoughts. He stole another glance at the photo frames with their lack of photos of Tina in them, and coupled with what Alice had just said, he immediately had the impression that Alice didn't have a good opinion of her daughter-in-law. Whilst he wanted to divert his questioning at this stage, he decided not to. Instead, he stored her comments and let her go on.

'That day I paid their house a visit it was Tina's day off, and ordinarily I wouldn't have gone, but I'd heard the rumours again about her messing around and I was hoping to catch her out with her fancy man…'

As soon as Alice said this, Hunter determined that he needed to interject. There had been only brief mention in the case file that it was suspected that Tina had an illicit relationship, and it may well provide the answer as to who the stranger was that Denise Harris saw at the Bannister home the day before their disappearance and George Evers the week before. He said, 'Can I just interrupt you there, Alice? You've just mentioned that Tina was having an affair with someone. Is that correct?'

'Just one of many,' she harrumphed. 'I warned David the moment I clapped eyes on her. She was a looker all right, but I knew that Tina Henshaw was trouble. There were rumours about how flighty she was years before our David got smitten by her charms.'

This information was a complete surprise to Hunter. He glanced at Maddie, raising his eyebrows, and then returned his gaze to Alice, picking his thread back up. 'Do you know, or have an idea who she was seeing?'

'I was told there were a few. I know that just before they disappeared she was seeing someone when she worked behind the bar of The Tavern. Apparently, it was common knowledge that she was *at it* with him. The only person who didn't know was David, until one of his workmates told him he'd seen her with him. I know he had words with Tina about it. Strong ones. He made her leave.'

'We have on file that police were called to their house over a domestic row three weeks before their disappearance. Was it to do with that?'

She shrugged her shoulders. 'David wouldn't say too much about what happened about that. He was embarrassed about the police going to the house. He'd never been in trouble in his life. It could have been, although she'd left the pub a couple of months before they had that row. You'll know more about that than me.'

'I'm afraid I don't, Alice, that's why I asked. What happened back then would have been recorded on paper, so I think it's been destroyed now. Can you remember what he said about it?'

'He said nothing at first. I found out they'd rowed and the police had been called from a neighbour, and I confronted him about it. He wouldn't tell me anything to begin with, but I eventually got something out of him. He said he'd hit her. I was mortified, I can tell you. In all of my twenty-two years of marriage, my John's never laid a finger on me. I had a right go at him there and then, and he admitted that he'd hit her after she'd attacked him. He said he'd confronted her about the affair and she told him it was lies. They had an almighty bust-up, and she went for him and he slapped her across the face. David said he'd apologised and he told me that the police had warned him that if there was a next time, he'd be locked up.' Alice paused, taking in a deep breath. 'That detective, St. John-Stevens, kept going on about that row, trying to make out our David was a wife-beater or something. He wasn't, I can assure you. It was Tina's fault, that. All of her fancy goings-on came out after they disappeared.'

'So did the police find out who she'd had her affair with?'

'Detective St. John-Stevens did. He confirmed it was a man from David's work.'

'Did he tell you his name?'

Alice shook her head. 'No, but we found out later. The bloke was given his cards. Went off to work for another building supplier. A delivery driver. I heard he got killed in an accident on the motorway about five years ago.'

Hearing that news disappointed Hunter, and then he remembered that George Evers, David's work colleague, had tipped him off about seeing Tina with another man and wondered if it was the same man. He stored his thinking for later and said, 'Well, that's filled in details about the domestic incident at their home and the reason behind it. But that was three weeks before they all disappeared. You wouldn't happen to know if Tina was still seeing this man just before she disappeared, would you?'

'She wouldn't admit to David that she was seeing him. We only found out it was someone from his work when the police investigated them going missing. It wouldn't surprise me if she was, though. Tina was a bit too free around men. Like her mum, she loved to be the centre of attention. That's why she liked working behind the bar. If it had been up to me, our David would never have married her. I mean, look what's happened.'

Although understanding the way she felt, Hunter didn't respond. Instead, he nodded. He said, 'Were you made aware that a man had been seen at the front door of their house the day before they disappeared?'

'Detective St. John-Stevens told me about that and asked me if I knew who it might be. I told him about what Tina was like and the rumours, and that also that one of David's work colleagues had tipped him off about her seeing someone, but he came back a few days later and said it wasn't the man from David's work. He'd eliminated him, he told me. He was at work during the time that man had been seen at the house. Detective St. John-Stevens said it might have just been an innocent caller. No one had actually seen him go into the house or come out of it. When I asked Denise, the neighbour across the road, about it, because I found out it was her who'd seen him, she told me she hadn't actually seen the man go in, just standing at the door.'

'Denise Harris, you mean?'

Alice nodded sharply.

'I've seen the statement she gave to an officer, Alice, and she's on my list to talk to, but I've just checked to see if she's still living there and nothing's coming up on the voters list. You wouldn't know if she's still there, would you?'

Alice shook her head. 'She's moved. She moved years ago now. Not long after what happened. Her husband got his redundancy from the pit and they bought a B&B in Bridlington. Me and John went and had a weekend stay there about ten years ago. We've only been away that once since they went missing. I can't relax anymore. It's always at the front of my mind as to what happened to them, especially little Amy, poor thing.'

Hunter was silent for a few seconds, watching Alice's face. With a look of sympathy, he said, 'Sorry to hear that, Alice. I can't imagine what it's like for you not knowing what's happened to them.' Hunter paused, letting his sentiments rest in her thoughts, then he said, 'Just going back to Denise Harris, you wouldn't know if she still has the B&B, would you?'

'I don't. I kept in touch with her for a few years after our visit, sent her a couple of Christmas cards, but things just fizzled out. I haven't been in contact with her for probably eight years now.'

'You haven't got the address, have you?'

'I have it somewhere, but I don't know if I can put my hand on it right now. I'll have to search for it.'

'That's all right. It's not urgent. You have a search when we've gone, and when you find it just give me a call.' Pausing, he continued, 'I know I've side-tracked somewhat, Alice, but I assure you it has helped my enquiries. Can I now take you back to the day when you discovered David and the family missing and called the police?'

For the next twenty minutes Alice reiterated what she had put in her original statement. There were no deviations and no further revelations. After thanking her, Hunter handed over his contact details and told her he would be back in touch. As he made his way back up the driveway with Maddie, he was planning his next steps.

CHAPTER FIVE

Back at the office, Hunter was writing up his notes from the interview with Alice Bannister; it had thrown up some interesting possibilities and given him fresh lines of enquiry. If, as Alice was suggesting, her son hadn't killed his wife and daughter and committed suicide, his knowledge and experience told him that no one can just disappear these days. Everyone leaves their footprint, be it on technology, through phone or computer, or through financial dealings at banks, post offices or other financial institutions, and even if they had changed their names there were methods to trace them if they were alive.

Primarily, Hunter wanted to know for certain if since July 1991 any of them had accessed any means of funding, and if that wasn't the case, he would know that they were definitely dead and they could change their game plan. *Maybe ask for additional helping hands.* Though when he gave that another thought, realising it was St. John-Stevens he had to approach, he wasn't very confident, especially when he had to tell him it was to follow up one of *his* cases. Knowing the person his new boss was, Hunter knew he would see that as criticism of the investigation he had undertaken and instantly throw up barriers. So, for now, he decided he was going to keep things under wraps.

List completed, he handed it over to Maddie, who had been itching to get started since they had got back, and while she made a start, he did a voters list check for Denise Harris. Within five minutes, he struck lucky. According to the recent list Denise was still living at The Seahorse B&B in Bridlington.

He googled the name, found their website within thirty seconds and dialled the telephone number. After five rings his call switched across to voicemail and he left a message, briefly explaining he was carrying out a review of the disappearance of the Bannister family and wanted to go back over the statement she'd given to police in 1991, and after leaving his contact number, he hung up. For a moment, his eyes rested on his computer screen. There was nothing else he could do until she got back to him. He checked his watch. It was just after 1 p.m. Lunchtime, and his stomach was telling him he needed more than a sandwich.

Stepping into the canteen, he spotted Grace at a table with Mike Sampson. She instantly acknowledged him with a wave and big smile, and Mike pulled out the chair next to him and indicated for Hunter to join them. Suddenly he felt guilty for not having made any attempt to contact his team since his quick exit from MIT. He made his way across to them, checking that St. John-Stevens wasn't around. Seeing he wasn't, Hunter laid down his mobile on their table, told them he was going to get some food and went over to the serving area. He opted for steak pie, chips and mushy peas and made his way back to them.

'I've been meaning to text you, Hunter,' Grace opened, 'but we've been so busy on this job. We're all pretty gutted with what St. John-Stevens has done to you.'

'Me too. I still feel like decking the twat,' Hunter said, setting down his plate of food.

Grace and Mike both let out a laugh.

'How's it going? You're working with Maddie Scott, aren't you?' said Grace.

'You know her?'

'Not that well. I've chatted with her on a couple of courses I've been on. And I worked with her once on a rape when I was in CID. I know she's very bright, got a degree in sociology or something, but also can be a bit scatty at times. Didn't her daughter get thrown from her horse and get badly hurt?'

Hunter smiled. 'To say you don't know her that well, you don't miss much, do you, Grace?'

'That's because we don't talk all that shite that you men talk about. We learn stuff,' she replied with a smug grin.

'I think it's called gossip, Grace,' Hunter scoffed, breaking into his pie and forking some into his mouth. Chewing quickly and swallowing most of his mouthful, he continued, 'How's your case going? Still no sign of Rasa, whatever her name is? I saw the TV appeal.'

'Katiliene. Rasa Katiliene,' Grace responded. 'Still not found her. We now believe she's dead. We traced her to The Comfort Inn on the day she went missing, and that's the last place we can trace her to. She went there to meet a punter, the man on the TV appeal, and we're now trying to trace him.'

'Do you know who he is?'

'You've seen the quality of the footage. It's not that good, though we believe it's someone called Luke Riley. He's from Wakefield originally. He's a registered sex offender. Done time for raping a sex worker in Leeds.'

'And what's also interesting,' interjected Mike, 'is that he was found not guilty eighteen months ago of the attempted murder and attempted rape of a street worker in Huddersfield after he picked her up in his car and took her to some waste ground, where he tried strangling her after she refused unprotected sex.'

'Cut and dried, then?' Hunter asked.

'Well, he's our main suspect at the moment,' Grace answered. 'But we've other lines of enquiry. We're still trying to trace her pimp, a guy called Matis Varnas, who's from Lithuania. We believe he and his partner Ugne brought Rasa here from Lithuania. We've been told they're renting a place in Rotherham and we're making enquiries there.'

'What about The Comfort Inn, where she was last seen? Doesn't it have CCTV?' asked Hunter.

'Funny you should say that,' answered Mike. 'The camera on the floor covering the room she rented and a camera covering the back of the motel were interfered with. Somebody stuck duct tape over the lenses. We think whoever took Rasa took her through the cleaner's entrance at the back.'

'Wow! Organised, eh? Fair bit of work to do, then?' said Hunter.

Both Grace and Mike nodded.

'How are you doing in your new job? Got anything exciting?' asked Grace.

Hunter swallowed his food. 'Got one interesting job. Don't know if it's going to go anywhere, though. A missing family back in nineteen-ninety-one.' He sought out Grace's eyes. 'The Bannister family? Remember the case?'

Grace momentarily lifted her eyes to the ceiling. 'Hmm, vaguely. I was at training school with you when that happened, and I can remember it being talked about on shift when I got posted to Barnwell. Dad, mum and daughter if I remember, wasn't it?'

Hunter nodded, setting down his knife and fork. 'That's them.'

'But wasn't the talk that the dad killed them both and then drove off somewhere with their bodies and committed suicide?'

'Supposedly, Grace, but they're still officially listed as missing because they haven't found the bodies. I've just picked up the case and started doing a review of it. All I've done at the moment is spoken with David's mum, and she's strongly of the opinion that David wouldn't have harmed them. Especially his daughter. She's very critical of the investigating officer. And you'll never guess who was the detective who investigated it?'

'Go on,' Grace responded.

'None other than St. John-Stevens.'

Grace's mouth dropped open.

'Does he know you're reviewing it?' Mike asked.

Hunter shook his head. 'Not yet he doesn't. I'm going to do all my enquiries before I tell him.'

'He's going to love you if you find anything wrong with his investigation.'

'I'm trusting you to keep schtum 'til I've finished. My career's taken a bad enough nose-dive as it is.'

Grace mimicked zipping her mouth. 'My lips are sealed.' With a grin, she added, 'Keep me posted, won't you?'

'You two will be first to know,' Hunter answered, returning to the remains of his pie, chips and mushy peas.

'By the way, talking about St. John-Stevens, have you heard?' said Grace.

'Heard what?'

'Someone's scraped his car in the car park. He's on the warpath. He's been checking cars for the last hour.'

Hunter swallowed hard. 'Has he found who's responsible?'

'Not as far as I'm aware. He came back to the office in a foul mood. It's a brand new Merc, apparently. He's only just bought it. Threatened if he found out who'd done it, they would be moved back into uniform.'

Hunter lowered his head to suppress a grin. There was no way now that he was going to confess. This had just made his day.

Wearing a grin that only an atom bomb would remove, Hunter stepped back into the office in a very buoyant mood.

Maddie greeted him with, 'Denise Harris rang whilst you were having lunch. She quizzed me about the case and asked why we wanted to talk to her after all this time. I've not said too much, only that we're reviewing the original investigation and speaking with the witnesses who gave statements. I've said you'll call her back.'

'Thanks, Maddie,' Hunter replied, making his way across the room to the kettle. 'Fancy a cuppa?' he asked. He shot a quick glance at Maddie and instantly decided that he was not going to mention who owned the Merc she'd scraped. If she asked any questions, he'd simply tell her that he'd sorted it and leave it at that.

'Love one. Just finished my sandwich.'

'How have you got on with those tasks?' he asked, switching on the kettle and dropping teabags into two mugs.

'Sent off requests for the financial checks and emailed the liaison officer at Work and Pensions. I've also emailed NHS England to see if any of them received any medical care or have visited a GP since nineteen-ninety-one.'

'Nice one, Maddie. I never thought about the NHS. Good work.' Hunter finished making the tea and handed over one of the mugs. 'Fancy a trip to Brid tomorrow? How does that fit in with your daughter? We might not be back on time.'

'I can make arrangements with my mum. She'll pick Libbie up from school and give her her tea. It'd be good to get out of this place, and it's years since I've been to Bridlington.'

'Good, Brid it is, then,' Hunter said, putting down his mug and picking up the phone. He dialled Denise Harris's number and she picked up after only two rings.

Denise Harris asked lots of questions, a couple similar to what Alice had asked, enquiring if they had found the family, and whether they had information as to what had happened to them. Hunter repeated what Maddie had already told her, that he merely wanted to go back through her statement and ask further questions, and bringing the conversation to an end he arranged for him and Maddie to be there just before lunchtime the following day.

After that he returned to the lists of actions he had drawn up. One of them was chasing up forensics. He had bullet-pointed the samples Scenes of Crime had collected from the Bannister home and wanted to check if they still had the blood samples. He was especially interested to see if any swabs had been retained of the stains on the vinyl floor covering the kitchen. He recalled extensive cleaning with bleach had been carried out, corrupting the blood grouping, but he knew that advanced techniques to recover DNA would overcome that issue. As he dialled the number of the forensics evidence manager at Wetherby, he had his fingers crossed that they were still in storage. His call went to voicemail, and softly sighing he gave relevant details of the case to enable a check and left his contact details.

For the last hour he re-read Denise Harris's statement, fixing the main points in his head in preparation for their visit tomorrow, had another look through the case file to see if there were any letters from Alice Bannister — there weren't — and finished by studying the crime scene photographs of the Bannister home. As he stared at the photos taken of the kitchen floor where forensic lighting highlighted the significant blood staining that bleach had failed to remove, it brought to the fore what Alice had said about her son — that David wouldn't do anything like that — and wondered what forces were behind the family's disappearance. There was also another driving force encouraging him to investigate the mystery — St. John-Stevens — and although he knew it was wrong to place his focus on the DCI, it would be good to embarrass the man in return for what he'd done to him.

Hunter and Maddie left the office just before ten, heading out to Bridlington. Traffic wasn't bad, and they covered the seventy-seven miles in under two hours. They found The Seahorse, a large Georgian house among a row of similar terracing, but double-yellow lines at the front and residence-only parking in the surrounding streets forced them to double back into town and park up in a long-stay car park a good quarter of a mile from the B&B.

It had been a few years since Hunter had been here, and he was saddened to see how run-down the resort had become. As they skirted the town centre, he noted the number of pound shops and charity shops there now were in comparison to a decade ago and couldn't help but think of how differently he had seen this seaside town as a young boy. Back then it had seemed thriving and bustling, the ancient town centre full of character.

Coming out of his reverie, he found himself approaching The Seahorse. The house was built over three storeys, in a desirable position facing the promenade, and Hunter recalled from the website that it had ten rooms that started from £75 per night up to £100. It was an imposing building painted cream and white, and as he neared the front door he saw it had a coveted AA award for best B&B. He was already impressed as he pushed open the door. He entered a wide hallway with switchback staircase and original black and white tiled flooring, and yet with white and light grey painted walls and matching décor it had a more contemporary look than traditional flair.

From a doorway to the right, a medium built, auburn-haired woman, dressed in a white blouse and dark blue slacks appeared. She greeted them with a welcoming smile.

'Denise Harris?' Hunter enquired, holding up his ID. Out of the corner of his eye, he saw Maddie doing the same.

'Detective Sergeant Kerr?' she returned and shook his and Maddie's hands. 'We'll go through to the dining room. We don't do lunches, so it's empty.' Denise took them into the room to the left of the hall that looked out over a rectangle of community lawn to the promenade. It had a large double bow window that gave a very good view of the sea. The room was light and airy, and tables were set for two with white linen tablecloths. Looking around the well decorated room that followed the grey and white theme from the hallway, Hunter wasn't surprised it had won an award.

Denise showed them to a table and pulled up a chair from another table. 'Can I get you a drink? Tea, coffee, juice?' she asked.

'Tea would be lovely,' Maddie replied.

'Same for me, thank you,' Hunter responded.

Denise left the room, reappearing five minutes later carrying a laden tea tray. She set down the teapot, milk jug and three cups and stirred the tea in the pot. 'You set me thinking after your phone call yesterday. It's been such a long time since David and Tina and little Amy disappeared. I used to think about it a lot, but I haven't given it a thought for years. Your phone call brought it all back again last night.' Denise put a little milk in the cups and poured three teas.

'It's nineteen years since it happened,' Hunter responded, taking one of the cups and adding a spoon of sugar.

'Nineteen years. My, how time's flown. We left the street two years after that happened. My Alex got his redundancy from the pit and we bought this place. Been here seventeen years now.'

'You've got a nice place,' Maddie responded, slowly roaming her eyes around the room so that Denise could see.

Hunter guessed that Maddie's gentle introductory chat was to put Denise at ease. A relaxed witness was far better than a stressed one. They could focus and remember more.

'I know I asked you yesterday on the phone, but what's made you look at it again after all this time?' Denise enquired.

'Since the success of the Rotherham Shoe Rapist case — you might have seen it all over the news — we've started reviewing all the key undetected cases to see if there are any new leads worth following up. This is one of them. We just want to make sure we haven't missed anything from the original investigation, and the reason we've come to see you is that you were a main witness and we're here to go back through your statement. We're especially interested in the man you saw at the Bannisters' front door the day before they were reported missing. Can you remember that?'

She picked up her cup two-handed, nursing it. Tight-lipped, nodding slowly, she said, 'That detective who was dealing with it came to see me several times about that man. He kept asking me if I could have made a mistake about the day I'd seen him, and checking I was sure that I couldn't recognise him. To be honest, in the end, I got a bit confused with all the questioning. I don't know if I was any use to him or not.'

'It can seem a bit daunting, Denise. As I say, you were an important witness and that detective would be just trying to see if you might remember something else which could have identified who the man was.'

'But I couldn't. I told him that. He had his back to me all the time and his collar was up. I didn't see his face.'

Hunter watched Maddie take her journal from her bag and turn to a fresh page. As she took out her pen, he said, 'It is a long time ago now, Denise, and things won't be that fresh, but would you mind just going back to that day before they all went missing? Just say what you can remember. I won't prompt you about what you put in your statement back then; all I want you to do is just go through that day. Only tell me what you can remember, okay?'

Hunter watched her nod, her gaze fixing his, though it looked as if she was staring right through, and he guessed she was trying to recapture the images from that day before she started to talk.

Bringing back her focus, she said, 'I remember it because I was doing my cleaning and washing that day. That's how I came to see him when I did. I'd done our bedroom and bathroom and then come down to start on the front room. I was doing the hoovering near the window, and that's when I saw him at their door. He was just standing there.'

'You never saw him arrive?' Hunter asked.

Shaking her head, Denise answered, 'No, he was already there. I saw him knock at the door, wait a few seconds, then he looked to the side alleyway and back to the door.'

'So, you saw him for a good few seconds?'

'Yes, it wasn't long. I went back to the hoovering and roughly a minute or so later, I saw he had gone.'

'So you don't know if he went into the Bannister house or if he walked away?'

'No.' She shook her head.

82

'And it wasn't David?'

She shook her head again. 'No. It wasn't David. David had fair hair. This bloke's hair was darkish brown. He had his collar up, hiding his face, but I could see the top of his hair. Anyway, I saw David come home about an hour later, so I know it wasn't David.'

Her comment stirred Hunter up from his chair. 'What? You saw David come home an hour after you saw this man at their front door?'

'Yes. As I said, I was also doing my washing that day and the first load had just finished. I was cleaning the window at the time and was just going to leave it to hang out the washing when I saw David come home. He let himself into the house.'

Hunter had not seen anything in Denise's statement about what she had just said, though he remembered that the summary had made mention of David going home. He said, 'Roughly what time was this?'

'Lunchtime. I hung out the washing, finished cleaning the window and then went in the back for a cuppa and a sandwich. I finished the rest of the washing and did the kitchen. Then Alex came home and we had our tea.'

'So, you didn't see the man or David again that day?'

'No. We didn't go back in the front room until after we'd had our tea. We put the TV on to watch the early evening news, if I remember.'

'Denise, your statement doesn't say anything about what you've just said about seeing David coming home when he did. All it mentions was you seeing that bloke at the front door of the house.'

She threw him a puzzled look. 'Well, I told that detective that. That's what I said about him confusing me. He was asking me if I'd got it wrong and that it was just David I'd seen, but I hadn't. The bloke had darker hair than David, and I saw David dressed in his work clothes that day. This bloke had on a dark overcoat.'

Hunter stroked his chin, thinking through what Denise had just told them. After a few seconds he asked, 'Was there anything else from that day that you told the detective who came to see you?'

'You mean about the man getting into the car in the alley I saw later that night?'

'Man getting into a car?' Hunter jolted upright.

'Yeah. In the alleyway next to Tina and David's house. It was parked by their wall.'

There had been no mention of any man getting into a car in the case file. Hunter said, 'Tell me more about this, Denise?'

'Well, as I say, it wasn't until later that evening, and I didn't see properly because it was starting to get dark and there's no streetlight near the alleyway. It must have been about half-nine-ish. I was just closing the curtains and I saw it parked there. It stuck out because I'd never seen it there before, so I was a bit curious.'

'Did you get its number?'

'I never thought to. It didn't look suspicious, and there was a man just getting into it. I thought it might be someone from David's work, delivering something. David was always doing odd jobs around the house, and sometimes for other folk at weekends. He helped my Alex re-point the back wall and re-build our outhouse.'

'And it definitely wasn't David's car?'

'No. I know David's car. He always parked it at the front of the house. Although he hadn't parked it there that night. He'd left it a few doors away. He'd parked it there when he came home at lunchtime and never moved it.'

'And, you've didn't recognise this car?'

'No. Never seen it before.'

'What about the man getting into it?'

'I couldn't see him properly at all. Like I say, it was getting dark and there're no streetlights near the alley. He was just a figure.'

'Can you tell me exactly what you saw him do from the moment you saw him?'

'Well, as I say, I was just closing the curtains and he was there, getting into the car. I saw him get in and shut the door and then he just sat there. The car didn't move. I told Alex there was someone sat in a car next to David's house, and he came and had a quick look and said it was probably one of David's work mates, and for me not to be nosy, so I closed the curtains. It wasn't there when we went to bed, because I looked out of the window before I closed the bedroom curtains.'

'And there's nothing about this figure you saw getting into the car that stood out, that would help describe who it was?'

Denise seemed to think about it for a few seconds, then shook her head, answering, 'No.'

'And anything about the car that stood out?'

'Other than it was a Peugeot, no.'

'A Peugeot? How do you know that?'

'I didn't know what type it was. It was my Alex who said what it was. He said he could tell because of the badge on the grill.'

'Did you mention this to the detective, or detectives who came?'

'Only one detective came. A young fellow. He took my statement and he took one from Alex. He came back again a couple of weeks later and kept asking me if I could be mistaken about it being David's car and if the man could have been David getting into a different car. In the end I got all confused. After all, David went off in his car, didn't he? That's what the detective said, that they had done all their enquiries, and that they believed David had killed Tina and Amy and driven off with their bodies and committed suicide by driving into a river or lake somewhere. He wrote another statement for me about what I'd seen.'

Hunter spun all this new information around in his head. He knew that interviewing techniques and the taking of statements had changed dramatically over the years to enable a more accurate account to be obtained. But even if there had been doubt as to the identity of the person or the vehicle seen in the alleyway next to the Bannister home the night before they were all reported missing, it still should have been mentioned somewhere. The same went for David Bannister being seen going into his home one hour after the sighting of the stranger at the front door of the house. This was very sloppy detective work that needed correcting. There were leads here that needed following up.

CHAPTER SIX

On his way in to work Hunter stopped off at a convenience store, grabbed some milk and picked up a copy of the local weekly newspaper. The lead story was the abduction of Rasa Katiliene, and on the front page was a picture of her leaving the pub with the heavy-set man she was last seen with. They hadn't named him or found out that he was a convicted sex offender who had also been cleared of the attempted murder of a street worker, but they made it clear that he was sought in connection with Rasa's disappearance and the police were appealing for the public's help. It made for a powerful local story, and Hunter dropped it on the front seat of his car to read later. He had his own headline story to deal with for the next few hours and didn't need the distraction.

The moment Hunter got in to work he boiled the kettle, made himself a drink and settled down to the tasks at hand. Two things were at the top of his list: to see if he could find the first statement of Denise Harris and the statement of her husband Alex, which mentioned the man seen getting into the Peugeot parked in the alleyway beside the Bannister residence; and to see if he could find George Evers, the man who had tipped off David Bannister about the sighting of Tina with one of their work colleagues. He was puzzled why there was no statement from him on file, especially since St. John-Stevens had gone to the trouble of checking his alibi during the time period of the sighting.

Hunter also wanted to know the identity of the work colleague who Tina had allegedly had an affair with, despite Alice telling him that she believed the man had been killed in a motorway accident. Hunter decided he would give the task of finding Denise and Alex Harris's statements to Maddie, and he would try and track down George Evers. He picked up the phone and rang the Intelligence Unit. As he only had a name and no other personal details, his first check was to see if a George Evers from Barnwell was on the system. He was told there were several George Everses listed, though none from Barnwell. Hunter thanked the call-handler and hung up.

His next port of call was the voters list. He got twenty-seven hits countrywide, none from Barnwell. *This isn't starting well*, he told himself, rubbing a hand over his face. He had already learned from a phone call yesterday that the building suppliers George Evers and David had worked for no longer existed; they had been bought out by one of the major retail building suppliers over a decade ago, so that avenue of enquiry was dead. He had just begun printing out the addresses of the twenty-seven George Everses when Maddie strolled into the office. For the first time that week, she didn't appear harassed. In fact, Hunter thought she looked remarkably relaxed and fresh, and she had make-up on.

She put her bag on her desk, slipped off her coat, started up her computer and made her way across to the kettle, announcing, 'I could murder a cuppa.'

'Everything okay this morning?' Hunter asked.

'No dramas, if that's what you mean. And I've set my handbrake this morning,' she replied with a hearty laugh. 'By the way, did you sort out the owner of the Merc? Who does it belong to?'

Hunter gulped. For a split-second he was tempted to tell her a lie, but then dismissed that idea and answered, 'It belongs to the new DCI.' He felt his stomach flip, and swallowing the lump in his throat continued, 'The scratches are hardly noticeable, so unless he asks me point-blank, I'm not going to say anything. And if he does ask, I'll say it was me, like we discussed,' he added, seeking out her eyes. 'I suggest we keep this just between ourselves.'

Maddie met Hunter's gaze. 'Well, as long as it's not going to cause any further problems for you.'

'Further problems?'

'What he's done. Why he's put you here.'

Hunter cocked his head. 'So there are rumours flying around, are there?'

Maddie blushed. 'Well, there are, but if it's any consolation, Sarge…'

'Hunter,' he interjected.

'…Hunter, everyone's on your side. They think it's well out of order, what he's done. And I did check back with Grace, because I wanted to know the truth and I knew she'd tell me.'

'And what did Grace say?'

'She told me exactly what had gone off on Sark, with that guy Billy Wallace, and that the DCI had used Guernsey's investigation to get his revenge because he'd tried to get you suspended over the gang-shooting of one of your informants, and his decision had been overturned by Detective Superintendent Leggate. That's what she said.'

Hunter released a smile. 'All in my favour, thankfully, and I wholeheartedly agree with what she told you. And now that's aired, as long as you can work with me, then I'm sure we'll make a good team.'

'Definitely.'

'Good. Now, has anything come back from all those enquiries you've made?'

'NHS England have replied. The Bannisters haven't accessed any medical services since the sixteenth of July, nineteen-ninety-one. Well, at least under their names, they haven't. I've also made a request for their medical records from the practice they were registered with to see if there's anything in David or Tina's record that might have triggered David's actions,' said Maddie.

'Okay, that's a good start.'

'And no child allowance has been collected for Amy since that date and there have been no financial transactions. Their bank account was closed down in nineteen-ninety-eight following a court request by Alice. The seven-year ruling, as you know.'

Hunter nodded. 'Well, that just about confirms that they are more than likely dead. Which, of course, the file suggests, and all of what you've just said seems to support that conclusion. But what's concerning me is why none of the enquiries you've just done are shown in the file. I know we didn't have the internet back then, but phone calls and requests could still be made for everything you've mentioned. There are just so many gaps. And now we've started reviewing it, those gaps are bugging me. I'm especially concerned about the lack of detail in the summary and the lack of statements for what we now know are important features of the case. It points out that something tragic happened that day because of the family's disappearance, but what it's left out is the sighting of two strangers that could be linked. Sure, it mentions the one at the front door at lunchtime, but it's missed out the one seen getting in a car parked in the alleyway next to their house that same evening. And although there is the possibility that the one at the front door could be David's work colleague that Tina was having an affair with, we know from the file that St. John-Stevens alibied him for that day, so who is the man seen in the evening, and why is he not given a mention in the file? It doesn't make sense. We also have the forensic evidence taken from the house that suggests someone was attacked, and I have to say that's another thing that's puzzling me.'

'What do you mean?'

'Well, SOCO found evidence of significant traces of bloodstaining in the kitchen that had been cleaned with bleach. If we go with the presumption that David did kill his wife and daughter and that the deed was carried out in the kitchen, why bother to clean it up if you are then considering killing yourself? People usually clean up the scene when they want to hide what they've done. And why didn't David leave a note? The majority of suicides do. They usually want to explain why they've done what they've done. The other thing is there's no mention of any bloodstained weapon found at the house. He must have used something.'

'Maybe he took the weapon with him.' Maddie shrugged her shoulders. 'But I see where you're coming from. Why go to the fuss of cleaning up the mess and taking away what you've used to kill someone with, if you're then just going to top yourself? What you're saying, Hunter, is that David wouldn't have needed to do any of that if suicide was on his mind.' She paused a moment and continued, 'But the argument to contradict that is that anyone who's just killed their wife and daughter is not going to be thinking logically. We know from our experience that in the majority of cases, most people who kill simply flip and are not thinking straight.'

'But how many murder suicides have you come across where the killer has cleaned up after themselves before they've committed suicide?'

'None that I know of or have heard of. I'll give you that.'

'None, exactly. For me, if he's gone to all that trouble of cleaning up in the kitchen, it would have been for the reason of covering up his crime. There are two ways of looking at this. The first as the file suggests, that David killed his wife and daughter, drove away their bodies and then he committed suicide by driving into a lake or river. Or the second, that someone else killed them all, cleaned up the mess, and then drove away with their bodies and dumped or buried them and made it appear as if David had flipped, killed his wife and daughter, and then gone off and committed suicide.'

Maddie nodded. 'There's also a third.'

'Oh, what's that?'

'That David did kill them and then cleaned up the mess in order to cover his tracks but whilst he was dumping their bodies, say by driving into a lake or river as suggested, he had an accident and went in with them and drowned.'

'There is that. I never thought of that. It is a possibility, I suppose.'

'It is, but it's also obvious from your second suggestion that you think that someone else killed them.'

Hunter nodded quickly. 'Definitely. Those two strangers spring to mind. Were they two different people or was it the same person?'

'We've raised a lot of issues here, and come to several conclusions as to what happened, but we've only second-hand knowledge of the case. The person who has all these answers is St. John-Stevens. You need to sit down with him and ask him these questions.'

Hunter's face set tight. 'Me? What? And point out to him his sloppy detective work?'

'That's not something you're going to say to his face, are you?' Maddie said with a cynical grin. 'According to the file, the evidence points to David Bannister killing his wife and daughter and then killing himself, but we've uncovered things that challenge that judgment. What we now know is that there is a least one other person, who has not been identified, as far as we know, and he was seen next to the Bannister home on the day they disappeared.'

'I have someone in mind for the stranger.'

Maddie's eyebrows raised. 'Who?'

'Does the name Dylan Wolfe mean anything to you?'

Maddie shook her head.

'Dylan Wolfe raped three woman and stabbed his girlfriend back in nineteen-ninety-one. One of the women he raped died from a heart attack, and he was charged with her manslaughter. She lived only four streets away from the Bannister home, and he committed that rape in November, five months after their disappearance. His other two victims lived less than a mile from the Bannisters as well.'

'I'm presuming this Dylan Wolfe was caught.'

Hunter gave a quick nod. 'Me and Barry Newstead arrested him. He got life.'

'Wasn't he interviewed about other offences he might have committed?'

'Although he initially confessed, he "no commented" all through his interview at the police station. Barry went to see him later in prison, but he just turned his back on him. Wouldn't say a word. Barry told me that he was convinced that Dylan had committed more offences.'

'But his attacks were all on women, you've just said. And they were rapes.'

'There was one attack which wasn't rape. He stabbed his girlfriend. And he tried to stab me when I arrested him. It was only my police radio that saved me. Dylan was not just a rapist but a nasty, violent man.'

'So you think he could be responsible for killing David, Tina and Amy?'

'I think it's something we should look at. I know from first-hand experience what he was capable of back then. And their home was certainly in close proximity with his hunting ground. We haven't bottomed who the stranger was at their front door on the day they disappeared, and we know David came home at lunchtime that day. What if he disturbed Dylan raping Tina? We know there was a disturbance of some kind in the lounge from the smashed photo frame. Let's say David and Dylan fought and Dylan stabs David and kills him in the kitchen. That would account for all the blood. Dylan then tries to clear up the mess and then later that evening brings a car, parks in the alleyway, loads their bodies away and them dumps them all somewhere. Then he comes back for David's car and dumps that. Denise Harris told us she saw a car in the alleyway next to their house that her husband identifies as a Peugeot and not David's, and when me and Barry arrested Dylan he was working in a car dismantlers yard at Kilnhurst, just a mile from their home. The yard would be a great place to hide David's car and then break it up.'

'You've put forward a credible scenario, and given what you've just said about his other victims all being in relatively close proximity, he's certainly worth looking at. But we're going to have to do some leg-work and digging before we go and interview him in prison, especially if he's already refused to talk during one visit.'

'That's why I'm trying to track down George Evers, David's former work colleague, who saw Tina talking with someone in a pub and then saw a man leaving her house. They might be the one and the same person, or they might be two different people. I want to show him Dylan Wolfe's mugshot from when he was arrested back in nineteen-ninety-one and see if he recognises him.' Hunter paused a second, letting Maddie digest his proposal, then he said, 'There's another factor as well that's swaying me away from David killing his wife and daughter.'

Maddie gave him a questioning look. 'What's that?'

'Remember his mum told us that David doted on his daughter and would never have harmed her? Amy had not done anything wrong and she was certainly too young to be a witness. Why would he kill her if he thought the world of her? Surely he would have just left her in the house to be found? Or even took her round to his mum's before killing Tina and killing himself?' Hunter shook his head. 'There are just too many question marks over this case, Maddie.'

'Well, I've already mentioned the DCI is the man you need to speak with to get some of these answers. Why don't you go and talk to him?'

'What, and get my head chewed off because he thinks I'm calling him incompetent? No, I've had enough grief from him for one week. I'm also still waiting for a response from forensics. I'll see what they come up with, and I'll see if I can track down George Evers, and then if there are still gaps, I'll approach him.'

Hunter set to work on tracing George Evers, and of the twenty-seven he had listed, he found phone numbers for fifteen. His plan was to call the one living nearest to Barnwell first and then work his way outwards. If *the* George Evers wasn't among any of these, then for the twelve he hadn't telephone numbers listed for, he would send an email to their nearest police force requesting an officer pay them a visit until he tracked down his man.

Within a quarter of an hour, he had spoken with three — none of whom were the right George Evers — and left a message for a fourth, and then he was distracted by his computer pinging, letting him know he had an incoming email. Glancing at the screen, he saw it was from the forensic lab at Wetherby and he broke away from his task to read it. The news was what he had been hoping for. The Forensics Evidence Manager replied that the department still held all the samples relating to the Bannister case, which included swabs from the kitchen.

Hunter rested his chin on his hand, musing over the news. He knew that testing for DNA was very much in its infancy in 1991 and had only been requested in the most serious of cases back then. The 'missing' category placed on the Bannister casefile hadn't warranted spending on that procedure. Added to that, bleach had been used to clean up the blood, thereby deeming the sample badly corrupted. Since then, however, techniques to separate and harvest samples, not only from blood but other trace evidence such as sweat or saliva, had vastly improved. This advancement meant he could test his theory about Dylan Wolfe's involvement, and the result would either support or destroy it. He had no option now but to go and see St. John-Stevens, as he held the budget to approve the analysis.

Maddie wished him good luck with a cheeky smile, and Hunter made his way along the corridor to the opposite wing where his old office was. He was buzzed through by a detective from the Public Protection Unit, who gave Hunter a cautionary look as he ambled past, heading for St. John-Stevens' office. Hunter saw his silhouette seated at his desk through the green smoked glass panels, and he tapped on the door and went in.

St. John-Stevens raised his head slightly, looking over the top of his glasses. He had a thick document in front of him. 'DS Kerr, to what do I owe this pleasure?'

Sarcastic twat, Hunter thought to himself, biting his lip. He replied, 'Have you got a couple of minutes, boss? I just want to run something past you.' He knew he preferred to be called sir, so Hunter deliberately avoided using the term.

St. John-Stevens removed his glasses and gave him a steady glare. 'Is this going to be a long conversation? I've got a busy schedule today. I have to be at headquarters in three-quarters of an hour for a Gold Meeting. Can this wait?'

'Well, I suppose it can, but I don't think this will take long.'

'Look, if it's about your move to the Cold Case Unit, we've already had this discussion. I've done this because I have your welfare to consider...'

'It's not about that at all,' Hunter interrupted. 'No, I'm quite enjoying myself. It's nothing like I anticipated. I'm getting myself involved in some really juicy cases and Maddie Scott is a lovely detective to work with.' Hunter paused, watching the DCI's face as his reply sunk in. He saw from his look the DCI hadn't been expecting him to say that. He thought he looked quite irked by it, which instantly pleased him. Buoyed, he continued, 'It's one of those cases I've come to see you about. I've just had a reply from the forensics lab after I made a request to see if some blood samples had been retained from a crime scene. I want permission to get those analysed for DNA.' Hunter avoided telling him what the case was.

'What's the case?'

'Well, it's been filed as missing persons presumed dead, but following enquiries, I believe something's happened to them.'

'You mean murder?'

'That's a lead I'm following.'

St. John-Stevens held his glasses between finger and thumb and began rolling them. 'Interesting. Where's the person missing from? Local?'

Hunter nodded, clenching his teeth.

'When was this?'

'Nineteen-ninety-one.' Hunter felt his guts flip.

'Nineteen-ninety-one,' the DCI responded, jerking up. 'I was a temporary detective back then in Barnwell. What are they called?'

No avoiding it now. 'David, Tina and Amy Bannister.'

'The Bannisters?'

'From Wath Road.'

'I know where they were from, DS Kerr. That was my case.'

'Yes, I know that, boss.'

'And don't call me boss. I prefer sir.'

Hunter could see his face was starting to go red.

After a short pause, the DCI said, 'And why are you looking at that case?'

'Because I'm reviewing it.'

'You're doing what?'

Hunter saw that St. John-Stevens' face was now beetroot. He had expected this and hoped to be able to avoid mentioning the case. This was the last thing he needed. He replied, 'I've started reviewing it and found a few leads that I think warrant following up.'

'Leads! Such as?'

'Well, as I say, bloodstains at the scene. You'll probably remember that someone had cleaned up an awful lot of blood in the kitchen with bleach and that it wasn't tested for DNA back then because the technique was still in its infancy.'

'That's because I knew it was from Tina, after David killed her.'

'But we don't know that for definite. The report says the sample was corrupted by the bleach and so it wasn't tested. We can now do a DNA test, and that would prove if it belonged to Tina or if it was from someone else.'

'And who else would it belong to? I carried out that investigation thoroughly and the conclusion was that David had killed his wife and his daughter and then killed himself, dumping himself and his family in one of the lakes or rivers around here.'

'Yes, I've gathered all that from the summary.' Hunter could already see he had agitated the DCI and held back on disclosing the information he had recently unearthed.

'So, are you challenging my decision then, DS Kerr?'

St. John-Stevens' voice was now several pitches higher. Hunter guessed they would be able to hear him in offices back down the corridor. He answered, 'No, I'm not by any means, it's just that a couple of things have cropped up that have given me another angle I'd like to explore.'

'Another angle?' the DCI spluttered. 'And what exactly is this other angle?'

'That they were possibly murdered by someone else, who then cleaned up after them and dumped the bodies and David's car somewhere different to where you believe.'

'What? This stops now, DS Kerr. I spent weeks on that case. I followed up every lead. I interviewed the Bannisters' families, their work colleagues, neighbours and friends and at the end of it I came to a credible decision, based on evidence and not some fanciful idea that you are now presenting. This ends here and now. You do not waste any more valuable time following up a lead that will go nowhere. And as for your request to get the blood sample analysed, I am not wasting my hard-pressed budget on a detective who quite clearly is not up to the mark. I think that incident on Sark has affected you a lot more than you're pretending.' St. John-Stevens leaned forward. 'My instruction to you, DS Kerr, is to file the Bannister case and do no more unnecessary work on it. Do you understand?'

'Yes.'

'Good. And don't let me see or hear any more nonsense from you, or you will leave me no other option but to place you on restricted duties. Do I make myself clear?'

'Very.'

'Good. Now don't waste any more of my time. Some of us have important work to do.'

Inside, Hunter was a seething ball of fury. He could feel his fingernails digging into the palms of his hands as he clenched his fists tighter. At that moment, all he wanted to do was punch St. John-Stevens' lights out for demeaning him. Taking a deep breath, he turned and walked out of the door, trying his best to remain calm.

Hunter stomped back along the corridor to the Cold Case Unit, his head thumping and his heart racing. He needed to let off steam, and when he found the office empty, he slammed the door shut and kicked his waste bin across the room, scattering its contents. For several seconds he looked at the mess, taking steady breaths to calm his anger, and then telling himself he should clean up before Maddie returned, he picked up his dented waste bin, collected the scattered paperwork and returned it to its place beside his desk. It was then he spotted the post-it note stuck to the screen of his computer. It was from Maddie. He pulled it off and read it.

Had to rush off. My mum just rang me. She's got to my house and found water all over the kitchen floor from the washing machine.

Sorry, I'll make up my time tomorrow. Maddie x

As he read it again, Hunter felt his fury subside. Her latest dilemma suddenly put his issues with St. John-Stevens into perspective. He had only been working with Maddie for four days and this was the third calamitous situation she'd had to cope with. He recalled Grace's comment about Maddie being bright but scatty and shook his head. She wasn't scatter-brained by any means, but she certainly had a habit of courting disaster. He screwed her note into a ball and binned it. There was no way he was going to ask her to make up her time with her present circumstances. He was confident she would put in the time when it was needed.

Dropping down onto his seat, he let out a sigh as his eyes zeroed in on the Bannister file. His thoughts drifted back to the conversation he'd just had with St. John-Stevens, and within seconds his rage bubbled to the surface again. *Fuck him!* There was no way he was going to close this case with so many questions unanswered, especially now he had a theory about what had happened and a lead suspect he wanted to talk to.

A plan quickly formed in his head, and although he knew he was risking his career by carrying it out, he knew it was something he needed to do for his own peace of mind. Picking up the case-file, he took the bundle across to the photocopying machine and fed in the paperwork, churning out duplicates. Separating the originals from the copies, he removed the crime scene photographs, reassembled the original file, put a fresh band around the cover and placed it in his out tray with a note attached — *for filing*, just in case St. John-Stevens came spying. Then, compiling a duplicate file, he added the crime scene photos, put a new cover around it and hid it away in his briefcase, setting the lock and placing it out of sight beneath his desk.

Feeling good about what he had done, Hunter fired up his computer and settled back in his chair. His first job was to find which prison Dylan Wolfe was incarcerated in so he could arrange a visit to question him about the Bannisters' disappearance. Whilst he knew that in 1991 his former colleague, Barry Newstead, had attempted to interview him about other crimes he may have committed and Dylan had refused to talk, Hunter hoped that the passage of time might now make him more amenable. He rattled off an email to his contact in probation with the request and then returned to his task of tracking down George Evers.

By 3.30 p.m. Hunter had ticked off his list of Georges living in Yorkshire, speaking personally with six and sending off two emails — one to West Yorkshire and one to East Yorkshire — with a request to visit the remaining two. By that time, his concentration was shot, his focus straying, and deleting his history in case St. John-Stevens came prying, he closed down the computer, picked up his briefcase and left.

CHAPTER SEVEN

Travel-weary, Kristine Oxborough stepped off the train from Kings Cross onto Doncaster station platform eagerly seeking the information board for her connecting train to Barnwell. She found the screen by the exit stairwell and cursed as she saw she had missed her train by three minutes and the next one wasn't for another forty-five minutes. When she saw it was the last one for the night, she was relieved the delay on the train from London hadn't been longer. Now she would at least get home before midnight. It had been a long day. She had been on the go since 5.30 a.m. and she could feel her energy levels almost drained. Dipping into her coat pocket, she took out her phone and rang her husband. He answered on the third ring.

'Darren, you wouldn't believe the journey I've had. It's been a nightmare. There was an accident on the tube so I had to catch the eight o'clock and then some pissed up idiots decided to kick off just after Grantham. We've been stuck at Retford for the best part of an hour waiting for the Transport Police to take them off. I've just missed my connection and the next one gets me in at quarter to twelve.'

'Do you want picking up?' Darren asked.

'No, it'll mean getting the kids up. I'll get a taxi. Hopefully I'll be home at midnight.' Before hanging up, she added, 'I need a drink after the day I've had.'

Her husband let out a short laugh. 'I'll put a bottle of white in the fridge. I'll wait up.'

Kristine hung up and descended the stairs, taking the underpass to platform 3b to catch her train home.

Platforms 3 and 4 were joined, and Kristine found well over a dozen people milling around, some of them in high spirits from a night out. Two couples in particular, who looked to be in their mid-fifties, were especially loud and lively. She decided to give them a wide berth until the train came and plonked herself down on one of the seats, pulling her coat around her as cold air blasted across the platform, sweeping back her hair.

For the next half hour she scrolled through social media, looking up from time to time as the couples were still performing to the crowd. The hangers-on around them were chipping in with a quip here and there that sparked off more drunken antics from the four, and Kristine just hoped that once they were on the train they would settle down. She was in no mood to party after the day she had just had.

Bang on time, the two-carriage train screeched in and once she saw the drunken party all take the front coach, she took one of the back seats in the rear, going back to her social media, keeping her head down. Shuttling away from the station, the engine quickly picked up speed and the ten-minute journey to the first stop seemed to fly by. The revellers departed at the third station, leaving Kristine and a man and woman on the train. They all got off at Barnwell.

Kristine followed them over the footbridge to the front concourse of the station, where she saw that a car was waiting for the couple. As she watched them climb into the back and drive away, she wished it was her. All she wanted now was to kick off her shoes that were pinching her feet, have a couple of glasses of chilled wine and then have a nice hot shower before climbing into bed. As she looked around, she saw the car park was empty. She looked at her watch. It was quarter to midnight and she knew that all the buses had now stopped. Home was a mile away and she didn't fancy walking with her aching feet.

She took out her mobile and phoned the first taxi firm in her contacts. It rang and rang, but no one picked up and so she ended the call and tried the second. It was answered within seconds, but the call handler told her that a taxi couldn't get to her before half-past-midnight, and quickly working out that by that time she could be home, she thanked him, didn't book and ended the call.

Frustrated, Kristine cast her eyes around the deserted car park, told herself she could still be home before quarter past if she put in a spurt and set off, walking fast. By the time she had got to the end of the street, she was blowing hard and clawing for breath, and dropping her pace a fraction she crossed the road and took a shortcut across the fields in the direction of home.

Halfway along the street, it started to rain. It was only a drizzle, but by the time she was halfway across the fields, her hair was plastered to her face, droplets teeming down her cheeks onto her neck and trickling beneath her blouse. Worse still, the field was getting soggy and her shoes were letting in water.

'Bloody hell. What a day. The sooner I'm home, the better,' she mumbled to herself as she came to the exit. It was as she stepped out of the field that she suddenly got an uneasy feeling. As if she was being watched or followed. She quickly looked back, but the steady stream of rain made seeing difficult, and all she could make out were lines of dark trees against an even darker backdrop. She jogged across the narrow lane and headed toward the footpath that skirted past the old chapel, taking her into her estate. *Another ten minutes and I'll be home.* She'd made this journey dozens of times and never thought anything of it, yet tonight she found her surroundings quite eerie. *Probably because of the lateness of the hour and the lack of people around*, she told herself, giving the front of the chapel a quick glance and straining her ears. All she could hear was the rain sizzling through the leaves of the trees lining the path before her.

The last part of her journey was in total darkness, and a cold prickly sensation ran down her back. She didn't like it one bit, and looking quickly around she jogged onto the path. The trees' canopy of autumn leaves offered her some respite from the rain and for that she was grateful, for her coat no longer offered any protection — her blouse was damp and sticking to her. She was relieved when she emerged from the path and could see the road that took her into her estate. She looked both ways and crossed the road.

Kristine had just stepped up onto the kerb when a flash of lightning lit up the sky, making her jump. Her breath caught in her throat as she clutched at her chest. 'Jesus,' she hissed through gritted teeth and set off again. *I can't stand much more of this. Thank God I'm nearly home.* Lowering her head, ready to make a final dash, she picked up the sound of a vehicle coming from her right, and glancing sideways her gaze was met by a blaze of headlights that stung her eyes, causing them to close. She snatched away her head.

For a few seconds, she was blinded. All she could see were flashes behind her eyes and as she blinked them open, she became aware of the car slewing to a halt a few yards away. She turned to see a tall dark shape emerge from the driver's side, skip around to the back where he sprang open the boot and then sprint towards her. It was in that split-second she saw the werewolf mask he was wearing and her heart leapt. She spun quickly, about to make a run for it, but he was on her in a second, one hand around her chest, the other clamped over her mouth. Kristine tried to scream, but it caught in her throat and panic swept in.

A second later, he had yanked her off her feet and was dragging her backwards. It suddenly dawned on her why he had flipped open the boot. She tried to struggle, pulling at his hands, but they were clamped tight. He was restricting her breathing, frightening her. And then, just as he was starting to force her into the boot, she heard the yells.

'Oi!' Quickly followed by, 'What are you doing?'

She thought it sounded like two different voices and she knew it was help arriving. She kicked backwards with her right foot, her heel catching her attacker's shin, her shoe shooting off. The man yelped, loosening his grip, and then he threw her to the ground. Kristine landed heavily, her face and hands both hitting the wet ground at the same moment, the jarring pain immediate. As she franticly pushed herself up, a spray of water whooshed over her, soaking her through. At the same time she could hear a car screeching and skidding away, followed by someone shouting, 'Are you all right love?' and 'Phone the Police.'

CHAPTER EIGHT

The alarm woke Hunter at 6.30 a.m., and by the time he got to work his stomach was churning with hunger, so he headed straight for the canteen. Walking through the doors, he spotted Grace standing at the counter. He sidled up to her.

'I hope that's not a full English you're having,' he said, nudging her.

She turned. 'Oh, morning, Hunter. And what are trying to say about me having a full English? Are you having a dig at my weight?'

Hunter held up his hands in surrender, a large grin lighting up his face. 'I wouldn't dare.'

'And you'd better not. Anyway, you can talk; this is the second time in a week I've seen you in the canteen.'

'That's because it's the only way I can see my old partner now I've been locked away in isolation.'

Grace let out a laugh, and before she could reply, she was handed a plate of poached egg on toast by one of the canteen staff. Offering Hunter a generous smile, she held out her plate of food. 'You'll be pleased to see, I'm still looking after my figure.'

Seeing her beaming smile reminded him how much he missed that greeting in the morning. He responded, 'That looks nice. I haven't had poached egg on toast for ages.' He placed an order for the same and then turned to Grace. 'Have you got ten minutes?'

'Sure, briefing isn't until eight.'

They made their way to a nearby table and as they sat down, Hunter said, 'I just wanted to catch up with you.'

'As long as you're not asking for money,' Grace grinned. 'Do you mind if I eat while we talk?' she added, cutting into her egg.

Hunter watched the yolk of Grace's egg cascade onto the toast, making him feel even more hungry. He said, 'I just wanted to be nosy and see how the case I was pulled away from is going. I haven't seen anything on the news recently.'

'That's because it's not going well. We're more than confident that she's dead now, I'm afraid. We found her mobile, bag, and the hoodie she was last seen wearing in a dumpster at the back of the Comfort Inn. The last contact with her was on the day she was last seen booking in there. No one's seen her since.'

'What about the sex offender from the CCTV?'

'Luke Riley! He walked into Barnwell nick yesterday morning with his solicitor. Me and Mike interviewed him. He admitted he'd been with Rasa on the day of her disappearance and had paid for sex with her in a room at The Comfort Inn. He said it was a regular weekly arrangement they had, but he said he left her there at just after two and then drove to KFC at Parkgate shopping centre for something to eat. He's handed over his phone for us to verify his location, and we've now got an action to check out CCTV there. There's always the possibility he could have killed her and put her in his boot and then drove there, but if he did, he was acting pretty calm, going there for food after he'd just killed her. And, to be honest, I got the feeling he was telling the truth. If he was lying, he was a bloody good actor. However, St. John-Stevens thinks otherwise. He fits the profile and he was the last person to be with her. So, he's still number one suspect.'

'What about the couple from Lithuania who brought her here? Didn't her friend who reported her missing say that the bloke had assaulted her?'

'We did a raid on the house they've been renting in Rotherham. We guess they saw the news and they've buggered off back to Lithuania. Border Control have confirmed that they flew from Manchester the day after it was on the news. We've got Interpol on their case.'

'That's it?'

'For now. Forensics have recovered the duct-tape that had been placed over the security cameras at the motel, but we won't know for a few weeks if there are any prints or DNA on it. And we've not got any other CCTV footage of Rasa leaving the motel or nearby. There are no other cameras overlooking the rear of the place, so if whoever took her did so via the cleaner's entrance, as we believe they did, then we've got nothing.'

'Seems like you're in for the long haul, then?'

Grace nodded and put some egg and toast into her mouth. At the same time, Hunter's breakfast arrived and he started tucking into it.

After a couple of mouthfuls he asked, 'How're you settling in with St. John-Stevens?'

Grace quickly finished chewing and said, 'He's okay. Not as switched on as Dawn, and he can be a bit up his arse, but I've known worse. We all still think it's awful what he's done to you. Anyway, why do you ask?'

Hunter swallowed his piece of toast. 'No particular reason. I had another run-in with him yesterday. I had to disclose I was reviewing that case of his regarding the missing family back in nineteen-ninety-one.' Hunter gave her a summary of his conversation with St. John-Stevens.

When he'd finished, she responded with, 'Oh dear,' pushing aside her empty plate.

'Worse than "oh dear," telling me I had to drop the case. There are so many gaps, Grace. If I'd have dealt with a case like that, I'd expect to be disciplined for neglect of duty.'

'So, what are you going to do? Drop it?'

Hunter stared across the table.

Grace's mouth formed a smirk. 'That look tells me everything. You're not going to, are you?'

'I will, once I'm happy that everything has been done properly. I have someone that I want to eliminate.'

'Oh! Anyone I know?'

'The name Dylan Wolfe ring any bells?'

'That's a blast from the past. The same Dylan Wolfe who stabbed his girlfriend and raped those women back when we were in our probation?'

Hunter nodded. 'One and the same.' Grace had been with Hunter when they had found Dylan Wolfe's third victim unconscious on Barnwell Craggs after she had just been attacked by him back in 1991. He had bashed her with a rock and only survived because a passer-by disturbed him.

'You and Barry arrested him, didn't you?' It was a rhetorical question. She added, 'Didn't he get life?'

Hunter nodded. 'I'm going to arrange to visit him in prison and interview him. I just want to satisfy myself that he wasn't involved. There's also one other witness at least to talk to.'

'Well, I wish you luck. And I hope St. John-Stevens doesn't find out.'

Hunter finished his breakfast. 'I'll deny all knowledge,' he said, scraping back his chair. 'It was good to catch up, Grace. We should do this more often.'

Maddie was in the office shortly before 8 a.m., dumping her coat and bag on her desk and then turning on her computer. 'Good morning,' she said brightly, picking up Hunter's dirty mug. 'Fancy a cup of tea?'

Hunter watched her striding towards the kettle. 'Get your washing machine sorted out?'

She turned with a guilty look on her face. 'Sorry about that. The hose split at the back. An engineer's coming this morning to sort it. I've got my mum waiting in for him.' She turned on the kettle and shuffled together two clean mugs. 'You must wonder what on earth you've got for a partner. I bet Grace didn't give you this much trouble?'

Hunter returned a warm smile. 'You've had a tough week, Maddie. We all have those. Next week'll be different, I'm sure.'

'Bloody well hope so,' she replied, crossing her fingers. 'What did you get up to after I'd gone? Dare I ask how your meeting went with the DCI?'

'It didn't go well. He told me to drop the case.'

'What, ordered you to?' Without waiting for an answer, she added, 'And the second question is, are you?'

'I've bundled up the file and it's in my out tray.' Hunter decided not to tell Maddie about photocopying the file. He had only been working with her a week and didn't know enough about her to give her his trust. He continued, 'I'm just going to finish off my enquiry with George Evers to satisfy myself. And I also want to satisfy myself about Dylan Wolfe. We've got a family who disappeared in nineteen-ninety-one who lived four streets away from a victim of a serial rapist-cum-killer, and although the circumstances and MO of this crime are different to the ones Dylan Wolfe was convicted of, who's to say he wasn't disturbed by Tina's husband while he was attacking her?

I'm still not happy with the cleaned-up bloodstains in the kitchen. That's bugging me.'

'That's fine with me,' Maddie said, handing Hunter his hot drink. 'As long as you don't implicate me. I can get myself in enough trouble as it is, without any help, thank you.' While scrolling through her emails, she lifted her eyes. 'Speaking of the name Wolfe — have you heard about the attack on that woman last night?'

Hunter shook his head. 'No.'

'Apparently a man wearing a werewolf mask tried to abduct a woman coming from the railway station. Pulled up in his car and got the boot open. He was trying to drag her in there when two blokes coming from the pub disturbed him and he got away. If it hadn't been for them, who knows what would have happened to her? Terrible, isn't it? She must have been absolutely petrified. What's the world coming to, eh?'

'Has that been on the radio this morning?'

'No, I've just been talking to one of my colleagues in CID. They've got the job.'

'Well, I hope they catch him.'

'Definitely.' Maddie returned to her screen, clicking rapidly on her mouse. After a few minutes, she exclaimed, 'Goodness me!'

Hunter looked across.

'You will never guess what I've just received!'

'I'm not a mind-reader, Maddie.'

She smirked and said, 'Only got an email from the practice the Bannisters were registered with. They've sent me PDFs of their records. I've just opened up Tina's, and there's something here we didn't know.'

'Oh yes? Well, spit it out then, Maddie.'

'She was pregnant. Six weeks pregnant, according to her notes. She went to see her GP just a few weeks before she disappeared to ask him for an abortion.' Lifting her eyebrows, she continued, 'She disclosed the baby wasn't her husband's.'

'What?'

Maddie nodded. 'That's what's here on her notes.'

'When was this?' Hunter watched Maddie's eyes slowly moving down the screen.

After a few seconds, she looked up. 'According to the date, it would have been two days before the police attended their home following their domestic.'

'That's why they rowed? David either found out or she confessed and he told his mother something different.'

Maddie nodded. 'It would be a good bet.'

'Crikey, Maddie. And that now makes it more imperative that I trace George Evers to see if we can find out who the stranger was that he saw Tina talking to in the pub. And it also throws a different light on the stranger that Denise Harris saw at the front door of their house on the day they all disappeared. Have I got this all wrong about Dylan Wolfe? Could it have been the father of Tina's unborn baby?' Hunter rapped his fingers on the desk. 'We can't ignore this, Maddie, despite what St. John-Stevens says. This information is far too important.' After a short pause, Hunter added, 'I just can't understand why St. John-Stevens wouldn't have done these enquiries in the first place. To me, this is just basic stuff.'

Hunter continued to work on tracing George Evers. After having no luck with those listed as living in West Yorkshire, he moved across the border into Lancashire and on his second telephone call he found him. George was now retired, and Hunter quickly learned that following the buy-out of Barnwell

Building Supplies, George had initially worked at the new company's nearest base in Barnsley, and after spending two years there he'd managed to swing a transfer to their Preston branch, where he originally hailed from. George was still living in Preston, near the army barracks. Once Hunter told him the purpose of his call — that he was reviewing the disappearance of the Bannisters — and that he wanted to talk with him about the unknown man he saw talking to Tina, George was more than happy to oblige. Hunter arranged to drive across straight away, taking his postcode, before ending the call.

'Result,' he called, looking across at Maddie. 'Found George Evers living in Preston. How do you fancy going to talk with him? It's less than a two-hour run.'

'Right now?' Maddie replied, looking up from her computer.

'No time like the present. And the quicker I see him, the quicker I can sort the case-file.' Hunter paused, holding Maddie's gaze. 'Unless you're worried about St. John-Stevens finding out.'

'I'll just tell him you ordered me,' she grinned, turning off her computer and grabbing her coat and bag. 'I'll just ask my mum to pick up Libbie, in case we don't get back in time.'

While Maddie called her mum, Hunter went into Dylan Wolfe's intelligence file to see what photos they had of him; for his own clarification, he wanted to see if the stranger George had seen Tina talking with could have been Dylan, and if not, then at least he could rule him out of the investigation. There were only two photos of him, front and side view head-and-shoulders shots, which Hunter instantly recognised as the ones that had been taken the day after his arrest in 1991, after he had been brought back from the hospital.

As Hunter studied Dylan's sewn-up, bruised face, it triggered the event in his memory; he and Barry had found him in a borrowed car, hiding out in the grounds of the old coking plant at Manvers. He'd tried to escape but had lost control of the car, crashing it upside down in a ditch. His face had hit the windscreen, busting it up pretty badly. Hunter had been first to his aid, finding him hanging by his seatbelt, crying out, 'I'm going to die.' He wasn't, but he had broken ribs and his face was badly smashed up, requiring a lot of sutures. He had been twenty-five back then, and Hunter wondered what he looked like now. Would he be badly scarred or would his injuries be hardly noticeable? Hunter printed off an A5 copy of the mugshot, clipped it onto the front of the Bannisters' duplicate file and slid it into his briefcase.

They reached Preston a good half hour before midday. George Evers' terraced cottage was just a few streets from the army barracks, and they found a parking space close to his house.

George answered the door within seconds. He was a stout man of average height with a thick head of iron-grey hair and a ruddy complexion. Hunter and Maddie showed him their IDs and he took them into his lounge, where he had a fire burning. Feeling its heat, Hunter realised why George's face was so red.

'The wife's just nipped out to the shops. We've run out of milk, I'm afraid, so I can't offer you a drink,' George said, relaxing into an armchair and offering them the sofa.

'That's okay, Mr Evers; if I drink any more tea, I'll need more than a few toilet breaks on the way back. Anyway, I don't think this will take too long. We only want to ask you a few questions,' Hunter replied, taking up his offer of the sofa. Maddie sat beside him.

Going through the same preamble he did with Alice Bannister and Denise Harris, he explained the nature of their enquiries and the reason behind them and continued, 'We have on record, George, that it was you who told David Bannister that you suspected Tina was involved in a liaison with one of your work colleagues. Is that right?'

George was silent for a moment, then he said, 'I don't want to speak ill of the dead, Detectives, but everyone knew what Tina was like. I felt sorry for David, the way she used to muck around like she did, because he was a lovely fella. Worked so hard and doted on his daughter. Always talking about her, he was. When I heard the rumours that Terry was sniffing round Tina and then saw him going into the house that day while he was on his delivery round, I thought I should tell David about it. It just wasn't right.'

'Can I just stop you there, George?' Hunter interjected, leaning forward. 'You've just mentioned the name Terry there.'

George nodded. 'Yes. Terry Whitehead.'

'That's the name of the colleague from your work who was having an affair with Tina?'

'Well, I wouldn't describe it as an affair. My understanding is he was just calling in for sex. That's what Tina was like. Or so I understood from the rumours I heard.'

'Did you give the detective who spoke to you back in nineteen-ninety-one Terry's name?'

For a few seconds George returned a perplexed look. He answered, 'Yes. I spoke to one of them on the phone when it was on the news that they'd disappeared. I told them what I've just told you, and someone came out and took a statement from me.'

'I'm sorry about this, George, but your statement's not in my file. It must have got mislaid. This is the first time I've heard Terry Whitehead's name mentioned. I've spoken with David's mother and she told me that she'd been told that someone from David's work had been involved with Tina, but she hadn't been told his name. All she was able to tell me was that she believed this man had been killed in an accident about five years ago.'

George gave a quick nod. 'Aye, that was Terry. Once it all came out about what had been going off between him and Tina, no one would have anything to do with him and he left. He went to work as a lorry driver for a firm in Rotherham, as far as I recall. And, like you've just said, I also heard he'd been killed in a motorway pile-up a few years ago now.'

'I'm sorry to have to ask you all these questions, George, but as I say this is the first I've heard all this, so if you wouldn't mind I'd like to go back over what you can remember and what you told the police when you made a statement.'

George shrugged his shoulders. 'Sure, if it'll help. But there isn't that much to say. As I say, it was just rumour I heard at first, and if I hadn't had to make that emergency delivery that morning, I would never have seen Terry going into their house.'

'So, you only saw this Terry Whitehead fellow going into Tina and David's house on the one occasion?'

George gave a sharp nod. 'Yes. And I only saw him then because one of our regular customers needed some urgent supplies, and the gaffer asked me to take the delivery because our three delivery drivers had gone out. It was to a builder who had his yard a few streets away from David's house. I saw our lorry first and wondered what it was doing there, and then when I saw Terry going into the house, I knew the rumours were true. I remember thinking that it was a good job the gaffer hadn't asked David to make the emergency delivery because there'd have been hell to pay for Terry. I didn't tell David straight away about what I'd seen. I had a word with the missus first about it, and she asked how I would feel if it were me, and so I told him a couple of days later. I know him and Terry had words, and I know he had words with Tina about it.'

'Yes, we know about that. The police were called.'

George screwed up his face. 'That's news to me. I know they were called when David and Tina had a row about the second man I saw her with.'

'A second man?' Hunter gave George a puzzled look.

'Yes. A couple of months later I happened to call in at The Tavern at lunchtime, and she was in the snug with a young man. They didn't see me, and after what had gone off with Terry I didn't want to get into a scene with Tina, so I skedaddled straight out of there.'

'And you told the detective investigating their disappearance that?'

'Yes, when he came to take my statement.'

'Did you know this man Tina was with, in the pub?'

George shook his head. 'Like I told the detective, I'd never seen him before. Looked to be a businessman of some sort.'

'Why do you say that, George?'

'The way he was dressed. He was in a shirt and tie and had this posh overcoat on. Like one of them Crombie's.'

'Did you get a good look at him?'

'Not really. As I say, as soon as I saw them together, I left. He was sort of side-on. All I can remember is that he looked to be roughly mid-to-late twenties, clean-shaven, with short dark hair.'

'And when you say together — I know it was only a matter of seconds you saw them, but could it have been a business meeting of some sort, or did you have the impression it was something more intimate?'

'Well, she had this serious look on her face but she was leaning in to him, as if they were having this hushed conversation. And she had her hand on his leg, so I thought, "Aye, aye, there's something going on again here between him and Tina." As I say, I didn't want to get involved, so I left. I told David the next day I'd seen Tina with the bloke, but I didn't say what I'd seen, you know, her hand on his leg. That was on the Friday when I told him, and on the Monday, when he'd come into work, he told me the police had come out because he and Tina had rowed over what I'd seen. She said I was telling lies. I told him I'd definitely seen her with him, and I know he believed me.'

'And you say this was a few months after you'd seen Terry Whitehead going into her house?'

George nodded. 'Two months at least, from what I recall. It was just a couple of weeks before they all disappeared.'

'I know it's a long time ago, George, but if you saw a photo of this man, showing how he looked back in nineteen-ninety-one, do you think you would be able to recognise him?'

George gave a quick shrug. 'It was a long time ago, and as I say I only saw him for a few seconds, and his face was sort of side-on, but I can try.'

Hunter took out the photographs of Dylan Wolfe from his briefcase and showed them to George. 'Do you think he looked like this?'

He gave a short laugh and responded with, 'He looks like he's been in the wars.' Then, studying them for the best part of a minute, he handed them back to Hunter, commenting, 'The age looks about right, but the hair's not right. I think the guy I saw Tina with had darker hair. And the nose doesn't look right either. I'm sorry.'

Feeling disappointed there was no recognition of Dylan Wolfe, Hunter replied, 'Don't apologise, George. Now, if you wouldn't mind, I'd like to take another statement from you about what you've told me.'

For the next hour, Hunter wrote down George's reflections on his sightings and circumstances surrounding his former work colleague, Terry Whitehead, and the stranger he had seen with Tina in the Tavern pub in the weeks prior to the family's disappearances. When he had finished, Hunter couldn't help but think that the description of the stranger in the pub, especially the mention of the dark hair and dark overcoat, had some similarity with the man Denise Harris had seen at the front door of the Bannister home on the day of their disappearance.

Saying goodbye and thanking George, Hunter made his way back to the car, deep in thought. A shadow moved through his mind. Something was disturbing him. Something about this whole investigation didn't feel right. Too many things that he felt were important had been missed out, or ignored. He needed to think carefully about his next steps.

CHAPTER NINE

The weather forecaster last night had said temperatures were going to plummet overnight and that there would be a sharp frost. *She wasn't wrong*, Hunter thought to himself, seeing his car covered in a patina of white as he left the house, shivering as he popped the locks. Climbing in, the coldness of the leather seats forced another shiver through his body, and quickly firing up the engine, he cranked up the heater to max and switched on the front and rear demisters. Watching the windscreen slowly clear, he switched radio channels to take in the local seven a.m. news. It was just starting.

'In the news this morning, police are hunting a man who attacked a thirty-eight-year-old woman the night before last. They say a man in dark clothing and wearing a werewolf mask tried to drag her into his car just before midnight but was scared off by two men who heard her screams and came to her aid. Police are warning women out on their own at night to be extremely vigilant and to report anything suspicious on 101… Other news this hour. Detectives are no nearer to discovering the whereabouts of missing Rasa Katiliene, who disappeared over two weeks ago…'

And I'm trying to discover the whereabouts of a whole missing family who disappeared nineteen years ago, Hunter told himself, reversing off the drive.

He drove into work steadily, his thoughts drifting from what he had learned yesterday to his next move. Visiting George Evers had raised new lines of enquiry that he simply couldn't ignore, even though St. John-Stevens was telling him to drop the case. *Is he for real?* The man's whole investigation had been shambolic. He knew St. John-Stevens would have had very little training as a detective when he took on this case, but any cop with an ounce of common sense could see that things he had been told warranted further investigation. Instead, it looked as though he had just swept them under the carpet. Had he just come up with a theory as to what had happened and run with it, or had it just been too complicated a job for him to deal with? *Well, I'm not filing it until I'm happy with it, so you can put that in your pipe and smoke it, St. John Stevens.*

By the time Hunter got to work, he was resolute about his next steps. He was going to talk to his former colleague and uniform mentor Roger Mills, now a police pensioner, who had been first at the scene when Alice Bannister had reported her family missing. Roger would be able to guide him through the crime scene photos and recount what he had seen and found that day. He might even be able to give him answers to some of the questions he had about St. John-Stevens' enquiry.

As he drove into the office car park, Hunter saw that there were still lots of spaces, and having already decided he was going to be in and out as quickly as possible, he chose a space close to reception. Leaving his briefcase tucked out of sight and locking his car, he nipped up the stairs to the office, did a quick computer check to see if Roger was still living at the same address as the one he had retired to, and leaving Maddie a note saying that he should be in just after nine, he jogged back down the stairs to the car park and headed out. Slowing for the barrier, he spotted St. John-Stevens' Mercedes coming towards him, and avoiding eye-contact, he increased his speed, checking his mirrors once he had passed to make sure that the DCI hadn't turned to follow. He headed off to the Dearne Parkway, where he took the route to the village of Elsecar, where Roger had a bungalow.

As Hunter pulled up outside, he saw the lounge light blazing and a car on the drive covered in frost. *He's up and in*, he told himself, grabbing his briefcase and opening the door. He'd thought he would be. He knew from their past working together that Roger was an early riser — a habit from his previous career as a soldier. Hunter made his way down the drive and rapped on the side door. Roger appeared within a few seconds, throwing open the door.

Looking surprised, he said, 'Hunter! Long time, no see.'

Hunter knew that Roger was in his late fifties now, but he could see he still hadn't lost any of his military bearing. Ramrod straight in the doorway, Hunter could see he'd put on a few pounds around the waist, but his shoulders were still broad and he looked the picture of health with a tan.

'To what do I owe this pleasure? You haven't come to spoil my retirement and tell me that one of the scrotes I've had dealings with wants to make a complaint after all these years, have you?' he added.

Hunter smiled. 'No, nothing like that, Roger. I've come to pick your brains.'

Standing to one side and ushering him in, Roger replied, 'Not as sharp as they used to be, I'm afraid, but come in. I'll stick the kettle on.'

The warmth of Roger's kitchen was very welcoming. Hunter could smell cooking and saw a frying pan on the hob with bacon on the go.

Roger caught his eye. 'I'm just making myself a bacon butty. I'll stick some more rashers on.'

'That's all right, Roger. I don't want to keep you too long,' Hunter replied, even though his stomach was telling him different.

'Nonsense. I've got all the time in the world. The wife's gone to work, and it'll be nice to catch up. I hardly see anyone these days.'

Hunter slipped off his coat. 'Well, if it's not too much trouble for you, that'll be greatly appreciated. I only had time for a cuppa this morning.'

'Go through to the lounge. I'll make us a butty and a brew, and you can fill me in on what you want.'

Hunter rested his coat over the back of the sofa and plonked himself down, opening his briefcase and taking out the duplicate Bannister file. And, while listening to Roger shifting around in the kitchen, he picked out the crime scene photographs, separating them in preparation for their discussion.

Within ten minutes Roger stepped into the lounge, handing Hunter a bacon sandwich on a plate and a mug of steaming tea, saying, 'Get that down yer.'

For the next fifteen minutes, in-between mouthfuls, Hunter and Roger caught up with what they had been both up to since Roger had retired. Hunter told him about his transfer from CID into the Major Investigation Team, some of the cases he had been involved in and what had happened most recently on Sark. In return, Roger filled Hunter in on what he had been up to since his retirement five years ago. Hunter learned that he had initially taken a part-time job as a driver for Tesco but quickly got fed up with the mundane work. After two years of working for a firm fitting electronic trackers on farm plant equipment, he'd decided to retire completely, using most of his lump sum from his pension to buy a one-bedroom apartment in Tenerife, where he and his wife intended on living over the winter period when she retired next summer. 'That's where we've just come back from. We've spent the last month decorating and refurbishing the place,' Roger added. He confessed he hadn't heard about the Sark incident, saying, 'Well, it sounds as though Billy Wallace won't be missed, and it'll be one less for the tax-payer to have to fund.'

'I wish it was as simple as that. Guernsey police are conducting an investigation.'

'But it sounds to me as if you have nothing to worry about. He tried to kill you all and you acted in self-defence. Section three of the Criminal Law Act and all that, eh?'

'There are other forces at play as well, though, Roger, that are making things difficult for me.' Hunter told him about DCI St. John-Stevens and his enforced transfer to the Cold Case Unit.

'The same St. John-Stevens who was in fast-track and did a short stint as a detective at Barnwell?'

'One and the same,' nodded Hunter. 'That's why I've come to see you. I'm reviewing one of his cases that appears to be a bit of a botched job as far as an investigation goes, so I want to pick your brains about it to see if I can clear up some of the things that are worrying me.'

Roger screwed up his face in bemusement. 'An investigation with St. John-Stevens? I never worked on anything with him. He wasn't at Barnwell for that long a time as I recollect.'

'The Bannister case ring any bells?' Hunter finished the last mouthful of his bacon sandwich and rested his empty plate on the arm of the sofa. 'That was lovely, by the way,' he added, wiping a crumb from the side of his mouth with the back of his hand.

'The family who disappeared?'

Hunter nodded sharply. 'That's them. I've spoken with David Bannister's mum, Alice, who told me she was the one who reported them missing and you were the first person at

126

the scene. I know from the file that was your only role in the matter, so I just want your first-hand experiences of that day, if you can remember.'

Putting his own empty plate to one side, Roger replied, 'Crikey, Hunter, you're taking me back here. I can remember the job, but I can't remember dates or anything.'

'I can help you there, Roger. It was nineteen-ninety-one. It was in July that year. I came out of training school at the beginning of October, and you were my tutor. We dealt with the body of June Waring, who suffocated whilst being raped by Dylan Wolfe, that year. Remember?'

Roger slowly dipped his head. 'Got it. I've fixed it in my head now,' he said. 'What do you want to know?'

'Just what you remember about going to the house. What you saw. What you did. That sort of thing. I'll ask you questions from time to time.'

'Okay.' Roger lowered his eyes for a moment. 'I remember our shift was on afters and we'd only just finished briefing when the call came in. It wasn't a priority one, but I do remember it quite clearly because it was a whole family being reported as missing. When I got to the Bannister home, Alice was in a bit of a state. She said she'd called round, and found both doors unlocked and no one in, and that she'd rung her son's works and been told he'd not gone in that morning. She said that his car wasn't parked on the street where it normally was. She then told me she didn't know if there'd been an accident or if they'd been burgled, because she'd found signs of a disturbance in the lounge.'

'Can I just stop you there, Roger? You said that Alice told you that the doors were unlocked. Were they open?'

'No. I asked that same question when Alice told me. She said she'd knocked on the front door first, and when there hadn't been any answer, she'd tried the door handle and the door was unlocked, so she'd called out, expecting her daughter-in-law to be there with her granddaughter. When she'd got no answer, she'd let herself in, gone along the hallway into the kitchen, and found the back door unlocked, so she'd opened it and looked into the yard. When she'd seen they weren't there, she'd gone upstairs, checked the two bedrooms and bathroom and found the house empty, and thinking that her daughter-in-law might have just nipped round to the neighbours or to the local shop, she'd gone into the lounge to wait for her, and that's when she found the table overturned, the photo frame smashed and what she believed to be blood on the hearth. She had then rung the hospital to see if any of the family had been treated or admitted, but they hadn't, and that's when she had rung us.'

'That's very much the same as what Alice told me,' Hunter responded. He picked out a crime scene photograph of the lounge and showed it to Roger. 'Is this what you saw in the lounge?'

Roger held the photo, cast his eyes over it for several seconds and handed it back to Hunter. 'Yes. As you can see, a small side table's been overturned and the hearth rug's all crumpled. That photograph frame you see smashed on the floor had apparently been on the mantelpiece according to Alice, and as you can just make out, there are splashes of blood on the hearth. It wasn't a lot, but it led me to believe that something had happened. A struggle or a fight of some sort. What you can't see in that photo is a number of cigarette butts and cigarette ash on the carpet to the left-hand side of the hearth. Alice told me that David's wife occasionally smoked and used an ash tray that was on the mantelpiece. That was gone. She described it to me as one of those green onyx ones that were popular at the time. I instantly got a bad feeling, what with the bloodstains on the fireplace, that it had been used as a weapon. Alice also showed me where the house phone had been ripped from its socket. That's when I asked for CID attendance. Before they got there, I searched the entire house, thinking I might find bodies. I also looked outside in the yard and outhouse. It was whilst going through the kitchen I smelt the bleach and saw bits of staining on the floor. I later learned from SOCO that bleach had been used to clean up blood from the kitchen floor.'

The information about the ash tray was new to Hunter. Nothing about that was in the covering report, or in any of the statements in the file. He asked, 'And St. John-Stevens joined you?'

'Yes, him and Keith Saker. Remember him?' Roger answered, his mouth breaking into a cynical smile.

Hunter certainly did remember Keith Saker. Grace had had a run-in with the bombastic, overweight detective when they had been probationers; she had thrown two mugs of tea over him one evening following his sexist behaviour towards her. It had resulted in her being the talk of the station and Keith Saker never living it down.

Hunter broke into a smile himself. 'That's a blast from the past. I'll never forget Grace putting him in his place that night he made those comments to her.'

'And richly deserved as well. He was an arrogant twat. She did us a great favour that night. Many of us had wanted to do something like that to him over the years. He treated uniform as if they were incompetent and he was the best thing since sliced bread, and yet he was nothing but a lazy arse who lived on his past reputation because of a couple of good jobs he'd been involved in. Everybody applauded her actions that night, even the gaffers, but no one told her that because she was in her probation.' Roger paused, giving Hunter a look of sad reflection. 'I'm told he's in a bad way now. He's got dementia and is in a nursing home.' Pausing again, he continued, 'He was an arsehole all right, but he doesn't deserve that.'

Hunter agreed with a curt nod, and after a few seconds of silence he said, 'So, just going back to when you were at the Bannisters' home, before CID came, was there anything else you did, or anything you can remember about the scene?'

'Besides what I've already told you about what I saw at the scene, there were other things that made me think something bad had happened to them, and that the family just hadn't upped sticks and left. Firstly, the wife's bag and purse were on the side in the kitchen. Alice pointed that out to me. There was also some money in a drawer. Thirty quid, if I remember. Not a lot, but something you wouldn't leave. And I found David's wallet in his bedside cabinet with a few quid in it and his bank card and a credit card. And remember, I said the back doors were unlocked. Well, the keys were in the door, on the inside. And, of course, there was a strong smell of bleach and bit of staining on the kitchen floor.'

'I've seen mention of the bleach in the file, and I know SOCO did tests and said that a fair amount of blood had been cleaned up with bleach.'

'The smell was really noticeable, but the strange thing was SOCO never found an empty bottle. Whoever cleaned it up took away the bottle.'

Hunter mulled Roger's response over for a couple of seconds and said, 'I've been told the blood was more than likely Tina's?'

'The wife's?'

Hunter nodded.

'The names have slipped my mind after all this time. I remember Alice, the mum, because I spent quite a bit of time talking with her, and I also remember David's because Alice flipped when I asked her if she knew if he had been depressed or suicidal lately. She asked me what I was insinuating, and told me all about her daughter-in-law's fancy men and what he'd had to put up with since they'd been married. I had to calm her down. In fact, I was glad when CID turned up and my role was over. And more so, I couldn't wait to get out of there when I saw who it was turning up. I didn't have much time for either of them. St. John-Stevens was another arrogant prick. More degrees than a right angle but not an ounce of common sense, and he spoke to you like a piece of shit.'

'Nothing's changed,' Hunter responded, thinking out loud. Following a short pause, he asked, 'Anything else, Roger?'

'There was one other thing. And it set me to thinking that there could have been a visitor there just before their disappearance.'

The stranger Denise Harris had seen at the front door? 'Oh yes, what was that, Roger?'

Roger picked out one of the crime scene photos and turned it so Hunter could view it the right way up. It was a wide-angle shot of the Bannisters' lounge, taking most of the room in. Roger jabbed a finger at the coffee table next to the sofa. On it was a single cup. 'That cup was half full with coffee. It was cold and had a film on it. Next to it was a ring stain where another cup had been. And in the kitchen, I found a cup on the draining-board, which looked as though it had been washed. SOCO arrived just before I left, so I told them about it and they dusted it for prints, but there were none. They said it had been washed with bleach, just like the floor. It was clean as a whistle.'

'Did St. John-Stevens and Keith Saker know all this?'

Roger nodded. 'Yes, they were there. I said to them that it looked like someone was covering up something bad that had happened there. And I asked them if they thought the family had maybe been killed or abducted or something like that, and that arrogant little shit St. John-Stevens said to me, "You should know it's too early to come to conclusions like that, officer. There are a lot of enquiries still to be made by us detectives. Then we'll make that decision." I could have knocked his fucking head off his shoulders; he was only a bloody CID aide with five years in.'

Hunter let out a sharp laugh. 'Like I say about him, Roger — nothing's changed. Except he's up a few ranks now.' Hunter studied the photo of the cup on the coffee table. Although he'd viewed the photographs several times, he hadn't studied the cup on the table with any scrutiny before. Lifting his eyes, he said, 'Anything else, Roger?'

'Not that I remember in the house. There was the fact that David's car had gone. He usually parked it just outside the house, but it wasn't there and we never found the keys for it. The day after the family were all circulated as missing, a car the same make as David's was found burned out in an old limestone quarry, near Sprotbrough, but we were later told it wasn't his, and as you know the final theory was that David had killed his wife and child during a row and then committed suicide by driving into a river or something.'

'That's what it suggests in the file,' Hunter answered in a low voice.

Roger studied Hunter a moment. 'The way you say that is the same way I felt when I was at the house. I was convinced something bad had happened in that house and that whoever had done it had started covering up their crime and then been disturbed. I thought maybe it had been Alice who disturbed them when she turned up, especially with the doors being unlocked and the keys still in the back door. Maybe they nipped over the back wall into the alleyway. I did some looking around and most of the shift were turned out to do a local search of outbuildings and the nearby industrial estate, but we didn't find anything. I did have a quiet word with Keith Saker a couple of days later, and he said that they still had a lot of enquiries to do and had a number of theories and they were looking into all of them. I was surprised when I heard that it was believed David had killed his wife and daughter and then topped himself.'

'Having not been involved in the original investigation, I can't say how they came to the decision that made them close the enquiry so early, but what I can say is that while I've been reviewing it, there have been so many things I've found out that I feel should have been mentioned in the final report. I can't think why they have been left out or not followed up.'

'Like what?'

'Well, for starters, a lot of what you've just told me isn't in the report.' Hunter then told him of the information that George Evers had given them and also Denise Harris's sighting of two strangers the day before they were reported missing.

Roger scrunched his eyes. 'It does make you wonder why none of that was mentioned, doesn't it? Are you thinking it's some kind of cover up?'

'I can't see what they would want to cover up or why. Like I said earlier, I'm thinking at the moment that it's just a botched job. St. John-Stevens wasn't experienced enough at the time to conduct an investigation of that type, and Keith Saker was just an idle good-for-nothing who would sooner be propping up the police bar than doing his job. I'll tell you what I did initially think. That the stranger Denise Harris saw at the front door and then later getting into the car in the alleyway next to the Bannisters' could have been Dylan Wolfe, because his first victim only lived a few streets away as you recall. But when I showed George Evers the mugshot of him from nineteen-ninety-one, he didn't recognise him.'

'And you've no idea who those two men are?'

'No. Never been identified as far as I'm aware. And as far as the report goes, it doesn't look as though St. John-Stevens has done anything to find out who they were. Under normal circumstances I would just ask him straight out, but as he's told me to drop the case, I've got to do some digging around without him finding out, before I decide what to do with the review.'

'Well, good luck, Hunter. Sorry I couldn't help you.'

'You've been a great help, Roger. And it's also been good catching up with you and seeing you look so well. I'm envious. I'm just hoping me and Beth will be as comfortable and have the time you have when I retire.'

Roger pushed himself up from his chair. 'Don't wish your life away, Hunter.' He picked Hunter's plate up from the arm of the sofa and slotted it on top of his own. 'And let me know how you get on if you find out anything. I would be interested to know what happened to the family. It has been one of those jobs that's niggled away at me over the years.'

Hunter got back to the office just after 10 a.m. Maddie looked up from her computer as he strolled in and greeted him with, 'The boss has been in here asking after you. He's called in twice in the last ten minutes to see if you're in yet. I told him a little white lie: that you'd been in but had to pop out to get some milk.'

Hunter sighed heavily. 'Thanks, Maddie. I came in early to do an address check for Roger Mills, my old tutor, who took the missing report about the Bannisters, and then as I was leaving to go and see him, he was just coming into the car park.'

She raised her chin, forming a silent 'O' with her mouth.

'How did he sound?'

'Not impressed. Told me that you had to ring him as soon as you came in. Oh, and he's taken the Bannister file.' Maddie pointed at Hunter's out tray, which was now empty.

'Bollocks.' He took off his coat and shoved his briefcase under his desk. 'I'll get us a cuppa first before I ring him. It'll give me time to come up with a good excuse as to where I was going when he clocked me.'

Maddie shook her head, issuing a tight smile. 'Anyway, was it worth it, going to see your old tutor?'

Hunter shrugged his shoulders. 'Yes and no. He was able to set the scene for me, but what he told me doesn't really take me any further forward, only gives me more to think about.' He gave her a potted version of his and Roger's conversation while he made them both tea. As he handed Maddie her drink, he said, 'I don't know where that takes us, to be honest. I've got lots of unanswered questions, but the only person who can answer them is St. John-Stevens, and as you know he's told me I've got to drop the investigation, so he's not going to be any help.'

'I've thought of a couple more avenues,' Maddie responded.

Hunter set down his drink. 'Oh, what are those?'

'See if we can find out who Tina's close friends were at the time and speak with them to see if she revealed anything. And there's nothing in the file to suggest anyone spoke with her parents. We could see if they're still around and have a chat. I could speak with Alice for that information. Also, her GP. We've got a copy of her record to show she was six weeks pregnant and that she had asked for an abortion because it wasn't David's, but that's only a summary of her visit and discussion. What if she disclosed to her doctor who the father was and he chose, for confidentiality purposes, not to enter it onto her record?'

Hunter clapped his hands. 'Maddie, that's brilliant. Yes, give Alice a ring, but first get onto the practice immediately and see if her doctor's still working there.'

She gave him a broad smile. 'Done that already. Spoke to the practice manager and she told me that the surgery that Tina visited is now part of a four-surgery practice. It was bought up ten years ago when the leading doctor retired. But Tina's doctor, Dr Bhatia, is still around. I told the practice manager a little bit about our investigation and asked if she still had Dr Bhatia's details as we'd like to speak with him, and she's going to contact him and ask him to ring me.'

'You beaut. Well done.'

'I thought that would cheer you up.'

Hunter had just sat down and taken a sip of his tea when his phone rang. He squeezed his eyes shut and growled, 'I bet this is St. John-Stevens.' Opening his eyes, he snatched up the handset. 'DS Kerr, Cold Case Unit,' he said with an exaggerated note to his voice. It was the receptionist downstairs. She told him a small parcel had just been delivered and asked if he could come down and collect it.

The parcel Hunter retrieved was an A4 padded envelope with his name and Barnwell MIT on a typewritten label. As he made his way back in the lift, he gently squeezed the envelope, trying to feel through the padding. He could make out that it contained something solid, about a foot long, and with several nodules, and he attempted to open it but it was sealed at both ends with Sellotape.

'Personal parcel for me,' he announced to Maddie as he stepped into the office. He sat down at his desk, took out a pair of scissors from his drawer and snipped away the top of the envelope. Peering inside, he thought for a moment that he saw a doll, and intrigued, he tipped the figure onto his desk. It *was* a doll. Female. It was a cheap version of a Barbie, the kind from a low-budget store, wearing jeans and a pink hoodie, but the weirdest thing was the arms and legs were fastened with black plastic builder's ties that had been trimmed, and the head was covered by a miniature clear plastic bag, the type that was resealable. Hunter stared at it for several seconds, occasionally looking across at Maddie and then returning his mystified gaze to the trussed-up doll.

'What on earth…?' uttered Maddie.

'My sentiments exactly.'

'I can see it's a doll, but what's it supposed to mean? Does it mean anything?'

Hunter stared long and hard at the toy, his memory banks whizzing on overdrive. 'Not a damn thing,' he replied after a couple of seconds.

'Anything else in the envelope?'

Hunter looked at the typewritten label on the front of the envelope again, and tipping it up, gave it a shake. Out fell a sheet of folded paper. He set down the envelope, slipped on a pair of latex gloves from his desk drawer, and lifting the A4 sheet at one corner with finger and thumb, he unfurled it. On it was typed:

Detective Sergeant Kerr, I hope you don't mind my personal approach, but the thing is I feel I know you as if you were an old friend. I do have to say you have done ever so well for yourself. Married with two fine sons and now a Detective Sergeant. It has to be all those cases you've solved. Though I have to say you've not done so well with your latest case. There hasn't been anything on the news recently. Have you come to a dead end? Well, here's a little clue to help you on your way.

P.S. I'll see how you get on with this before I decide whether to send you another clue or not.

'Are they on about the Bannister case?' Maddie asked after Hunter had read it out to her.

Hunter placed the doll and the note into separate clear plastic evidence wallets and sealing them, he signed and dated the bags. For a few seconds he studied each of the items again, and then lifting his eyes, answered, 'No. I think this might be referring to the investigation being conducted by MIT. That Rasa, the Lithuanian girl, whatever her name is, that's disappeared. The envelope is addressed to me at MIT. Whoever sent them is obviously not aware of my transfer. I think this might be a clue as to what's happened to Rasa.'

'She's dead? Suffocated with a plastic bag, you mean?'

Firm-mouthed, Hunter slowly nodded. 'Either that, or this is from one of those freaks you get contacting you whenever there's a case like this. Though I'm more inclined to think that this is not some prank. I think they've sent that doll because they want us to understand it represents Rasa and what they've done to her. That note is their way of confirming that. Remember the CCTV they showed of her on the news? She had long blonde hair.' Hunter was already using the past tense when he responded.

Maddie shook her head. 'If she is dead, and that's how she died, that must have been horrible. I can't imagine what she must have gone through.'

'We know there's some evil people out there, Maddie,' Hunter replied, tight-lipped, adding, 'Having not been involved in the case, it would be interesting to see if she was wearing a pink hoodie and jeans on the day she disappeared.' He picked up his mobile, said, 'I'll get hold of Grace and see if she can talk,' and sent her a text. In less than a minute she had answered. Hunter read her reply and said to Maddie, 'She's out on an enquiry; she says she should be back in an hour and she'll pop into the office.'

Maddie acknowledged this with a nod. 'Are you going to show her the doll and note?'

'Yeah. I'll see if she thinks the same as me and then make a decision on whether it could be evidence or not. I don't want to give St. John-Stevens too much of a leg-up with the case, do I? It might make him look good.' He laughed at his own joke and then his mouth set firm. 'Sadly, the other side of this is that he might think I'm pulling some kind of stunt on him, given what he thinks about me.'

Maddie rolled her eyes. 'You men.'

It was half past eleven before Grace strolled into the Cold Case office. Mike Chapman was in tow.

'Wotcha,' Mike said, plonking himself down at one of the empty desks. 'Are you gonna stick the kettle on? I'm parched.'

'It's over there,' Maddie responded.

Mike harrumphed, pushed himself up and went to make the drinks.

Grace said hello to Maddie and then asked Hunter, 'What's up?'

He showed her the doll and note in the exhibit bags.

Reading the letter first, she then scrutinised the doll. Upon finishing, she looked up and said, 'Wow. When did you get these?'

Hunter jerked his chin towards the bags. 'They came in a padded envelope this morning addressed to me. I think they refer to your case. Whoever sent them thinks I'm involved in it.'

'And you think that this is might be a confession from the person who abducted Rasa? That they've killed her?'

'Either that or a prank. The letter hasn't got the best grammar I've seen.'

'On par with the statement-taking of some officers I know,' laughed Grace, angling her head towards Mike Chapman, who was just setting down four mugs of tea.

Hunter had just picked up his mug and was about to make a comment when the door burst open and in strode St. John-Stevens, his face flushed.

'I was told this was where I might find you all. My, this is all very cosy, having a chat over a cup of tea when there's work to be done.' He arrowed a finger at Grace and Mike. 'You two were given tasks from this morning's briefing.'

'We've done them,' Grace answered back sharply, jolting upright.

'Well, you should be handing them back to the DI and filling in your journals, not having a jolly old chinwag. This is not kindergarten.' The DCI planted his hands firmly on his hips. 'And as for you, Detective Sergeant Kerr: I left a message for you to contact me the moment you came in. That was two-and-a-half-hours ago.'

'I've been trying to ring you, boss. Your phone's been engaged,' Hunter lied.

'Not for two-and-a-half hours, it hasn't. And why didn't you come to find me, in that case? I'm only down the corridor. And how many times do I have to tell you I don't like being called boss?'

Hunter could see St. John-Stevens' face flushing even redder. He answered calmly, 'Did you want me for anything important, sir?'

'First, I want to know where you were you off to so early this morning?'

'Just nipped out to see a former colleague who's not been well. He took a bad turn while on holiday recently. I heard he might have had a heart attack, and I just wanted to make sure he was okay,' Hunter lied again.

'And who might that be?'

'Roger Mills. He was my tutor when I joined. He was in uniform.' Hunter watched the DCI's face contort with anger. He thought he was going to explode.

'I know who he is, and I'm hoping it was only a welfare visit and nothing to do with him being involved in the Bannister case that I told you to drop?'

Suddenly, Hunter felt good. This was the first time that he felt he had the upper hand with St. John-Stevens. Straight-faced and with a degree of satisfaction, he replied, 'Of course it was a welfare visit, sir. I never even mentioned the case. The file's been in my out tray for the past couple of days. In fact, didn't you pick it up this morning?' Hunter watched the DCI studying his features. He kept a poker face.

'If I think for one minute you've been behind my back, disobeying an order, I will have your badge. Do you understand?'

'Wouldn't dream of it, sir.'

The DCI gave Hunter a long, hard stare and Hunter held his gaze, not flinching. After a good twenty seconds, St. John-Stevens snatched back his glare, turned on his heel and stomped out of the room. As the door closed everyone looked at one another, and when they were confident he was out of earshot, they burst into a fit of laughter.

CHAPTER TEN

'Fuck! Fuck!' The man cursed to himself, pacing backwards and forwards inside the dilapidated portacabin. He kicked a chair, sending it crashing against the wall, before stopping at the grimy window, looking out across the yard. Last night's rain had filled the uneven tracks with water, the surface of which glistened with the waste oil that had gradually leaked from the dozens of rusting, scrapped cars stacked in threes, end to end. His eyes rested on the open shipping container outside. He could just make out the rear end of the burned-out Ford Escort sticking out of it, his focus zeroing in on the boot where he had hidden the Lithuanian prostitute's body. For a split second the image of her squirming and thrashing, her mouth sucking at the plastic bag over her head as she clawed for breath, flashed inside his head. He wondered if Detective Sergeant Kerr had received his package yet, and if he had, would he catch on to what it symbolised? He was sure he would, having read about the cases he had been involved in.

Once he had bought the doll, he had spent days scouring dozens of charity shops, shopping for similar clothes to the ones the prostitute was wearing so he could send the right message. He'd love to be a fly on the wall when DS Kerr opened it. Would it be on the news? Thoughts of the news triggered a vision of the night before last, when he'd messed up and almost got caught. Thankfully, the mask and false plates would make sure he wouldn't be identified, but he had to be careful from hereon in. The last thing he needed to do was make another mistake.

Hunter drove home in a dreamlike state, his thoughts bouncing between the parcel he had been sent anonymously and St. John-Stevens' obnoxious behaviour. *Why does it feel like I'm back at school every time I'm in his presence?* Although this time he had rattled the man with his responses, he could tell from the DCI's reaction that he didn't believe one word of what he had said, and he knew that at some stage he would be looking to get back at him. He had immediately warned Roger to expect a call from St. John-Stevens and told his former colleague what he had said to the DCI about doing a welfare visit. Roger assured him that he'd be more than willing to back him up.

By the time Hunter had pulled onto his drive he was wired with frustration, and entering his home, he threw his coat over the bannister, went straight to the kitchen and took out a chilled beer from the fridge. Flipping off the top, not bothering with a glass, he necked half the beer in one gulp, letting out a heavy sigh as he removed the bottle from his lips.

'Heavy day?' Beth said, appearing at the door.

'St. John-Stevens again.'

Beth went to the fridge and took out a box of mince. 'Spag bol for tea,' she said, tearing back the cellophane wrapping. 'Why don't you apply for a transfer? You don't have to put up with him. He's doing your blood pressure no good at all.'

Hunter took another glug of beer, and then wiping a dribble from the corner of his mouth answered, 'Because I'm not giving him the satisfaction of thinking he's beaten me, that's why.'

Beth stopped what she was doing, and turning to him, replied, 'Well, I've no sympathy for you, then. All I can say is that you're as stubborn as he is.'

144

Hunter finished his beer and set down the empty bottle. 'I'm going to get showered and changed.' He was about to step away when Beth glanced over her shoulder.

'Where do the empties go?' she said sternly.

Hunter shook his head and dumped the bottle in the waste bin. Then, walking away, he said with a grin, 'I don't know, I've St. John-Stevens on my back at work and Beth Kerr on my case when I get home.' Then he scurried away, letting out a laugh. As he climbed the stairs, he already felt better.

Before jumping in the shower, he dropped in on the boys. Jonathan was doing his homework. Acknowledging his eldest with a brief nod and saying he wouldn't disturb him, Hunter quickly moved on to Daniel's bedroom. He was on his Xbox. Hunter said the same to his youngest, turned down the offer to play *Call of Duty*, telling Daniel to lower the sound, closed his door and went into his bedroom to undress. After a quick shower, Hunter changed into his joggers and T-shirt and made his way back downstairs. Beth was adding Ragu sauce to the fried mince and onions.

'Can I help?' he asked, kissing her neck.

'You can set the table,' she replied over her shoulder and added, 'Your phone's been going. I think you've got a message.'

Hunter had left his mobile near the charger. He picked it up. The message was from Grace. She was asking if they could meet tomorrow, and she'd sent an image snapped from a frozen clip of CCTV footage that they had of Rasa Katiliene prior to her disappearance. As he studied the picture of the bleach-blonde Lithuanian wearing a pink hoodie and jeans, he had no doubt in his mind that the doll he had been sent was meant to reflect her characteristics, and couldn't help but think that it had to be Rasa's killer who had sent it. *But why me?* thought Hunter. *Who's toying with me?*

For the rest of the day, the mysterious sender of his parcel preyed on his thoughts, as did the contents, especially the letter. Its cryptic message hinted at someone from his past, and he spent the evening replaying every case over his nineteen-year career, trying to recall some of the conversations he had had with each of the villains that might earmark one of them as the sender of the note; but no matter how hard he tried to filter just one of them from his brain's archives, no one sprang to mind.

CHAPTER ELEVEN

6.45 a.m. Hunter smacked off the alarm, got out of bed wearily, and in the dark trudged to the bathroom, staying longer in the shower to refresh himself. He'd had another restless night, grappling with thoughts on who the mysterious messenger and probable killer of Rasa Katiliene was, but his overworked brain hadn't solved it. Dressing on the landing, he crept back into the bedroom, kissed Beth on the forehead, told her he'd see her later and tiptoed downstairs. He made himself a mug of tea and a couple of pieces of toast and then quietly left.

He drove to work with the radio turned down, pondering over what to do about the doll and note. If it had been his old boss, Dawn Leggate, he wouldn't have hesitated to hand them over so they could thrash out their relevance to the investigation, but he had no appetite to help St. John-Stevens. Once Maddie got in, he would talk it through with her and get her opinion. And he was meeting Grace later that day to discuss the matter. If she said that it could be a probable lead, he'd abide by her decision, even if it did mean helping his archenemy.

As Hunter entered the office, he was greeted with bright autumn sunlight pouring through the windows, arcing warm shafts of light across the room, and it instantly lifted his mood. The first thing he did was unlock his desk drawers and check the doll and note were still there. They were. Slipping off his coat, he booted up his computer and then drifted across the room, switching on the kettle, checking his watch. It would be another hour before Maddie got in.

He had just poured boiling water over the tea bag in his mug when his mobile rang. He thought it might be Beth, but he looked at the screen before answering. *Zita Davies*. Zita was a reporter with the local *Chronicle*. A couple of years ago, she had publicised his painting success at an exhibition at the Mall Galleries in London, resulting in him gaining representation by a reputable gallery in Lincoln, and in return he had given her the heads-up whenever a case had broken. A few years ago, she had given him a lead on a case that had helped them identify a female victim who had been murdered and dumped in Barnwell Lake. They had been in touch ever since with Hunter sharing his team's successes. As the deadline was looming for the weekly paper, he guessed she was ringing for an update on Rasa Katiliene's disappearance, believing he was involved in the enquiry.

Hunter answered the call, preparing to disappoint her. 'Good morning, Zita. To what do I owe this pleasure, as if I couldn't guess?'

'I'm afraid it's not a pleasant phone call, Hunter. I'm ringing you about the piece in the *Yorkshire Post* this morning.'

'*Yorkshire Post*! I haven't read the *Yorkshire Post* in years. What's the piece you're talking about?' His face screwed up with bewilderment as he talked.

'It's a piece about you. In fact, it's front-page news.'

'About me!'

'It says Guernsey Police are investigating you over the death of Billy Wallace on Sark.' Following a brief pause, she said, 'Is it true?'

Her information sent his brain into a spin. For a second he struggled to get out his words. Finally, he said, 'Zita, I need to see what it says.'

'Is it true, though?' she asked softly.

Even though Hunter trusted Zita, the bottom line was she was a journalist, and journalists were always looking for front-page news. What she had just told him was front-page news. Swallowing hard, he said, 'I'll need to see what they've put before I say anything.'

'I'll text you the link.' She paused again before adding, 'You will get back to me, won't you? My editor wants the story, and he's asked me to write it. I've got no choice, I'm afraid, Hunter. I'll do my best to give you a fair hearing, trust me.'

'I know you will, Zita. Let me read it and I'll come back to you.'

Seconds after ending the call, his phone pinged and he opened up his incoming message. Zita had sent the link to the *Yorkshire Post* feature. Watching it upload, Hunter could feel his stomach churning. When it appeared on the screen, it was as if he had been hit by a meteor. The headline was a straight lift from the book HUNTER KILLER. Without reading on, he knew from the title this was not going to be good. He read the leading paragraph.

Today, the Yorkshire Post *have learned that Guernsey police are investigating the suspicious death of escaped serial-killer, Billy Wallace, following a violent struggle with Barnwell Murder Detective, Hunter Kerr on the Channel Island of Sark.*

Hunter could feel the back of his neck reddening as he read on. The article was a blow-by-blow account of his and his father's encounter with escaped prisoner Billy Wallace, which included the part where Billy had fallen into the sea, stating: *police are still searching for his body.* The half-page spread finished with a standard police quote from the detective leading the investigation, saying that they couldn't comment further whilst enquiries were ongoing, which always made it sound as if the person was guilty. *That he was guilty.* Thankfully, there had been no mention of Jonathan. He had been spared that. This was not good. *How the fuck have they got wind of this?* The alarm bells started ringing in Hunter's head. *St. John-Stevens.* This was his way of hitting back. This could get him sent home on gardening leave until at least the Coroner's Inquest ended on Guernsey. He could be away from work for months. *Fuck!* There was only one way he would be able to find out who had leaked this story. As much as he didn't want to, he had to ring Zita back.

She answered almost straight away. 'Have they got their facts right, Hunter? Did this happen straight after his escape?'

'Not straight away, Zita, but it was not long after. It was back in September.'

'A month ago? Why didn't you tell me?'

'Because I knew what the headlines would be. Well, not as dramatic as the *Yorkshire Post*'s, but I knew they would be fairly dramatic. And anyway, you know this is sensitive. It's still an ongoing investigation. If I'd have told you, I would have been in serious trouble. In fact, if I say too much now, I could end up in trouble for prejudicing the enquiry.'

She snorted down the line. 'Bullshit, Hunter Kerr, and you know it. I always protect my source. I would protect you.' She paused a few seconds, and then solemnly she asked, 'Is there more to this story, Hunter?'

'God no, Zita. It was an accident. You know Billy's background. You followed his original trial two years ago after he had killed all those retired detectives up in Scotland and tried to kill my dad. As you know, he escaped from Barlinnie jail at the beginning of September, and because he'd tried to kill my dad it was decided that it would be best if we went somewhere safe until he'd been caught. We all went to Sark because that's where my wife's parents are living, and he somehow found out and followed us there. He tried to shoot us and I tackled him, and he went over the cliff. That's the story, Zita. Nothing suspicious.'

'Can I say Billy tried to shoot you? The *Yorkshire Post* haven't got that info.'

'That's what happened, Zita. My dad got injured by a stray bullet. Thankfully, not serious. Though, I'd appreciate it if you didn't quote me on that. As I say, I'm not supposed to say anything because of the investigation and the inquest coming up, but I need to defend myself against this story. They've made it sound as though I'm to blame.'

'You know I won't attribute the story or quotes to you. I'll make it read as though I've got it from a source on Sark.'

'I'd appreciate that, Zita.'

'Is there anything else you can give me?'

'There is nothing else, Zita. That's the story. He tried to kill us and I tried to stop him. He went over the cliff. That's it.' After a short pause, he said, 'I'd appreciate sight of it before it goes to print. I know I can't stop it, but I could amend any inaccuracies.'

'Done.'

'Oh, and just one more thing before you hang up. You wouldn't happen to know where the *Yorkshire Post* got the story from, do you?'

'I spoke with Andy, the reporter who wrote the story, and he told me it came from an anonymous source. I know him, and told him "bullshit," but he assures me it was. He sounded genuine when he told me. He said a man rung him up late yesterday afternoon and gave him the story. He told me the man wouldn't give his name, and so after he rang off, he made a phone call to Guernsey Police, who confirmed they were conducting the investigation. I believe him.'

'Thank you, Zita.'

'I'll get the copy across to you before it goes to my editor, so you can see what I've written. I'll tell it as it is, don't worry.'

'I can't do anything else except trust you, Zita. I'll return the favour, if I can.'

'I know you will.'

When she ended the call, Hunter opened up the *Yorkshire Post* story again and re-read it. There was nothing within the article to suggest the source, but in his own mind he knew who it was attributable to. He could already feel the rage bubbling to the surface. He needed to get out of the office before he did some damage.

Fighting back the need to burst into St. John-Stevens' office and throttle the life out of him, Hunter hurried down to the basement changing room, quickly changed into his training kit and entered the gym. It was empty, which pleased him, because it meant that no one would see the eruption that was about to explode from him. He headed straight for the punchbag, launching himself at it, delivering punch after punch at high speed, only stopping when he was forced to draw breath. As he wiped the sweat from his brow, his knuckles stung and drawing them back, he saw they were red raw. If he carried on any longer, he knew they would bleed and so he turned to kicking the bag, waist and chest high, karate style, until again he was out of breath. All of that had taken ten minutes but he felt better, and after finishing with another ten minutes of sit-ups and press-ups, he made for the shower.

As the warm jet hit the back of his neck, although wrath towards St. John-Stevens still ate away at him, he no longer had the urge to thump him. Besides, his knuckles were too sore to start throwing punches. He got dressed, and feeling a lot better he made his way back to the office where he found Maddie at her desk, just hanging up the phone.

'Morning, Hunter,' she addressed him brightly, her face a beacon of smiles. 'I dropped Libbie off early at my mum's, so I could chase up some phone calls regarding Tina Bannister.'

'That smile tells me you've had some success,' Hunter replied, sinking down heavily in his chair. Suddenly, he felt drained.

'I have,' she answered cheerily. 'First of all, I've spoken briefly with Dr Bhatia, Tina's GP. He sounds as sharp as a knife for someone in their eighties. He remembers Tina well and is prepared to talk to us. I just wanted to fix a time and date with you before I arrange anything.'

'Good,' Hunter returned, gently rubbing his knuckles, which were now starting to ache. He was regretting hitting the punchbag so hard.

'And secondly,' Maddie interjected, before he could say anything else, 'that phone call I've just finished was with one of Tina's closest friends, a Julie Swift, who's now living in Manchester. Alice found her details in one of her old address books and left me a voicemail.'

'And has this Julie been helpful?'

'Not in terms of giving us a lead, she hasn't, but it was interesting getting another take on Tina.'

'Okay, share it then, Maddie.'

'Well, I've learned that she and Tina have been friends since comprehensive school. They sat next to each other in their first class and hit it off and then stayed in the same classes all the way through school. She told me that Tina lived with her mum in one of those council flats at Blenheim Place. She didn't know if her dad was around or not, and she did ask Tina once about him, but Tina told her she didn't know who her dad was and her mum would never tell her. Julie also told me that her mum was a waste of space. She spent more time at the pub than looking after Tina, and it appears Tina was very much left to her own devices. Julie told me that they would spend most of their time in the flat, playing music and drinking cider. Apparently, Tina's place was an open house most nights, and there was always a crowd in there.

'Julie told me that she envied Tina's freedom as a teenager, but she did tell me that on a few occasions, when they were alone, Tina told her she hated her lifestyle and wished she had a proper mum and dad like other kids, which made her feel quite sorry for her. Julie also told me that there was always a small gang of lads turning up at the flat, the majority of them from the year above at school, because Tina had a bit of a reputation for being easy with the lads. She said that when she got older and they started going to the pubs, she always felt that Tina behaved like she did around lads because of the lack of love she got from her mum, and that the sex was more about being wanted than anything else.' Maddie broke off, pulling a sad face. 'I feel quite sorry for Tina. It looks like she probably carried that on into her adult life from what we've learned from Alice and George Evers.'

Hunter took in what Maddie had told him and said, 'Did you ask her about any of these lads who came to the flat?'

'Yes, she gave me a couple of names that I can chase up. She said that once they left school, they all lost touch. She'd occasionally bump into a couple of them, mostly on nights out, but as far as she was aware Tina didn't date any of them. David was the first person Tina had a serious relationship with.'

'Did Julie know David, then?'

'She knew him from school, but he was never part of their crowd. She said he was so quiet at school that you wouldn't give him a second look. She and Tina bumped into him at Christmas time, nineteen-eighty-eight, in the Stute working men's club. Tina was drunk and spilled her lager over him, and they just got chatting. She said the pair ended up snogging by the end of the night, and the next thing she knew Tina and David were an item. She was a bridesmaid at their wedding in eighty-nine.'

'Did you ask her about their marriage and mention the affair she had with David's work colleague?'

'I did. She said David was lovely and obviously besotted with Tina. On the other hand, she didn't speak too highly of Tina. She said she felt a bit sorry for David because of what Tina was like. She thinks David wasn't exciting enough for her and believes that was the reason she still flirted in the company of other blokes. But she did say that once Tina was pregnant with Amy, she seemed to settle down. Julie never saw Amy born because she was going out with the man she's now married to, and he got a teaching post at a school in Hyde, so she moved away there with him. She last saw Tina at Amy's christening. She said she spoke to her a few times on the phone after that, right up to the month before she disappeared, but she says she had no idea about her affair. And Julie did sound surprised when I told her about it. She thought Tina had changed. She told me that Tina talked an awful lot about Amy, and she was of the opinion things were good between her and David the last time she spoke to her.'

'Tina obviously covered things up from what we now know.'

'Obviously.'

'So, we're just left with speaking with her GP about her pregnancy?'

Maddie nodded.

'Okay, we'll do that and see where it takes us. I can't think of anything else we can do. Ideally I'd like to get the samples tested from the Bannisters' kitchen and I'd like to speak with Dylan Wolfe, if only to eliminate him, but St. John-Stevens made it abundantly clear both those things are out of bounds. We've a number of leads but we're unable to pursue them. It's so frustrating.' Continuing to gently rub his knuckles, Hunter faced Maddie and said, 'Now I need to tell you about what's happened this morning.' For the next five minutes, he told her about the article in that morning's *Yorkshire Post* and his discussion with the reporter at the *Chronicle*.

When he'd finished, she said, 'Oh, I'm so sorry, Hunter. I thought my life's torrid at the moment with Libbie, but you're going through a worse crisis than me, especially with what St. John-Stevens has done to you as well.'

Hunter held her gaze. 'Between you and I, Maddie, I can't prove it, but I think he's behind the article. I can't think how else they would have got hold of the information they have. The incident has been on the Guernsey news and there's been a piece in the papers, but there was no mention of me in those. The other reason I've mentioned this is because over the next few days there might be a fair few phone calls from reporters, and I'd like you to answer them and tell them I'm on holiday or something. Would you do that, please?'

'Absolutely. No problem, Hunter.'

'Thank you. And now we'd better get on with some work. While I see what emails I've got, can you ring Tina's old doctor back and fix up an appointment to see him? Shall we say tomorrow afternoon?'

Maddie nodded. 'Will do.'

While Maddie made her phone call, Hunter dealt with his emails. He had dozens, many of them in-force spam — courses available or policing announcements. One from his contact at the probation service, regarding his request for information about Dylan Wolfe, caught his eye and he opened it. It ran to a good few paragraphs, the opening an apology for not getting back to him promptly, explaining he had just returned from a holiday in Santorini with his partner, and initially Hunter relaxed into the personal tone of the note, but then the next few paragraphs became business-like and made him sit up. He perused them again, making sure he had read the content correctly, and upon finishing he sat bolt upright, stating loudly, 'Bloody hell, he's out!'

'Who's out?' Maddie responded, darting her gaze across the desks.

'Dylan Wolfe. I've just had an email back from Probation. Dylan was released on licence five weeks ago to a bail hostel in Sheffield, and guess what?'

'I'm guessing you're going to say he's done a runner.'

'You bet. I need to message Grace and speak with her. I've got a feeling about him not only being involved in the Bannisters' disappearance but Rasa Katiliene's as well. I think he could be behind that package I've been sent.'

In the 18th century George and Dragon pub in Wentworth village — Barnwell MIT's usual venue for social gatherings and after-work drinks — Hunter and Grace slipped off their coats and seated themselves at a table in the snug with a round of drinks.

'Well, this is like old times,' Grace said, raising her glass of chardonnay.

Hunter gazed across the table, watching her taking a sip of wine. She was wearing a pink blouse and blue slacks, and her dark hair was braided the way she used to wear it when she started the job back in 1991. The date triggered a vision of him and her in uniform out on patrol, dealing with their first major job together. They had come across a break-in at an engineering firm and while checking out the scene had discovered the intruder still on the premises. He had tried to escape and they had ended up in a fight. Grace had been on the receiving end of a punch Hunter had ducked away from, and then he'd hit her with a blow that had been intended for the burglar. They had got their man, but she had ended up with a black eye and bandaged wrist, something she still reminded him of from time to time during lighter moments. Since then, they had both married and had children — she two girls, Robyn and Jade — and after two career breaks to look after them during their early years had returned to work in CID. He had been in Vice, Drug Squad and CID and gained promotion. Two years ago, Grace had joined him in MIT and ever since they had been partners. *Bloody good partners.* Together, they had put away some pretty nasty monsters in those two years. But all that had changed following the arrival of the new DCI. Hunter dragged his thoughts back and replied, 'It was until St. John-Stevens came along.'

'Now, now, don't be bitter, Hunter,' chided Grace. 'We all know what a remarkable and caring leader he is.'

Her comment sparked a snigger.

'So, you think he's the one who leaked to the press?' Grace continued, rolling the stem of her wine glass between finger and thumb.

'It's got to be him. I can't think of anyone else who would want to cause me this much grief. He's had it in for me from day one, because Dawn had the temerity to challenge his decision over the shooting of that informant I had gone to meet that night with Barry. He said I was to blame, but Dawn argued I wasn't and had me reinstated.'

'But that's no reason to go to these lengths. Are you sure you're not being paranoid? Couldn't it have been Guernsey Police who gave the story?'

'There's been nothing in the Guernsey press for weeks. And when the original story was released, there was no mention of a British detective involved, or my family. The DI in charge of the investigation told me they would hold back on that as long as they could and that more than likely it would only come out at the inquest.'

Grace pursed her lips. 'Well, if it is him, it's a pretty vicious way of getting back at you.'

'What did he say the other day, when he thought I was going behind his back over the Bannister case? He said he'd have my badge.'

'But you are going behind his back over the Bannister case. There's no *thought* about it.'

'That's beside the point.' Hunter broke into a grin and she tittered.

'Anyway, enough of St. John-Stevens, you said you needed to see me over Rasa Katiliene,' said Grace. 'Is this following on from our conversation the other day about the note and doll you received before we were rudely interrupted by St. John-Stevens?'

Hunter gave a quick nod. 'I think I know who sent me the note and doll, and if I'm right he would be more than capable of killing Rasa.'

'Wow, who is it?' asked Grace.

'I'm guessing you haven't got anywhere with the investigation?'

'The only person we've got in the frame is the sex offender Luke Riley, who admitted going to The Comfort Inn with her and paying her for sex. And he's only in the frame because he's the last known person to have seen her and St. John-Stevens hasn't got anyone else to look at.'

'What about the Lithuanian couple who trafficked her here? Wasn't she badly assaulted by the man, and didn't they flee the day after the TV broadcast about her disappearance?'

'We've managed to trace them. They're back in Lithuania. Sure enough, they fled back home immediately after the appeal went out on TV, but they've told detectives that was only because they feared the British police would blame Rasa's disappearance on them and lock them up in a British jail. The couple have admitted to bringing her into the country illegally but denied it was for prostitution, and the man has admitted to assaulting her but says it was because Rasa stole money from them. They're currently locked up in prison for trafficking, and Mike and Tony are going over there next week to interview them.'

'But didn't you tell me that whoever abducted Rasa stuck tape over the lens of a security camera in the corridor so they couldn't be seen and used the exit doors at the rear, where there are no cameras, to take her out?'

'They did.'

'Well, if that's the case, why would this Luke Riley guy admit to going to her room and having sex with her if he'd gone to the trouble of covering the security cameras to avoid being seen?'

'You're talking with the converted, Hunter. A few of us have said that to the DCI, but he's adamant we should be continuing to look at Luke Riley. He's got some of the team running about all over the place, looking at his background and what he's been up to since Rasa was taken.'

'Do you know what? That's exactly what I think has happened with the Bannister case Maddie and I are reviewing. He came up with the theory that the husband killed his wife over her infidelity, and then his daughter, and then committed suicide by driving into a river somewhere, and stuck with it without compromise, dismissing all other evidence that would challenge his assumption.'

'You're basically saying he's a useless twat,' Grace said with a dry look.

Hunger sniggered. 'I wasn't going to use those words, Grace, but you've summed him up nicely.'

They laughed, taking the moment to have a quick slurp of their drinks.

Putting down her glass, Grace said, 'So who've you in mind for Rasa's disappearance and for sending you the note and doll?'

'I think it could be Dylan Wolfe.'

'I thought you were looking at him over the Bannisters' disappearance?'

'I was, but I now think he could be connected to Rasa's disappearance as well.'

'But he got life. He's still locked up.'

'He did get life, but I learned yesterday he had been let out on licence to a bail hostel in Sheffield five weeks ago, and he's done a runner from there. He's out and about somewhere and now wanted for return to prison. I firmly believe he's responsible for Rasa's abduction, and it wouldn't surprise me if he's killed her the same way that he's shown with the doll. And that letter I got now makes sense. Before he was sent down at court, he said to me, "You've not seen the last of me, PC Kerr." All prisoners have access to the internet at some stage, and although it's monitored, no one would give him a second look for following local news. He would have easily been able to find out what I've been up to in recent years, as the letter suggests. My name's been in the *Chronicle* a good few times over the high-profile cases I've been involved in, and then there's my painting success, where my family was mentioned.'

Grace locked eyes with Hunter for a moment. Then she said, 'The way you're presenting Dylan Wolfe, he certainly sounds a credible person of interest we should be looking at. But you know the next thing I'm going to say, don't you? Do you have actual proof it's him? And secondly, why would he send the letter and give himself away?'

Hunter pursed his lips. 'I don't have proof, Grace. It's a gut feeling, I'm afraid. I just remember what he was like. How he treated those victims. They were like prey. When me and Barry interviewed him back in nineteen-ninety-one for the two rapes and attempted rape, one of the things we quizzed him about how he had targeted them, but he refused to tell us. We found from our enquiries that all three of his victims used the same working men's club where he drank regularly. Two of them were regular drinkers there themselves, and one went there once a week to play bingo. The other thing we found, if you remember, was that Dylan wore a ski mask during his attacks. We found that mask at his girlfriend's when she reported the assault on her by him. We believe that's one of the reasons why he stabbed her. Out of revenge.' He paused and added, 'And on the subject of the mask he wore, that also brings me on to the attack on that woman the other night, when the attacker tried to drag her into his car.'

'The man wearing the werewolf mask?'

Hunter nodded sharply. 'I know I could be stretching my imagination a bit too far, but the press nicknamed Dylan the Wolf Man because of his surname, and it would be the ideal thing to wear, if he's into leaving clues, like that doll and note I've been sent.'

Grace stopped drinking, staring intently at Hunter.

He was about to mention Dylan Wolfe's possible link to the Bannisters' disappearance that happened just months before he was caught, when he became conscious of a presence looming over their table. He looked over his shoulder and was faced with a smug-looking St. John-Stevens. Hunter's stomach flipped. *This is all I fucking need*, he thought to himself.

'My, this is a comfortable little gathering. This little tete-a-tete wouldn't be about me by any chance, would it?'

'You're suffering from an inferiority complex, boss. We're actually debating who the little shit might be who leaked the Sark incident to the press. I was just telling Grace here what I'm going to do the person once I find out who it is.'

Hunter issued the DCI a mocking grin while Grace fought hard to stifle a smirk.

'And what might that be, Detective Sergeant Kerr?'

'Oh, they'll find out. No need for you to worry your little head about it for now.'

The DCI puffed out his chest. He looked furious. 'What did you just say to me? This is insubordination, Sergeant Kerr. I shall be writing you up for a discipline first thing tomorrow. You won't even have a job in cold case by the time I've finished.'

Hunter slammed down his beer glass, the colour draining from his face. 'Shall I tell you what you are going to do, SIR? Right now, you are going to make your way back out of the door you've just come through and drive away from here and leave me in peace. I am off duty, as is my colleague, and if you write any such thing, I will make a formal complaint to Professional Standards that you are bullying me in the workplace and harassing me by following me around when I am off duty.' Hunter scraped back his chair and stood up to face his angry-looking, red-faced DCI. 'Do I make myself clear, SIR?'

Grace gripped Hunter's wrist. 'Leave it, Hunter,' she said through clenched teeth.

St. John-Stevens was forced to step back in order to aim a finger at Hunter. He spat out, 'I'll see you in my office first thing tomorrow, Detective Sergeant Kerr,' turned on his heel and stomped to the door.

As the DCI left, Grace said, 'Flipping 'eck, Hunter, if you hadn't made an enemy of him before, you have now.'

Hunter sat back down, exhaling deeply. 'Fuck him! He'll give me a bollocking, that's all. He'll be scared I'll take my threat to Professional Standards. He knows the accusations I've made could have lasting repercussions for his precious career.' He picked up the remainder of his drink and downed it in one. 'I'll get us another round.'

CHAPTER TWELVE

Hunter's head started thumping the moment he woke up. Slowly opening his eyes, his gaze lingered on the bedside clock. It was a blur, and then his sight adjusted. 7.10 a.m. He groaned. It felt like cotton wool was stuck to the insides of his mouth and as he stirred to get out of bed to get a drink, his stomach roiled. As he took a deep breath to stop himself vomiting, his forehead started to sweat.

'Oh, you're alive then?'

He looked up to see Beth putting down a mug of tea on his bedside cabinet, and he made an attempt to push himself up but his head spun and bile lurched into his throat. Swallowing hard, he groaned. 'God, I feel terrible.'

'I'm not surprised. You fell in the door last night.' Beth moved across to the dressing table and started to put on her make up.

Hunter shut his eyes, his thoughts drifting back to yesterday evening. He could remember after his fourth pint Grace telling him he should slow down, but he was so wound up over St. John-Stevens he went on to whisky. Fatal. And now he was paying the price. He dragged himself up the bed and took a drink of his tea.

'I bet you don't even remember how you got home?' Beth said, applying eye make-up without looking around.

Hunter thought about it. After a couple of seconds, he said, 'Grace dropped me off.'

'I know. I spoke with her while you were being sick on the drive. She told me to tell you she would be here about quarter to eight to take you to work, so you'd better get your skates on.'

Hunter finished his tea before hauling himself out of bed into the shower. As he dressed, he could hear Beth below getting fractious with the boys as she chivvied them to get themselves organised for school. Normally he would have hurried down to support her, but this morning the least bit of movement was too much effort. As he made his way downstairs Beth was at the front door, ushering out Jonathan and Daniel.

She threw him a stern look and said, 'I'm dropping them off at your mum and dad's, they're taking them to school, and Grace will be here in five minutes, so you need to get yourself sorted. I'll see you tonight.' And with that, she left.

As the door slammed shut, Hunter mumbled, 'Sorry,' and made his way into the kitchen, where he filled a tumbler with water, added Alco-Seltzer and drank it down in one.

He had just dragged on his coat when he heard a car horn beep, and opening the front door, he saw Grace waiting in her car at the top of the drive. Picking up his briefcase and trudging up the driveway, he climbed into the passenger seat.

'Good morning,' she said brightly. 'And how is my favourite Detective Sergeant feeling this morning?'

'Shit,' Hunter answered, buckling up his seatbelt.

'Well, you've only yourself to blame. I did warn you.'

'You sound like Beth.'

'She given you a hard time as well?'

'Not exactly. It's what she doesn't say that's worse. Do you women take a course in how to make your husbands feel dreadful?'

Grace let out a laugh, and pulling away from the kerb, said, 'I was going to drop you off for your car, but my guess is you will

166

still be under the influence, so I'll take you straight to work and you can make arrangements to pick it up later, okay?'

'Yeah. I think you're right. That's the last thing I need at the moment. I've got to face St. John-Stevens when I get in and I'm in no mood for him whatsoever.'

'I wouldn't worry about him. He'll probably want to make it known that he's in charge, but it's like you said last night: he'll not dare take it any further because we were off duty and he had no right hassling you like he did. He's a career man, after all. He'll not want that to be put in jeopardy.'

'Well, I'll get myself sorted out with a brew and bacon butty and go and see him after morning briefing.'

'What are you going to do about the doll and note you got? Are you going to mention your theory to him about Dylan Wolfe?'

'I think at this moment in time, he'll not be interested in anything I have to say. You know my thoughts about Dylan's involvement, so I'll hang on to it for a few days and make some enquiries to see if I can track him down. And in the meantime, you can make your own discreet enquiries, and if you get anything then you can let me know.'

'Done.'

Hunter walked into the office carrying a warm bacon sandwich and a mug of strong, sweet tea and found Maddie at her desk on her computer. She greeted him with a friendly smile and pointed at a folded newspaper on top of his keyboard. He saw it was a copy of the *Chronicle*, and without picking it up guessed it contained Zita's article. He set down his sandwich and cuppa, picked up the paper and whipped it open. The front-page headline was KILLED IN THE LINE OF DUTY and the opening paragraph read:

Today, the Chronicle *has learned that Detective Sergeant Hunter Kerr was forced to defend himself and his aged father when escaped psychopath, Billy Wallace — jailed for the brutal murders of five people two years ago — tried to shoot them on the island of Sark, resulting in him falling to his death.*

The account focussed on Billy's brutal killings two years previous, including the attempted murder of Hunter's dad, a little about his trial, how he had escaped from Barlinnie Prison to seek revenge against Hunter's family and how they had been forced to flee to Sark for their own safety. It concluded with several paragraphs on how Billy Wallace had managed to discover their whereabouts, had coerced the owner of a small yacht to take him there, and ended with how Hunter had acted in self-defence when Billy tried shooting his father, resulting in him falling backwards 150 feet into the raging sea. Zita had used the same quote from Guernsey Police as the *Yorkshire Post* to end her piece. The headline and article were far more supportive of Hunter, and he could feel himself getting emotional as he finished reading. He took a deep breath. Zita had done him proud. He owed her one.

'Either you're having an affair with her or you've paid a lot of money for that,' Maddie said with a grin.

Hunter looked across. 'What are you trying to insinuate?'

Maddie laughed. Then she said, 'Well, she's certainly come to your rescue with that.'

'And nothing more than I deserve.' Hunter set down the newspaper, took two paracetamols from his top drawer, and popping them into his mouth, he swilled them down with a good glug of tea.

'Feeling under the weather?' Maddie asked.

'You could say that. I drank too much last night and now I'm regretting it.' He told her about his meeting with Grace in the George and Dragon, and how St. John-Stevens had walked in on them and how he had reacted. 'I've got a bollocking coming from him once I've eaten and drunk this.'

'I don't know, ever since I've met you, all I've witnessed is you courting disaster with senior officers,' she responded mockingly.

'Only with St. John-Stevens. He's a pain in the arse.'

'And as for a bollocking, I don't think it'll be this morning. I saw him dashing out of the car park as I was arriving. He seemed to be in a hurry.'

'Probably plotting my downfall,' sniped Hunter and took another drink of tea and a bite of his sandwich. Gulping it down, he said, 'Well, if that's the case, shall we arrange to see Dr Bhatia about Tina Bannister and see where that takes us?'

Dr Bhatia had retired to a large bungalow in the tiny village of Cadeby, a place Hunter knew well; years ago, he and Beth would head there on a regular basis in the summer months, before Jonathan and Daniel came into their lives, calling in at the Cadeby Inn for a beer and a leisurely lunch. As he and Maddie entered the village, driving past the Inn, Hunter couldn't help but notice it had lost its country pub look and was now a fine dining restaurant. He stored it away in his memory with a view to giving it a try in the very near future.

Dr Bhatia's home was immediately right after the Inn, situated at the head of a small cul-de-sac that contained only six homes, all of them of substantial proportions. Hunter pulled up and cast his eyes over the large stone-built bungalow. 'Well, he's certainly done well for himself,' he said. 'I bet this cost him a few bob.'

Maddie picked her bag out from the footwell. 'Even a superintendent's police pension couldn't afford this. Oh well, we can dream,' she added, opening her door.

The doctor had the front door open before they had even knocked, greeting them with, 'I've been looking out for you. Come in, please.'

Hunter shook the doctor's hand. The man returned a firm shake, and as Hunter eyed him, he couldn't help but think how well he looked for someone in his early eighties. He was a good foot smaller than himself and quite rotund, but had a commanding presence about him, and with only a few wrinkles and a decent head of very dark hair, which Hunter guessed was dyed, he could have easily passed for a man in his sixties.

He welcomed them into the house, pointing them along a long corridor that led through to a large lounge that was filled with warm light coming through a bank of folding doors which opened onto a huge, well-maintained garden.

'This is a lovely room,' Maddie said, running her eyes over her surroundings and settling them on the view out to the garden.

'It's the main reason we bought the house. That, and the location. It's so quiet out here, and there are some beautiful walks.'

Hunter nodded, his eyes drifting to an array of colourful pictures made from fabrics and beads adorning the walls.

'Please take a seat,' Dr Bhatia said, pointing towards a three-seater sofa. He settled down in a comfortable-looking armchair. 'Can I get you a drink?'

'I'm fine, thank you,' Hunter answered and looked at Maddie as he sat down.

She shook her head. 'No thank you. We don't want to take up too much of your time.'

The doctor relaxed back into his chair, crossing one ankle over the other. 'You want to speak with me about Tina Bannister, you said on the phone?'

Hunter nodded. 'We just want to ask you a few questions about her, if you don't mind. We understand she was one of your patients?'

'Yes, her and her mother.'

'Do you remember them well?' asked Maddie.

'My memories are fading slightly these days, dear. Sometimes I can't remember what I did last week, but when it comes to my patients, I remember nearly everything about them. Most of my patients, I dealt with from the moment they were born, and sometimes, sadly, to the moment they died. I remember Tina, mostly because of her mum. She had a drinking habit, you see, and didn't look after Tina that well when she was little. Social Services were always ringing me about her.' He paused and said, 'Her mum died before she got to see little Amy. Cirrhosis of the liver and other drink complications. I did try to help her, but she just wouldn't listen.' His nut-brown eyes drifted up to the ceiling, as if in reflection. After a few seconds, his gaze was back upon Hunter and Maddie again. 'Have you found Tina after all this time? Is that why you've come to see me?'

'I'm afraid we haven't, but it's something we're hoping to do.' Hunter explained his and Maddie's role in reviewing the case and said, 'We want to ask you just a few questions in relation to what we have read in her medical notes, if that's okay?'

'What do you want to know?'

'You might well have been asked some of these questions before if detectives came to see you after Tina disappeared, but either nothing was written down, or we've lost what you told them with the passage of time. The file has been handled quite a number of times during, and since, their disappearance, so sorry if it seems we are repeating things.'

'I understand totally. That happens in the health service as well, as you probably know. And in answer to your question, a detective did come to see me after they all went missing. It was quite tragic, what he told me. And it wasn't just Tina he asked about. Both little Amy, and Tina's husband, David, were also my patients. I was asked about all of them.'

'Can you remember the detective who came to see you?' Hunter asked.

'It was a very young detective.' Dr Bhatia paused, pursing his lips. After a couple of seconds, he said, 'He had a double-barrel name. It's slipped my mind.'

'St. John-Stevens?' Hunter enquired.

'That's him. Yes.'

'Can you recall what he asked you about?'

'Oh yes. He wanted to know about Tina's pregnancy. You see, she had come to see me several weeks before her disappearance to tell me she had got caught and was pregnant and wanted a termination. I asked her why, and she told me because it wasn't David's. She said if he found out, that would be the end of her marriage and so asked me if I could arrange it. I had to tell her it wasn't something I could make a decision on, on my own — that it needed two doctors to agree, and that terminations were only usually given on medical grounds. I had to tell her the fact that it wasn't her husband's baby was not medical grounds. She was in a terrible state when she left my surgery.'

'Did the detective ask you anything else?'

'He asked me if she'd mentioned to me who the father was.'

'That's something we're interested in. Did you know who it was?'

'No, I'm afraid not.' The doctor shook his head. 'It was not something I discussed with Tina. It never got around to that anyway, because she changed her mind.'

'Changed her mind?' interjected Hunter.

'Yes, a few days before she disappeared, Tina came to see me to tell me she had changed her mind and that she no longer wanted a termination. She'd decided to have the baby.'

This news came as a complete surprise to Hunter, and whipping round his gaze to meet Maddie's, he saw she was masking the same astonished look as himself.

Hunter dropped Maddie off at the office to update her journal with details from the meeting with Dr Bhatia and then drove over to Chief Superintendent Michael Robshaw's house, to meet his former boss. Michael was pleased to see him and ushered him through to the kitchen, where he put on the kettle and grabbed a couple of mugs, into which he put tea bags. Hunter noticed that his former boss was no longer on crutches, but he had a distinct limp from the deliberate attempt on his life by Dawn Leggate's ex-husband.

'You're looking well. You seem to be moving around a lot better now,' Hunter said, pointing towards his injured leg.

'I'm still at the physio's twice a week and I'm getting out most days for a walk. The consultant told me my femur should be stronger than before now it's pin and plated, but he says I might always have a bit of a limp from the damage to my hip. I need to build my walking up for my forthcoming retirement,' Michael replied, ending with a half-laugh.

'The boss mentioned you were calling it a day. Are you ready for that?'

'You don't need to call Dawn "boss" in our two's company. Anyway, she's not your boss anymore.'

'More's the pity. I've missed her.'

Michael issued another short laugh. 'A little bird told me you're not seeing eye to eye with DCI St. John-Stevens.'

'Have you heard what he's done to me?'

'Moved you to Cold Case? Not much gets past me. I've still got my ear to the ground and my contacts.'

'I've had a few run-ins with him since he moved me as well, I'm afraid. I don't know why he's got it in for me like he has. I can only think it's since that incident with my informant when he got me suspended and then Dawn got me re-instated. It seems to be sticking in his throat and this is his way of showing he's now in charge.'

'Cold Case is not bad. There're a lot of unsolved cases that need a fresh review, and by someone with the right skills. To be honest, Hunter, I would have thought this was right up your street. And it's not going to be forever. St. John-Stevens is ear-marked for higher achievement. Two years in MIT and he'll be promoted and off to manage a district somewhere.'

'Isn't Dawn coming back, then?'

'Honest answer, don't know. Jack's trial is in two months, and whilst it's not her fault what he did to me, I'm sure Jack'll be blaming her and me for his predicament. And don't forget, when she came down here on the joint operation to capture Billy Wallace, she was still married to him. There's going to be the scandal of us two having an affair while we were conducting an investigation together. I'm sure Jack's barrister will give her a rough time when she gives evidence against him. It's not going to paint her in a good light.'

'The Force are not going to hang her out to dry, are they?'

Michael pursed his lips. 'I hope not. She doesn't deserve it. Dawn's a bloody good senior detective. If I've got anything to do with it, she'll be back on full operational duties within two months of the trial ending. I should still be in the job, albeit preparing for my retirement, so hopefully I can yank a few strings. We'll have to see.' Michael finished making tea and handed Hunter a mug. 'Do you mind if we talk in here? I prefer to stay standing. If I get settled down, my leg stiffens and it takes me ages to get going again.'

Hunter laughed. 'You sound like a pensioner already.'

Michael pointed a threatening finger and said with a grin, 'Careful what you say. I can make sure you're in Cold Case for the rest of your career if you're not kind to me.' Taking a slurp of tea and swallowing, he added, 'Anyway, what do you need to speak with me in confidence for, as you said on the phone? I can't pull any strings to get you out of Cold Case, if that's what you're here for.'

Hunter shook his head. 'No, it's not for that, boss. It's about a case I'm reviewing. I've got some very serious concerns about the initial investigation, especially regarding the officer involved in the case, and I didn't know where to take it.'

'Have you discussed them with DCI St. John-Stevens?'

'That's the problem, boss. He was the officer who investigated the job when he was a trainee detective. I have sort of aired my concerns about the case, and he had a go at me, accusing me of criticising his investigative skills. He's told me I have to drop the review. He's taken the file away from me.'

Michael stroked his bottom lip, letting out a drawn, 'Mmm.' Then, he said, 'I can see why you've come to me in confidence. Do you want to take me through the case and I'll see if I can give you some advice or not?'

Hunter took a quick swig of his tea, set down his mug, took out the duplicate copy of the Bannister file from his briefcase, and flipping open the cover, removed the original crime scene photographs he had kept, and spread them out across the work surface for Detective Chief Superintendent Michael Robshaw to view. Then he recounted his review of the investigation in chronological order, starting with the information from his former colleague Roger Mills, who had been first to the Bannister home after they had been reported missing. He gave Michael a blow-by-blow account of Roger's initial actions at the house, especially focussing on the many aspects that had been left out of the file's summary: the house phone ripped from its socket, the overturned table, the cigarette ash on the carpet in the lounge and the missing onyx ashtray that had possibly been used as a weapon. He showed his former boss the photograph with the specks of blood on the hearth. He then introduced the SOCO findings of the bleach-washed kitchen floor, where a large spillage of blood had been cleaned up, and also the bleach-washed mug left on the kitchen draining board that was possibly evidence of a visitor before the family's disappearance. That led him to Denise Harris's testimony regarding the stranger on the doorstep on the day before the family were reported missing, and also the mysterious person she saw getting into the driver's seat of the Peugeot car parked in the alleyway beside the Bannister house on the same evening, both of whom had never been identified. He finished with the information they had learned that morning from Dr Bhatia. As Hunter finished, he looked into the eyes of his former boss, awaiting his response.

For a long moment, silence ensued. Michael had a studious look on his face. Finally, he responded. 'I have to say, now you've gone through all this, I do remember the case. But only faintly. I remember it being on the local news and in the papers, but that's all I remember because I was a DI in Sheffield back then, so had my own case-load to focus on. The way you have explained things just now, I can see why you're concerned. All these matters should have been included in the investigation summary, especially because this evidence suggests a serious crime was committed and the speculation is that David Bannister committed a double murder and then committed suicide.'

'That's what I thought. It's what I would have expected.'

'But from what you have told me, with regards to the actions of St. John-Stevens, he does appear to have covered all the bases of a vulnerable missing persons enquiry.'

'I totally agree, boss. There were lots of boots on the ground very early on doing local searches. Roger Mills told me they did checks at neighbours' houses, and searched the nearby industrial estate, and also Underwater Search Unit was called out and they did searches at various locations where a car could be driven into the canal or river, but without gain. As I've mentioned, Scenes of Crime carried out a thorough examination of the house and even media appeals were done. Initially, everything was done by the book, but then, as the enquiry developed, the leads weren't followed up satisfactorily. For instance, the sightings of the two strangers on the day the family disappeared don't appear to have been investigated properly. For me, trying to identify who those individuals were would have been a priority. I wouldn't have made the speculation about David killing his wife and daughter and then taking his own life until I had been satisfied there were no other lines of enquiry.'

Michael Robshaw nodded in acknowledgment but didn't interrupt Hunter.

'Part of our review has been to check back with witnesses mentioned in the summary, and as I've said, they've told us things that I feel should have been put into the summary of the file but haven't been. Pretty important things to me.'

Michael Robshaw nodded again.

Hunter continued, 'We have made all the necessary checks to see if there is any possibility the family could still be alive and nothing's come back. The last record we have of any of the family was back in July, nineteen-ninety-one, so it does appear they are dead, but except for St. John-Stevens' speculation on paper, it's not backed up by physical evidence.'

'So, you think his theory is ill-judged?'

Hunter hunched his shoulders. 'It could well be the case that David did kill his wife and daughter and then took his own life, but for me St. John-Stevens' speculation is without foundation, especially given the information and evidence we've collected.' He paused, tightening his mouth, before adding, 'And I know I despise the man because of how he's treated me, but my thoughts about this are based on the facts and not what I think about him.'

Michael stroked his chin. 'I think you have a point, Hunter. This is not the way I would have expected the case to be presented. This is shoddy work from a detective, and I'm sure if the press got wind of what you have uncovered, there would be a lot of questions posed.' He paused and said, 'And you say you've gone back to St. John-Stevens and presented him with your findings?'

'About the stranger at the door, I did, and that's when he told me he'd bottomed who that was. He said it was one of David's work colleagues, but I now know it wasn't from the enquiries I've made. The timing's all wrong. The work colleague was warned off by David months prior to this. I haven't mentioned what Denise Harris told me, or George Evers, and also what we've learned this morning from Dr Bhatia, because he told me to drop the case. He doesn't know I'm still working on it.'

Michael slowly shook his head. 'And you don't need me to tell you that is not something you should be doing behind a senior officer's back.'

Hunter shrugged his shoulders. 'I know, but what would you do in my position?'

Michael issued a sardonic smile. 'Now you're putting me on the spot here, Hunter, asking me to side with you against a senior officer, and that's also something you shouldn't be doing with the Force Head of Crime.'

'I know that, boss, believe me. It's not something I'm proud of, but I just think the enquiry has still not run its course. There are too many unanswered questions and avenues to be investigated.'

'And I agree with that sentiment, Hunter. So, what do you want from this? Where do you think you can get the answers?'

Hunter then expounded his notion about Dylan Wolfe being a candidate for the stranger who was seen at the front door of the Bannister house and the possibility of him also being the stranger in the car in the alleyway, detailing his criminal background, and adding that Dylan's first victim only lived four streets away from the Bannisters. He put forward his own theory of Dylan targeting Tina, turning up at the house to rape her and being disturbed by David coming home that lunchtime, and it being Dylan who killed them all and dumped their bodies and then dumped the car. He finished by telling his former boss that Dylan Wolfe had been released five weeks ago and had since disappeared from his bail hostel. Hunter left out his recent receipt of the note and doll and his speculation that he was also involved in the abduction of Rasa Katiliene, for fear of sounding too fanciful.

When he had finished, Michael said, 'Fascinating. As much as I don't like theories without evidence, you've put forward a very credible alternative. Is there any physical evidence from back then which could support your theory?'

'SOCO did a thorough forensic examination of the house and lifted fingerprints and blood samples and also swabbed the kitchen floor, but as you know DNA testing was in its infancy and the samples weren't offered up for that analysis. I've checked with forensics and they still hold those samples. The ideal scenario is for fresh scientific tests to be carried out on those samples. I'm especially interested to find out whose blood was cleaned up in the kitchen. Roger Mills told me that the SOCO told him that the indications were that there had been significant blood loss in the kitchen, suggesting someone had been very seriously injured, more than probably killed, and if that blood is David's, as per my theory about Dylan Wolfe, then this would change everything and so I could justify reopening the investigation.'

Michael let out a blast of air. 'There's a big cost to that, Hunter, and the fact that there's no official investigation means there's no budget for that work to be carried out.'

Hunter held his former boss's gaze for a good few seconds before asking, 'Is there any way round this?'

'Crikey, Hunter, this is really putting me on the spot. My immediate answer, as Head of Force Crime, is no. Absolutely not.' Michael stared long and hard at Hunter, finally shaking his head and saying, 'I don't know, Hunter, if it was anyone else except you asking me this, I would stick to force protocol, but having listened to your story, I have a degree of understanding of what you want to achieve, and I share that feeling.' Michael paused and for several seconds was silent. After what seemed an eternity to Hunter, he said, 'I'm not making any promises, but leave this with me. I'll think it through and get back to you.'

On his way back to the office, Hunter called in at the street where the Bannister family once resided, parking opposite their old home, directly outside the front window of where Deborah Harris had lived so that he had the same view she would have had that day she saw the stranger at the front door of the Bannister house. He also wanted to see how good her observation point was, and how it had enabled her to see the stranger getting into the Peugeot car parked in the alleyway next to the house. As he ran his eyes along the front, and to the side where the alleyway was, he was more than happy with Deborah Harris's depiction of the two events and the descriptions of the individuals.

Before pulling away, he looked at the photograph Scenes of Crime had taken of the Bannister home back in 1991 and then returned his eyes to the current premises. There were significant changes, especially to the front, with new PVC windows and a new front door. Somehow, it now seemed soulless, and he wondered if that was his imagination running away with him or if it was something else. Something far deeper that he hadn't yet grasped. Had he missed something?

As his eyes settled on the front door, he thought about some of the conversations he had had with Alice Bannister during his follow-up calls. The most recent had been about the bureaucratic difficulties she had encountered disposing of the property because no bodies had been found and no one knew for certain what had happened to her family. With a sad and frustrated note in her voice, she had told him it had taken years of negotiations with her son's bank and building society, involving solicitors, before she had finally been able to sell the house. Now they had Claudia's Law, following the disappearance of Claudia Lawrence, for families of victims who had vanished, but back in 1991 that hadn't existed. Alice had said that when they had finally disposed of the house, all they had been left with was a few hundred pounds after years of pain and anguish and still no answer as to what had happened to her family.

Hunter suddenly remembered how he had felt that day he had been told they had found his girlfriend, Polly, murdered. It was the best part of a week before he'd learned she'd been stabbed, and from then on a whole host of ghostly visions of her being attacked by a stranger had visited him frequently for twenty-one years, only stopping when he had learned who her killers were and captured them. Until then, he'd repeatedly had feelings of anguish, despair and guilt. It was the reason why he had joined the police — to catch her killer and lock away the demons that haunted him.

With that thought, Hunter dragged his eyes back from the house and pulled away from the kerb to head into work. He hoped his former boss could come up with a way to help him try and resolve this case, if only for Alice to get closure.

Hunter checked his watch as he entered the building. It was coming up to lunchtime. He had put off speaking with St. John-Stevens long enough. It was time to face another one of his demons. He made his way up to his office, hoping he wasn't in, but as he tramped along the corridor his hope turned to despair upon seeing his dark shadow at his desk through the green smoked glass panels. Hunter rapped on the glass door, taking a deep breath.

'Come in,' the DCI shouted.

Hunter pushed open the door and stepped into the lion's den.

The DCI looked up from his paperwork.

'You wanted to see me,' Hunter said. The words seemed to stick in his throat for a split second before they came out. He was experiencing a degree of nervousness that he hadn't had thirty seconds ago.

'I thought I said first thing this morning.'

'Sorry, I've been busy. Time slipped away.'

St. John-Stevens' face flushed and his mouth tightened. 'When I say I want to see you first thing, I mean first thing. Not when you feel like it.'

Hunter stood to attention and took in another deep breath, holding it for a good few seconds before releasing it slowly. He didn't want the DCI to see he had him rattled. He replied, 'Do I need someone from the Federation for this meeting?'

'What's that supposed to mean?'

'Is this a disciplinary or a chat?'

'Don't be facetious, Sergeant Kerr.'

'I'm not being facetious. It's a simple question, sir.'

The DCI's face reddened further. 'You think you're smart, don't you, sergeant?'

Hunter was puzzled by that comment. He answered, 'No.'

'Know where I've been?'

Hunter's eyebrows knitted. 'No, but I'm sure you're going to tell me.'

'Headquarters. Discussing you.'

'And did it go your way?' Hunter spat out the words. He knew he shouldn't have said that, but he couldn't resist. He saw St. John-Stevens inhale sharply and watched his fingers claw at his desk.

The DCI answered, 'If it had, we wouldn't be having this conversation. Instead, you would be handing over your warrant card.' He paused, interlocking his fingers. 'Which I'm still working on, by the way.'

'I'm sure you are.'

'Your journalist friend did you a very big favour with her article in this week's *Chronicle*. You could say it saved your bacon.'

The nervousness Hunter was experiencing slowly dissipated. He realised the outcome he had earlier dreaded was instead going his way. With an edge of defiance, he responded, 'Had to counter the story you gave to *The Yorkshire Post*.'

For a moment, the DCI didn't respond. When he did, he said, 'Can I ask how you managed to get her to write her article in your favour? Are you in bed with the enemy, sergeant?'

Hunter issued a thin, roguish smile. 'She's just a friend.'

'A friend, you say. A special friend?'

'Just a friend. Something you don't have.'

The DCI quickly unclasped his hands, turning them into fists. His face turned purple. 'What!' he blasted.

'Are we done here, sir? I'm very busy.'

'You think you're clever, don't you, Sergeant Kerr? Well, let me give you this warning. You might have a few people fighting your corner for now, but that won't always be the case, sergeant. Soon I'll be up there, and boy, will you rue the day when that happens.'

Hunter stared long and hard at the DCI. He could feel anger rising to the surface. He needed to remain cool. He said slowly, 'Is that it, sir?'

'You need to know, sergeant, that if you take me on, you'll not win. And when you fall, there will be no one around to catch you.'

'I wouldn't bank on that.' Hunter slipped his mobile out of his pocket and held it up. 'I've just recorded this conversation. I'm sure the Federation solicitor will only be too pleased to hear it. I'm sure this constitutes bullying in the workplace. Now, unless you have anything else to say, I'll get on with my work.'

Hunter waited for a few seconds, and when the DCI didn't respond, he turned on his heel and left the office. He felt sick.

CHAPTER THIRTEEN

'God, I need a drink,' Hunter blurted, entering the office, yanking off his coat and tossing it over his chair. 'And not just tea.'

Maddie looked up from her computer. 'I'm guessing you've just come back from seeing the boss?'

'When will that man ever leave me alone?' he chuntered, picking up the kettle, shaking it and then switching it on. 'I think I've probably gained some respite for a few days at least.' Arranging two mugs, Hunter told Maddie about his mobile phone reveal.

She let out a laugh. 'You never did?'

'No, I didn't. But he's not to know I haven't recorded it. But I'll tell you what, when I saw the look on his face when I told him, it made me think that I should do that from now on. He can't keep treating me like this.' Hunter dunked the tea bags in the mugs of hot water, stirred them around for thirty seconds and slung them in the bin. Adding milk and sugar, he brought the tea back to the desks, and as he put the mugs down, he spotted a brown padded envelope in his top tray. He caught Maddie's eye and dipped his head towards it.

'Oh, that came half an hour ago. The receptionist brought it up. It looks like another parcel from that mysterious boyfriend of yours. Or should I say not so mysterious, if it's from Dylan Wolfe.'

Hunter eyed it for a few seconds, then took out a pair of latex gloves from his desk, pulled them on and picked up the envelope. It had the same printed label addressed to himself at Barnwell MIT. He turned it over, slipped the blade from a pair of scissors under the flap, slowly slit it open and gently tipped out the contents. The first thing to tumble out was a doll's plastic knee-length boot. That was quickly followed by two small pieces of bone that clattered onto the desk. Hunter ran his eyes over both items before casting a quick gaze across to Maddie, who was doing the same.

'Are those human bones?' she asked, not taking her eyes off them.

Hunter studied them for a few seconds and then answered, 'No, I don't think so. Too small. They look more like chicken bones to me. From a thigh.' He raised the padded envelope to check if there's was anything else inside, and seeing there was, dipped his hand inside, and with finger and thumb pulled out a folded piece of paper. Double-checking the envelope was now empty, he set it aside and opened the slip of paper. Out fell a picture from the folds. It was a black and white image of what appeared to be a terraced back yard with outbuildings. As he gave it curious scrutiny, the immediate thought entering his head was this was copied from a photograph of the Bannisters' rear yard, but in the absence of crime scene photos he would have to show it to Alice for confirmation.

'More clues?' asked Maddie.

Hunter read the typed note:

Dear Hunter, forgive the informalities again, but as I said in my last letter, I feel I know you like an old friend. Although 'friend' is not exactly the word I should use, but for now we'll keep things on a friendly footing. I'm disappointed to see nothing on the news about Rasa, especially as I went to great trouble to send you my last gift to help your investigation along. Maybe you and your colleagues think it's a hoax? Well, I can assure you it's not. She really is dead. She was such a spirited individual — put up quite a fight. It was delicious to see her draw her last breath.

Anyway, enough of my ramblings. Just to give you a further leg-up, these latest gifts are a clue to where you'll find Rasa's body. I do hope you work it out soon. She is starting to smell a bit. And when you do work out the clues, I do look forward to meeting you again. You and I have such a lot to discuss. I might even tell you about the others. Good hunting.

PS. 'Scuse the pun.

Hunter read it again, this time out loud for Maddie to digest. As he finished, he said, 'He's saying there are more. Jesus.' Hunter skim-read it a third time, and then took a few minutes, placing the note and items in four evidence bags.

'If these are from Dylan Wolfe, have you any idea who the others might be?' asked Maddie.

'Not a clue, although I told you that Barry always said he believed Dylan had committed more crimes.'

'The other question is, are the others bodies or rape victims?'

'I believe he's referring to bodies.'

'That's what I thought as well,' answered Maddie. 'And if that's the case, are the others the Bannisters?'

Hunter locked eyes with her for a moment. The same thing had entered his head. After several seconds of silence, he said, 'I need to think about what these clues mean. Chicken bones, a doll's boot and a picture of a terraced rear yard. The letter says these are to help us find Rasa's body. Is she buried in a back yard somewhere?'

'Are you going to let Grace know about this?'

'I'll give this some thought and message Grace later to fix up a meeting to show her what's been sent. Because of the nature of the note, I can't keep this to myself any longer, as much as I begrudge helping St. John-Stevens.'

From the balcony above the sports hall at Barnwell leisure centre, Hunter watched his eldest son, Jonathan, jiggle past a defender and unleash a shot that whipped past the goalkeeper in the five-a-side game below. That goal gave his team the lead with just two minutes to go and Hunter instantly let out a whoop of delight, proudly watching Jonathan throw a celebratory punch in the air as he jogged back to his own half. It was the first time during the last hour and a half of Barnwell FC's under thirteens coaching session his thoughts had focussed on the football. Until now, all he had thought about was the letter and the clues sent to him earlier that day.

He had left work and driven home with his deliberations all over the place, and wanting to block them from his thoughts once he got indoors, he had photographed the items with his phone and sent the images, together with a message to Grace, requesting a meeting early the next day. Then he had locked everything away in his briefcase, intending to focus on family matters, knowing it was Jonathan's coaching night. Yet, despite his best efforts, he had failed to switch off, the clues and puzzle washing around inside his head as he'd showered, changed, eaten his meal and driven Jonathan to training.

Even returning back home from the session, chatting with Jonathan about his gameplay and how he'd scored the winning goal in the final match, Hunter still found his thoughts drifting, mulling over the sent clues, his mind toying with whether they had been sent by Dylan Wolfe or not. As he emptied Jonathan's training bag, confining his football kit to the laundry basket, there was still no reprieve from his reflections.

The moment when he and Barry had first encountered Dylan in 1991 jumped into his inner-vision and began playing out like a TV drama; they had cornered Dylan at the old coking plant complex at Manvers the week after he had stabbed his girlfriend. Hunter had been tipped off that Dylan was hiding up at the old plant ready to flee to London where arrangements had been made for him to disappear, and he and Barry had driven down there to check out the tip-off. Hunter had found Dylan napping in a car and after disturbing him, Dylan had tried to stab Hunter in order to escape. His police radio had saved him, and following that attack there was a short car chase, ending with Dylan crashing his car and being badly hurt.

Once in custody, Hunter had learned that the car he'd been found in belonged to the owner of the car dismantlers where Dylan worked, and they had locked up the owner for assisting an offender. Unfortunately, they hadn't been able to prove that the car owner had helped Dylan to evade capture and he had been released without charge. Two years ago, Hunter had been told that the owner had died of a heart attack and his car dismantlers yard had been mothballed by his wife. He had seen it recently, its front gates chained and padlocked, a dilapidated eyesore at the edge of the industrial estate. As an image of the derelict dismantlers yard flashed inside his head, he grappled with recalling the owner's name. Suddenly, the man's nickname came to him. *Fat Bas. Now what was his name?* As he racked his memory again, it flashed into his brain and in that split second everything fell into place. Hunter hurried downstairs, took his phone off its charger and messaged Grace. *Think I know where Rasa's body is. Going to do a recce. See you tomorrow a.m.*

It took Hunter less than ten minutes to drive from his home to the derelict dismantlers yard that was once owned by Harold Barry Bones. It was starting to rain as he turned in to the industrial estate, and he drove down a deserted glistening wet road with his wipers repeatedly clearing the screen. Easing off the accelerator, he crawled past the yard's entrance gates, hoping to get a look through them, but corrugated sheets had been placed over the wire mesh, blocking any view. The only way he was going to be able to see into the yard was to find a gap in the perimeter fence, and not wanting anyone to see what he was up to — even though he was a cop, he was acting on the hoof — he drove around the corner, away from the main thoroughfare, turning off his lights as he pulled into the verge.

There were no streetlamps here and he sat in darkness, staring out through a rain-blurred windscreen, starting to think through his next move; if his thoughts were right and Rasa Katiliene's body was in the boot of one of the scrap cars in that yard, he would have to make a physical check — actually get inside the yard to carry out a search. *No good having second thoughts now, Hunter. You've got this far,* he told himself, suddenly having pangs of doubt about whether he was making the right decision.

Taking another look at the compound, he took a deep breath, reached into his glove box and took out his Maglite. *Let's go for it.* He removed the keys from the ignition, zipped up his coat and climbed out of the car. As he locked the door, he stood motionless, looking around his surroundings and listening. Somewhere in the distance a dog was barking in one of the compounds, but it was a good way off. There was no sound coming from the derelict dismantlers yard, so there didn't appear to be a guard dog, and he set off walking back towards the gates, keeping close to the fence. The corrugated gates were secured by a rusting chain fitted with a new-looking padlock. It was a good one that would take bolt-croppers to remove and he hadn't brought any. He cursed, took another look around and moved on, checking the fence as he went along. The top was covered by razor wire, so he had no chance of climbing over the top. His only hope was of finding a gap, and he found none at the front.

Around the next corner, things were looking better. Old wooden railway sleepers made up the fence here and many of those were in a bad state. A hundred yards along, Hunter found his gap. One of the sleepers had slipped to one side, and although it was a very tight squeeze, he was left with enough of a breach to slip through and once inside he switched on his torch. Staying next to the gap, getting ready to retreat, he whistled and strained his ears again, checking there was no guard dog. When there was no movement or barking, he swept his powerful beam around the yard. It was still very much as he remembered it nineteen years ago: dozens and dozens of scrap vehicles piled three-high in rows that stretched to the back of the premises, and to his left was the old reception block — a portacabin that had grilles over the windows. Beside it were two rusting ship containers, where he recollected car parts were stored.

The rain was starting to come down faster, and he knew it wouldn't be long before he was soaked. His jeans were already sticking to his thighs, so he decided to see what was in the containers, do a quick check of the portacabin, and then leave with a view to returning tomorrow when it was daylight.

He went to the furthest container. It was closed but it didn't look as though it was locked, and he yanked at the handle. It was stiffer than he'd anticipated — the rust causing the resistance — and it took him two strong pulls before he finally prised it from it from its barred position. Even then, it was just as stiff to pull open the doors, the hinges squealing as he hauled them apart. Finally, getting a wide enough gap, he poked in his torch. A strong smell of engine grease and petrol fumes hit the back of his throat, making him cough, and swallowing hard he scoped the inside. Vehicle parts were everywhere. Removed engine blocks covered the floor and smaller parts lined shelves fastened to the sides. He darted his beam around, but nothing jumped out at him as being suspicious. This was just a storage place for vehicle parts, nothing else.

Closing the door, Hunter moved on to the second container. As he flashed his torch across the doors, he saw this one was padlocked, and the chain and lock securing the handles appeared to be new. He studied them for a moment, weighing up whether to force them or not, considering the consequences should he find anything of evidential value. The defence would have a field day over the fact that he didn't have a warrant. But, while he contemplated walking away, the other side of his thoughts were telling him to go for it — if he found anything incriminating, he could always smuggle away the chain and padlock and say he found the container unsecured. Who was around to challenge that? Steadily, he circled the torch around the ground, moving it slowly outwards, looking for something solid to snap the lock. His beam found a long metal bar in the mud, and putting his Maglite into his mouth, clenching it between his teeth, he picked up the bar, inserted it between the chains, twisting and straining them tight, before putting all his strength into wrenching the links from the lock. It took a lot of heaving before the chain finally snapped, the padlock flying away with a clatter.

For a moment Hunter stood, unmoving, holding his breath, listening intently, but the only sound he could hear was the rain sploshing in newly formed puddles. He couldn't even hear the dog barking from earlier and taking a step forward, he slipped the chain out between the handles, twisted one of them outwards and tugged open the door. The ease with which it sprung open took him by surprise, and he almost stumbled backwards, only his tight grip on the handle saving him from falling onto his backside. As he took a step into the container, the stench hit him and he instantly knew what it was, because he had smelt it numerous times before. Death! There was something dead in here, and he could guess what.

Removing the torch from between his teeth, Hunter flashed it inside. The light hit the back of a car that looked as if it had been burnt out, and grey metal beneath blistered paintwork. The rear window was shattered and inside Hunter could make out the charred framework of the back seats. Pinching his nose, he swung his torch beyond the car. The ray hit the back of the container, picking out what appeared to be photographs and several old newspaper articles stuck up on the metal wall. He couldn't make out any of the details from this distance, but there was a big enough gap between the car and the sides for him to get closer, though first he wanted to check if he had got all the clues right. The smell told him he had. Targeting the boot with his torch, he stepped towards the car, pressed the boot release button and pulled it up.

The smell that hit him this time made him step back. It was horrendous. But what was even worse was the sight before him. He had found Rasa. She was bound by builders ties, hands and ankles, exactly like the doll he had received, and her head was encased in a plastic bag that almost shrink-wrapped her face. Her eyes were wide open, her look a mask of terror, leaving no doubt about the suffering she had endured in her final moments.

Pulling away his torch, Hunter stepped back outside. *I need to call out the troops.* He had just reached his phone in his pocket when an intense pain shot across the back of his head and he was propelled forwards, flashing stars blurring his sight. As he hit the ground, the lights went out.

All Hunter could feel was a throbbing ache in his head. It felt like it was about to burst with white flashes blurring his vision. He blinked hard, trying to clear his eyes, and that only increased the pain, causing him to stiffen. *What happened?* His thoughts were as fuzzy as his vision.

He tried to move but couldn't. His hands and feet were stuck. He squeezed his eyes shut and blinked a second time, swiping away a film of tears, and this time his sight recovered. He saw he was in a long room with dirty cream walls, and he quickly worked out the white flashes were coming from an overhead fluorescent light that wasn't working properly. When he spotted the grimy windows with grilles, he realised where he was. The portacabin in the dismantlers yard. At the same time, he realised why he couldn't move when his eyes dropped to his wrists and he saw that they were bound by plastic ties to the arms of a chair. His thoughts quickly flashed back to him finding Rasa's body and then the explosion of pain inside his head. Someone must have hit him from behind. He tugged at the tie on his right wrist, but it was fastened tight.

'Ah, so you're awake.'

Hunter snapped his head sideways, his eyes settling on someone sitting at a desk, a row of greasy green filing cabinets behind him. He was dressed in a blue boiler suit and was wearing a werewolf mask. Hunter could see the man had been working out with weights. He recalled Maddie telling him about the woman who'd been attacked by the man with the mask and knew this had to be the same person. He said, 'Dylan Wolfe?' and then swallowed hard. His mouth was dry.

The man slowly removed the mask, grinning as he did. As he pulled it over his head, Hunter saw it was Dylan, though he had changed dramatically since his last sighting of him. His face was criss-crossed by ugly scars, and his hair was thinner — he now had a widow's peak. Hunter's eyes rested on the red weals snaking across from one side of his face to the other.

Dylan wagged his finger, a wicked grin playing across his mouth. 'I knew you'd work out the clues. I wasn't wrong.'

Hunter's mind went into overdrive. He couldn't help but think of what had almost happened to him six weeks ago on Sark when Billy Wallace had pointed a gun at him. That had been bad, but somehow this situation seemed worse. He needed to buy himself time. Licking his dry lips, he responded, 'You know we can work something out, don't you, Dylan? If you untie me now, I'll never mentioned this happened.'

The smile grew wider on Dylan's face. He slowly shook his head. 'I can see what you're trying to do, Detective Sergeant Kerr, but that's not going to work. You and I have some unfinished business.' Suddenly, his face straightened. The look he returned was vengeful. 'You did this,' he spat out, arcing a finger back and forth across his face. 'And you're going to pay.'

Hunter's stomach emptied and he could feel a band tightening his chest. 'If you harm me, Dylan, you're never going to get out. Think sensibly about this.'

'I am thinking sensibly. I've thought of nothing else for nineteen years.'

Focus. Think what you can do. What to say. Hunter said, 'It doesn't have to be this way, Dylan. You're only making it worse for yourself. The police'll be here soon.'

Dylan let out a sharp, 'Ha,' then answered, 'No they won't. You came here alone. I saw you arrive. And you never had time to call them.'

Dylan arrowed a finger down at the desk, and Hunter could see he was pointing to his mobile.

'This is just me and you, Detective Sergeant Kerr. And do you know what's going through my head?'

'Whatever it is, Dylan, you don't need to do this. You don't need to make things worse for yourself. I know we can work something out.'

'I don't want to work something out. You've already ruined my life, and now I'm going to ruin yours.' Dylan pushed himself up and came from behind the desk, reaching into his boiler suit pocket. As he walked towards Hunter, he pulled out a plastic bag, shaking it from its folds.

Hunter's mind began racing, his heart pounding as fast as his thoughts. 'Don't be stupid, Dylan,' he shouted, straining to get free. His chair began to rock.

Dylan grabbed the back of the chair, halting Hunter's momentum. 'Do you know, I've watched several people die now, but the greatest thrill of them all came from putting a plastic bag over Rasa's head and watching her struggle. Boy, was that some buzz.'

'Dylan, there's still time to stop this.'

Dylan shook the plastic bag again, lifting it in front of Hunter's face. 'I reckon you'll last two minutes, tops. What do you think? I'm going to get such pleasure watching you suffer.' He opened out the bag and slipped it over Hunter's head.

CHAPTER FOURTEEN

'Hunter!'

The cry was somewhere distant at the back of his mind, and he thought he recognised it. The call came again, and someone, or something, shook his shoulders. This time he recognised the voice and he blinked open his eyes. 'Grace!' he cried, as her anxious face broke through the fogginess of his vision.

'Hunter. Thank God.'

'What's happened?' His head was still stinging and thumping. Then, everything came into focus. He remembered Dylan putting the plastic bag over his head and the panic it caused when he couldn't breathe. He remembered the taste of plastic as he sucked hard and then nothing else. He must have passed out. He looked around him. He was lying on the floor, no longer tied to the chair. Two young uniform cops were standing over him, concerned looks on their faces. He pulled back his gaze to Grace and said, 'How?'

Grace answered, 'I was having a drink with the team when I got your message, so I rang your mobile half a dozen times but it kept going to voicemail and I had a sense that something wasn't right, so I rang Beth. She told me you'd gone out. Told her it was something to do with work, and I guessed it was to do with those photos you had sent me earlier. I got them to put a trace on your phone and saw you were here, so I called for back-up and drove straight here. It's a good job I did.' She paused, taking a deep breath. 'I thought you were dead.' She gently punched his arm. 'Don't you dare do that again. You scared me.'

'Scared you? How do you think I felt? I thought I was a goner.' Hunter made an attempt to push himself up on an elbow, but he went light-headed, stars invading the back of his eyes, and he let himself back down.

'Just stay there, Hunter. An ambulance is on its way.'

'I don't need an ambulance. Once I get my breath back, I'll be okay.'

'One's on its way. Now don't argue.'

Hunter gave Grace a weak smile. He said, 'Dylan?'

'We got him. He tried to escape but the helicopter was up. They found him in the next compound.' She smiled. 'A guard dog bit him.'

Hunter started to laugh, but his throat was so dry it turned into a painful cough. 'Summary justice,' he said, closing his eyes for a moment and thinking what could have happened to him had it not been for Grace's quick thinking. He opened his eyes, and giving her hand a quick squeeze, he said, 'Thank you.'

'You owe me big time, Hunter Kerr,' she smiled cynically. 'And now do as you're told and wait for the ambulance. And don't argue if you have to go to hospital.'

'I promise, Miss,' he answered, crossing his chest.

Sitting up in a cubicle bed at Barnwell General, Hunter watched a nurse fit a blood pressure cuff around his arm. It was 10.30 p.m. In the hour since he'd been brought in, he had been assessed by a doctor, told he had a nasty cut on the back of his head that required suturing and then whipped down to the X-ray department. Now he was waiting for the results. As the pressure cuff started to squeeze his upper arm, he sought out the eyes of the nurse, wanting to ask questions as to his well-being. She was watching the digital read-out on the machine.

'How are you feeling?' she asked, not removing her gaze from the machine.

'Got a stinking headache.'

'Not surprised. That's a nasty cut you've got. We're just waiting for the doctor to view your X-rays and see if everything's all right, and then I can give you some paracetamol for the pain. Do you have any dizziness at all?'

Hunter started to shake his head, but that caused a fresh bout of pain, and wincing, he instantly stopped the movement. 'No, just a thumping headache.'

'There's a possibility you might have concussion, so I can't give you anything until the doctor's checked you over.'

The blood-pressure cuff slackened on his arm. The nurse studied the read-out and made a note on his chart. 'It's a little high, but nothing to worry about,' she said, removing the cuff. 'I'll take it again in an hour.' Hooking the chart over the end of his cubicle bed, she said, 'Is there anyone you need telling you're here?'

He was about to say Beth, when the cubicle curtains swung to one side and Beth appeared, a male nurse behind her. The male nurse said, 'Mr Kerr's wife is here.'

'Do you have a death wish or something?' she greeted him, and before he had time to respond, she added, 'Don't you think I've got enough on my plate at the moment, without worrying about you?'

Hunter noticed both nurses had adopted 'it's time for us to go' looks, which was reinforced when the staff nurse treating him said, 'I think we can leave you now your wife's here. I'll be back with the doctor as soon as he's free.' And with that, both nurses left.

Suddenly laden with guilt, Hunter answered, 'Who told you I was here?'

'Grace phoned me. Told me you'd been attacked by someone you were looking for. I spoke with the nurse when I got here, and he said you'd got a badly cut head that needed stitches and that you'd been down for X-rays. They're just monitoring you for concussion.' In the same breath, she continued, 'Let's take a look at the damage, then.'

Hunter lifted his head from the pillow and leaned forward. Beth loomed over him and started rooting gently through his hair. Even though he knew the wound had been cleaned, it stung as she parted the strands. He closed his eyes, holding his breath until she'd finished looking. As he rested his head, he asked, 'Is it bad?'

'No lasting damage. Your hair will cover the scar. He should have hit you harder, then he might have knocked some sense into you.'

'I didn't ask for this, Beth.'

'Didn't ask for this! You go off spinning me a yarn that you have something to chase up for work, and then I find out from Grace that you've been found at some godforsaken scrapyard with your head half bashed in, and that you'd gone there on your own, and you have the gall to say you didn't ask for this?'

Thank God Grace hadn't mentioned anything about him being tied to a chair and almost suffocated. He said, 'I thought the place was derelict. I didn't expect to find anybody there. He took me by surprise.' He watched Beth shaking her head at him.

'What am I going to do with you, Hunter Kerr? One day, you're going to give me a heart attack.'

He held her gaze, suddenly feeling very emotional as it hit home how differently things might have ended. It was a good thing Grace had had the intuition that something wasn't right

201

and had his phone signal traced. He swallowed hard. 'I'm really sorry, Beth.'

'You've got a lot of making up to do, Hunter.'

'I will. I promise.'

Breaking into a relieved smile, she slowly shook her head. 'Right, shall we see where that doctor is? Then we can get you home.'

Hunter awoke with a start, flinching at the sharp pain that came from the pull of the seven stitches at the back of his head. He rolled over onto his side and looked at the time on his bedside clock. 9.38 a.m. Surprisingly, he had slept for almost nine hours. It had to be the medication, he told himself with a smile. Last night they had got in just before midnight, and after seeing off his mum and dad with a short explanation of what had happened and a thank you for babysitting the boys, Beth had given him two co-codamol tablets with a generous measure of whisky. He had been so wired he thought he would have had trouble dropping off, but the whisky and tablets dulled the pain and relaxed him into sleep.

Now, despite the dull ache in his head, he felt remarkably refreshed, and throwing back the duvet he pushed himself out of bed and headed for the bathroom. He showered carefully, only dampening his hair, and dressed in his suit — he had to go to work, in spite of being told by the doctor he should take it easy for twenty-four hours.

Downstairs he found Beth in the kitchen. She didn't need to be at work until one o'clock. She turned as he entered, looking him up and down, and then threw him a scornful gaze.

'It was pointless the doctor telling you to take it easy today, wasn't it?' she said.

He finished tying the knot in his tie, drawing it up towards his shirt collar. 'I can't. There are things I need to do. Anyway, I'm only sat at a desk. It's not as though I'm doing heavy manual work.'

'Sat at a desk? I know you. You'll be off back to the scrapyard, I'll bet.'

'I won't. They won't let me anywhere near it. It's now a crime scene. I promise I'll stay at my desk. I'll take a couple more co-codamol and that will see me right. If I start feeling dizzy, I'll get Maddie to bring me home.'

Beth searched his face for a moment and then said, 'Make sure you do that, Hunter Kerr. I don't want you back in hospital. I've got enough on without looking after you as well.' She switched on the kettle and popped some bread into the toaster. 'What with Sark and now this, I don't know what I'm going to do with you. You're more trouble than the boys.'

Hunter let out a sharp laugh. 'Okay. Lecture over. I hear you loud and clear. I'll see what's happening and then get off early, if that's any help?'

'And I've heard that before as well,' she snorted, adding milk to two mugs.

Hunter gave Beth a peck on the cheek and took over making the tea. He remembered his phone was still at the vehicle dismantlers and said, 'Has anyone rung?'

'Grace,' Beth answered. 'She rang an hour ago and said that she's gone to the yard and that she'll be in touch later.'

Hunter nodded as he poured two teas.

Maddie fussed over Hunter the moment he stepped into the office, wanting to know the whole story, and while she made him a cuppa, he shared what had happened, after which he rang Grace on his desk phone. She answered on the third ring.

'Are you still at the yard?' he asked.

'Yes. Forensics are here. They got here half an hour ago. We locked the place down last night, and after briefing this morning me and Mike came down here with the DCI to make a start. Where are you?'

He told her he had just got into the office. 'What's St. John-Stevens like?'

'He's seething. And on the warpath. He's been quizzing me as to what I know. I told him I'd just got that text from you last night and showed it to him and left it at that. I haven't shown him the images from the second package you received. I've played dumb.'

'Do you think he believes you?'

'He can believe what he wants. I'm leaving it to you to make the decision what you tell him. I can get myself into enough trouble.' Lowering her voice, she said, 'I did remind him that I had fed in your suspicions about Dylan Wolfe and I could tell he was embarrassed by that.'

'He's certainly going to have to explain what he did about the information I've given. I'm going to play dumb myself about the packages and just say I thought that they were from a crank and that it wasn't until last night that I realised who they might have come from and what the clues meant. Half of that is true. In my defence, I'll tell the truth about him side-lining and ignoring me.' Following a pause, Hunter continued, 'Did you get a good look at those photos and newspaper articles pinned up on the back of the container where I found Rasa's body? I only got a glimpse of them last night, but I thought they might have something to do with what he was involved in back when I caught him in nineteen-ninety-one. They certainly looked old from what I could see.'

'Like you, I've only had a glimpse of them. Forensics are in there now and the container's sealed off, so I can't get a proper look. I've already asked them to get me some shots of them. I'll get them to snap some on my phone, and then I'll send them to you and you can have a look and see if they mean anything.' Her voice dropped even lower. 'St. John-Stevens is just heading my way so I can't say anymore, but just one thing before I go. The burned-out car they found Rasa's body in! They've done a chassis engine check and guess who it belongs to?'

'No idea. Go on, tell me.'

'None other than David Bannister. Your missing David Bannister.'

As Hunter spluttered, 'What!' before he could ask a further question, Grace ended the call and he was left looking at the dead handset with thoughts whizzing around inside his head.

Maddie caught his eye as she set down his mug of tea. 'Something up?' she asked.

Hunter told her what Grace had just said about David Bannister's car. 'I knew Dylan Wolfe was behind the Bannisters' disappearance. What did I say, eh?'

Maddie nodded.

Hunter was about to say more when he became conscious of someone entering the office. He turned sharply, straining the stitches in his head again, causing him to blink at the sharp pinch of his skin. He was surprised by the appearance of Detective Superintendent Dawn Leggate, and he greeted her with, 'Boss.'

'Yes, boss it is,' she responded, giving him a stern look. She set down her bag on his desk. 'Under normal circumstances, I should be giving you a bollocking for your escapades last night, but given that you've caught us a killer, and you got a nasty and permanent reminder of your foolhardiness, I'll leave it at that.'

Hunter watched his former boss's face lose its serious look to be replaced with a slight smile. Puzzled by her presence, a feeling of nervousness crept into his stomach. He said, 'This is a surprise.'

'For me as well, Hunter. You and I have Mr Robshaw to thank for that.'

Hunter's brows knitted together. 'Sorry?'

'He told me about your visit, what you told him about Dylan Wolfe and your hunch about his involvement in the disappearance of the Bannister family back in nineteen-ninety-one, and then we heard what happened last night, and the discovery of the Lithuanian girl's body in the family's burned-out car. I've been brought back to review the current investigation.'

'Gosh! Wow!'

'I've spoken very briefly with DCI St. John-Stevens and informed him what is happening, and now I want from thread to needle what brought you to the notion that Dylan Wolfe was involved in the family's disappearance and what you did with that information.' Dawn unbuttoned her coat, dragged up a chair and sat down. 'Before that, though, I bring good news.'

'I could do with some of that for a change.'

Dawn grinned. 'They found Billy Wallace's body yesterday on Sark. It was found washed up in a bay on the opposite side of the island from where you had your altercation with him. A post-mortem was done yesterday evening, and in spite of its state they are able to say that his injuries are consistent with the fall you described in your statement, and the pathologist has determined his death was by drowning, proving he was alive when he went into the water. I've spoken with a detective superintendent on Guernsey, and he assures me the investigation into Billy's death is now formally closed pending the inquest, which you will be notified of. Oh, and they will be releasing a press statement to that effect to stop any further speculation as to what happened on Sark.'

As Hunter's eyes rested on his boss's face, a huge feeling of relief washed over him

'Now show and tell me what you have on the Bannister family's disappearance and what connects Dylan Wolfe to it,' Dawn said, opening up her journal and clicking her pen.

Hunter took out the duplicate file and the crime scene photographs, spread out the photos in the order he would be delivering his information, and then repeated what he had told Michael Robshaw yesterday, slowing the pace whenever he saw Dawn making notes. As he came to the end of his account, he took out of his desk drawer the items from the two packages he had been sent, laying them out in their evidence bags over the top of the crime scene photographs.

Dawn stopped writing at this point, roaming her eyes over the items. When Hunter finished relaying how he had come by them, pointing at the tied-up doll, she asked, 'What action have you taken regarding these?'

'Well, I got the first package six days ago. At first, I wasn't sure what they were related to and if they had come from some nut-jack or other. It took me a couple of days to fathom out that it may have been related to the Rasa Katiliene, so initially, I didn't do anything, except bag them as evidence. Then, I learned from probation that Dylan Wolfe had been released on licence and had done a disappearing act from his hostel in Sheffield, and so I spoke with Grace and showed them to her and discussed the possibilities of the package coming from

Dylan Wolfe. She knew about the review I was doing into the Bannisters, and the theory I had about him possibly being involved in their disappearance, and so I discussed with her the possibility that he could have been involved in Rasa's disappearance as well, and that the note and items I'd been sent were related to that. She told me that the investigation into Rasa's possible abduction and probable murder was focussed on a convicted sex offender who had been the last to see Rasa. I told her I would hold onto them as exhibits, and asked her to feed Dylan's name into the enquiry, which I know she did.'

Dawn held up her hand to stop him there. 'Why didn't you feed it in yourself and hand over the evidence?'

'Under normal circumstances, I would have done. But Mr Robshaw's probably told you the issues I've been having with DCI St. John-Stevens. I'd already been told by him to stop the review into the Bannisters' disappearance even after I'd put forward Dylan Wolfe's name as a person of interest and shared my theory with him. I knew it was pointless approaching him, and I hoped Grace would be able to encourage the team to have a look at Dylan. When the second package came yesterday, I immediately sent the images to Grace and asked for a meeting to discuss what the clues meant. I'd fully intended handing all the exhibits over, but then, as you know, it came to me last night what they might mean and I couldn't resist going out for a look myself.'

'And I won't dwell any further on what my thoughts are about that.'

Hunter blushed. 'I wouldn't have needed to go out and do what I did if you'd have been in charge of the enquiry. I know you would have listened and actioned someone to look at Dylan Wolfe.'

'Well, I'm not going to respond to that. DCI St. John-Stevens is still heading up the investigation into the murder of Rasa Katiliene now we have found her body. My role is to conduct a review and nothing else. What I can say is that her body has been found in the boot of a car that once belonged to David Bannister, prior to his disappearance, which I'm guessing you probably know, given Grace is at the scene…' She broke off, smiling, and then continued, '…and that the work you have done as part of your review into the Bannister family's disappearance will now be handed over to MIT as part of their current investigation. Michael has told me, from your conversation with him yesterday, that the samples that were originally taken by SOCO in nineteen-ninety-one from the Bannister home are with forensics. I will be recommending, now we have Dylan Wolfe in custody, that those are now fast-tracked for examination.'

Hunter let out a happy sigh, shooting a sideways glance at Maddie, who had put just as much effort into the review as he had. Her face was glowing.

He returned his gaze to Dawn. 'Do Maddie and I get to be involved?'

'Not directly, I'm afraid, Hunter.' She saw his crestfallen expression and added, 'But that doesn't mean you are not involved as such. I will ensure your old team get the up-to-date file on the Bannisters, and that they liaise with you, so you won't be out of the loop. What I'm conscious of is that I don't want your relationship with St. John-Stevens to jeopardise the work that needs doing. Between us three and these four walls, the area I will be critical of in my report is that St. John-Stevens didn't take into account the information you had given him about Dylan Wolfe, delaying his arrest.'

Hunter nodded thoughtfully. After a few seconds of silence, he asked, 'Has Dylan said anything since he was caught last night?'

Dawn shook her head. 'Not as far as I'm aware. They will have bedded him down for the night. It's going to be lunchtime, I guess, before they do the first interview. He'll no doubt want a solicitor. My next job is to go and liaise with DCI St. John-Stevens at the scene and see what they have, and also break the news to him about bringing the Bannister case into the investigation. He'll probably already know that, with Rasa's body being found in David Bannister's old car. In the meantime, I want you to bundle the file and all the new exhibits you've got from Dylan Wolfe and prepare a full report for the MIT team. Okay?'

Hunter nodded, a self-congratulating smile spreading across his face.

It took Hunter two hours to compile his testimony detailing Dylan Wolfe's attack on him, after which he spent a further two hours going back through the Bannister file and his journal. He categorised the old and new evidence, handwriting a series of notes in preparation for drafting a new report and finished by bundling the exhibits from the two packages Dylan Wolfe had sent. At 12.15 p.m., with his head mashed, he put down his pen and announced to Maddie he was going for an early lunch and made his way down to the canteen.

Upon his return to the office, Maddie said, 'Grace has rung. She says can you ring her back.'

Hunter picked up the phone and called Grace's mobile.

She answered straight away with, 'Sorry I haven't rung. I'm still at the scene. It's been manic. They're just about to remove Rasa's body to take it to the mortuary and a low-loader's here to take David Bannister's car to the forensic drying room for examination. And Dawn Leggate's here. She's with the DCI.'

'Yes, I know. She was here to see me earlier. I didn't tell you when I messaged you yesterday, but I went to see Mr Robshaw on my way home from work, and told him about what had gone on with St. John-Stevens, and how he'd told me to close down my review of the Bannister case. I also mentioned that I'd earmarked Dylan as a suspect and asked him for some advice. After what happened to me last night and the finding of Rasa's body in David Bannister's old car, he's brought in Dawn to conduct a review of the investigation.'

He heard Grace let out a short laugh. 'No wonder the DCI's mooching around with a face like a smacked arse.' Breaking off for a second, she continued, 'The reason I've rung you is because of the photos and newspaper articles that are taped to the back of the container. I haven't been able to get a close look at them yet because of CSI working in there, but they have photographed them on my phone and I'm going to email them across to you. I've had a quick glance at the photos and they certainly raise questions as to whether Dylan might be involved in other attacks. The newspaper articles are referring to some missing women back in ninety-one. The names don't mean a thing to me. There are also a number of photos with them, which look as though they might have been taken by him. Many of them are discoloured with age and damp has got to them, but it does appear to me at first glance that in a few of the photographs the women are dead. There are a couple of them laid on the ground and from the way they're positioned, they certainly don't appear to be alive. There're also the local paper's pieces relating to those women that were raped back then, including that one you and I went to on the Craggs that night. Elizabeth Barnett.'

Hunter remembered that. He and Grace were not long into their probationary period as constables and had got called to attend a woman found unconscious on Barnwell Craggs. She was Dylan Wolfe's third victim. It transpired he had tried to rape her, that she had fought back and he had bashed her with a rock. For a week it had been touch and go whether she would survive or not. In the end, she gave evidence against him in court.

Hunter was about to respond when Grace said, 'I'm going to email everything to you and you can be having a look through while I'm finishing up here. I'll liaise with you when I get back to the office. Now Dawn's on the DCI's case, he won't be able to say anything when I pop in to see you.' On that cheery note, she hung up.

Within a minute the images taken on Grace's phone came through as several attachments to an email. Hunter counted eight in all and he clicked on the first jpeg file. It showed the montage of the dozen or so photographs together with the same amount of cut-out newspaper articles he had first sighted on the back wall of the container. It reminded him of an incident board when a major case was running, except there was no time-line sequence and there were no spidery lines connecting each piece. He enlarged it to get a closer look, but the photographs and newspaper cuttings lacked definition and so he was unable to read any of the headlines or get a more detailed view of the photographs.

He closed it down and opened another attachment. This one was of the front page of the *Chronicle*, and it featured the investigation into the death of sixty-four-year-old June Waring, instantly sparking a ghostly memory. It had been Hunter's first sudden death upon starting his career in 1991. A neighbour had called the police because June hadn't been seen for a few days. The rented terraced house she'd lived in had been locked when Hunter had arrived with his tutor, Roger Mills, and they had broken a downstairs window to gain access. Hunter had found her upstairs, tucked up in bed, dead. It was his first sight of a dead body, and June Waring's face had haunted his dreams for several nights thereafter. Following the discovery, he and Roger had begun enquiring into her lifestyle, quickly learning that June was an alcoholic with a history of mental and physical problems and initially it had been treated as a straightforward sudden death. Until the post-mortem. During that, the pathologist had discovered that June had been raped vaginally and anally shortly before her death, the brutal attack bringing on a cardiac arrest, killing her, and it had become a murder investigation. June Waring had been Dylan Wolfe's first victim. He had raped her, tucked her back up in bed, locked up the house and posted the key back through the letterbox to make it appear as if her death had been the result of a heart attack in bed. Had it not been for the thoroughness of the pathologist, Dylan might well have got away with it.

Closing down the attachment, Hunter opened a few more that featured articles from the local *Chronicle*. Among these attachments were stories relating to Dylan's second and third victim, sixty-six-year-old Anita Thompson, who had been battered and raped in her home, though she'd survived, and fifty-eight-year-old Elizabeth Barnett, whom Dylan had attacked on the Craggs when she'd been taking a shortcut home — the case he and Grace had got involved in. In these last two incidents, Hunter remembered how both witnesses had described their attacker as wearing a ski mask, and it had been that which had been his undoing. Hunter had been called to a domestic incident, after Dylan had attacked his girlfriend and fled, and he had found a ski mask hidden away in a wardrobe, sparking a major hunt for him. In an act of revenge, Dylan had returned to his girlfriend's flat and stabbed her several times, then he'd gone on the run.

A week later, Hunter had received a tip-off about where Dylan was hiding out and he and Barry Newstead had tracked him down and captured him. Visions of all those events flooded Hunter's thoughts and for a moment he found himself being transported back to 1991. It had been his first experience of encountering sleepless nights thinking about a case, a hardship that was to return time and time again and something that still occurred even with nineteen years' practice behind him.

Hunter finished looking at those attachments and opened a couple more. These were photographs. Twelve in total. They depicted what appeared to be elderly women in street scenes. From the background he recognised they were local. Five of the photos appeared to be of the same woman. There were two of her walking past some shops. In another two she was standing at a bus stop and in the final one the woman was coming out of the front door of a house. The door was green and Hunter tried to zoom in on the number, but it was just a blur. The other seven photographs appeared to be of a different woman and they all appeared to have been taken at various locations along Barnwell High Street. He recognised many of the shops in the background, the majority of which were now owned by different traders. Like the other photographs, the images were not of good quality and he was unable to identify who the woman was. She didn't look like any of the three victims he had been involved with. Closing that down, he opened the next jpeg. This was another newspaper article. The headline was a simple one — MISSING? — and he zoomed in on the opening paragraph, reading it quickly.

Police in Barnwell are appealing for anyone to contact them regarding the whereabouts of 79-year-old Alison Chambers, who has not been seen for seven days. She was last seen at a bus stop, a quarter of a mile from her home, after telling a neighbour she was catching a bus to Rotherham to do her weekly shopping.

Hunter lifted his eyes from the screen. Those words and the woman's name triggered something in the back of his mind. He returned his gaze to the computer, zeroing in on the date of the newspaper article. Friday 19th May 1991. Two months before he'd become a cop. He was about to read more of the feature when the name came to him. Her missing report had been one of the first case files Maddie had handed to him. 'Crikey me,' he blurted out, looking at his colleague.

'What's up?' she responded, lifting her eyes from her computer.

'Maddie, one of the first files you showed me was a missing woman called Alison Chambers. Does that ring any bells?'

She nodded. 'Yes, I put it into the out tray to go back to the archives for filing. Why?'

'Before I got clobbered last night, I noticed some old newspaper articles and photographs in the container I was searching at the vehicle dismantlers and Grace has sent me images of them. Several of them relate to Dylan's victims — cases that I was involved with when I first joined the police — and the crimes he went down for. But one of the images I've just opened relates to a missing person from nineteen-ninety-one, Alison Chambers, whose file you showed me on my first day here, and I think Dylan could have been involved in her disappearance.'

Maddie's mouth dropped open and she pushed herself up from her desk. 'I'll get it out of the tray.'

As Maddie stepped across to retrieve the folder from the top of one of the filing cabinets, Hunter returned to the computer, opening up the last attachment from Grace. This was another piece from a newspaper, but next to it were two separate photographs. Closing in on the photos, he saw that they appeared to be shots of an elderly woman lying in a shallow, muddy grave, although he couldn't make out her face. The hairs on the back of his neck instantly prickled. Hunter widened the image, settling his eyes upon the newspaper headline — WHERE IS CATHERINE? — after which he immediately dropped his sight to the opening paragraph:

Police are becoming increasingly concerned about 75-year-old Catherine Dewhurst who was last seen on Sunday, when she left her home on Park Close to walk to nearby St Margaret's church.

Hunter left his reading there, zoning in on the date of the article. It was published on the 28th April 1990. Catherine Dewhurst's missing file had also been one he had read on his first day working in Cold Case. He lifted his eyes from his screen, looking across the room, where Maddie was just picking out the folder for Alison Chambers. He said, 'While you're there, Maddie, can you get Catherine Dewhurst's file as well? I think we've found ourselves another of Dylan Wolfe's victims.'

Hunter opened the case files Maddie handed to him, selecting the typed copies of Alison Chambers' and Catherine

Dewhurst's missing reports, the first documents that headed up each file. Each of the reports had their photographs paperclipped to them, and after giving them a brief read-over to reacquaint himself with each of the disappeared women's stories, he rang Grace. She picked up on the second ring. 'Are you still at Bones' yard?' he asked.

She told him she was and said, 'The boss and the DCI are here as well. Forensics are just starting on the portacabin I found you in.'

A flash of what had happened the previous evening entered Hunter's inner vision, making him shiver, but he quickly pushed it away as he latched on to what Grace had just said, suddenly finding it amusing how she referred to Dawn Leggate as the boss and not St. John-Stevens. With a smirk, he said, 'I think you need to get a full search team down there, Grace.' He told her that he had just finished viewing the attachments she had sent him and summarised what he had uncovered with regards to the disappearances of Alison Chambers and Catherine Dewhurst. 'The photographs make it look like Dylan was following them around, learning their movements before he made his move. I wish we had found these when we caught him back in ninety-one. We did search the portacabin but not the containers because we were told that there were only engine parts in them. And to be honest, Grace, I hadn't enough experience to know what I was looking for.'

'Have you any idea whether Alison or Catherine could be the woman who was photographed in the grave?'

'No. I'm not familiar with either of them. I've got copies of their missing reports with their pictures attached, but the images you've sent are not of good enough quality to enable me to see which of the two, if either, it is. I'll send you images of the photos I have on their files and you can compare them with the ones from the container.'

'Yes, I'll do that. Forensics have taken them down and put them in exhibit bags, but I should be able to get a look at them. With regards to the search, I'll speak with Dawn and St. John-Stevens and tell them your thoughts.'

'I'm sure St. John-Stevens will have an issue with that, but if the boss agrees, he can't do anything about it. And especially as Rasa's body was found there, and the Bannisters' car is there. It wouldn't surprise me if their bodies are buried somewhere in that yard.'

'Dawn has already come up with that, Hunter.'

'Great minds think alike,' Hunter chuckled back.

'Show-off. Anyway, I can't be talking to you all day, some of us are busy.' Grace let out a short laugh and added, 'Send me the images of Alison Chambers and Catherine Dewhurst and I'll liaise with the bosses. I'll get back to you if I get something.' With that, she ended the call.

For a few seconds, Hunter stared at the handset before hanging up and looking across at Maddie. 'I'm going to go through these files and make some notes for when MIT have their briefing. Even if we can't be involved, we can prepare the information for them.'

Hunter sent Maddie home at her appointed time, staying on for a few hours reading through the files and making notes. He was also eagerly awaiting an update from Grace. When she hadn't rung by six o'clock, he tried her phone only for it to go through to voicemail. Leaving a message to say that he would be at home if she wanted to talk, he turned off the office lights and made his way down to the car park. As he was about to get into his car, he spotted DC Caroline Blake, one of the MIT

Family Liaison Officers, having a cigarette break in the smoking area, and he sauntered across to her.

'Hi, Hunter,' she greeted him, dropping the cigarette down by her side.

'Have you heard anything from Grace? I've just tried to get hold of her, but her phone's gone to voicemail.'

Caroline stubbed out the cigarette and binned it. 'Last I heard, an hour ago, was they had just ordered additional lights so that they could carry out a more thorough search of an area they've identified as a possible grave site. I'm guessing they're going to be working well into the night on this.'

A jolt of excitement lurched through Hunter's body, while at the same time a sense of disappointment overcame him because he wanted to be there. Quickly dismissing the thought, he asked, 'Has Dylan Wolfe said anything?'

'Not a word. Mike Chapman and Tony Bullars had an initial interview with him this afternoon, but they said he just sat there laughing all the way through. Wouldn't say anything about Rasa's body in the car or about attacking you. Even when they went through the attack on you, he just laughed. He's behaving like a psycho.'

'He is a psycho,' Hunter returned. 'Okay, Caroline, good luck. And tell Mike and Tony I asked after them.'

Caroline nodded. 'Are you in tomorrow?'

'Yes, eight o'clock.'

'I'll tell them to come and have a cuppa with you and update you. You never know, you might be back on the team now the boss's back.'

Hunter smirked. *Another colleague who's acknowledging Dawn Leggate as the boss.* 'I'll not raise my hopes. We'll see what tomorrow brings. Goodnight.' With that, Hunter made his way back to the car.

CHAPTER FIFTEEN

Hunter was fully awake by 6.15 a.m. the next morning, having had a restless evening and night. He had finally given up waiting for Grace to ring him at 10 p.m. and gone to bed feeling fractious, annoyed she hadn't contacted him to give him an update. Then he had tossed and turned, occasionally drifting off, but only for an hour or so on each occasion, waking up in a sweat with his heart hammering, as the vision of Dylan Wolfe putting the plastic bag over his head invaded his sleep. The last time he had dropped off had been just after 4 a.m. and then he had woken with a start again when he imagined he couldn't breathe. With his head back on his pillow, he drew in slow, deep breaths. Five minutes after quarter-past-six he turned over, turned off his alarm and got out of bed.

He pulled into the office car park just after 7 a.m., surprised to see quite a number of cars already there and the lights blaring on the first floor where MIT were based. *Something's happening*, he thought, grabbing his briefcase and closing the car door. He trotted up the stairs to the first floor and headed to MIT instead of his own office. He didn't care if St. John-Stevens was there or not. He wanted to know what was happening. The entrance doors to the MIT corridor were open, so he didn't need to wait for someone to allow him access. As he approached MIT, he clocked Detective Superintendent Leggate coming out of her old office. She looked his way and signalled him to come, propping open the door.

'Just the person,' she said as Hunter slipped past her. 'Take a seat,' she added, following him in.

'Where's the DCI?' Hunter asked, sitting down.

Dawn went behind the desk. 'Probably on his way back to the yard. We didn't finish until midnight, and I told him to start there this morning while I took care of briefing.'

'Have you found something?'

'You'll be pleased to know, we have.'

'A body?'

Dawn nodded.

'Where?'

'Buried behind the container where Rasa Katiliene's body was found. There's a gap between that and the fence, and pieces of old timber were piled there, but the moment we moved them we could see the ground showed signs of disturbance. We had to remove a section of the fence to make room to dig, and a couple of feet down we found a clothed skeleton. From the clothing we are able to match it to several of the photographs that we recovered from the container, so it looks like one of the bodies is either Alison Chambers or Catherine Dewhurst. We won't know until we get it down to the mortuary, and even then, we won't know unless we can get DNA from family members. You don't know if either victim has living relatives, do you?'

Hunter shook his head. 'We never conducted a review of them. Maddie and I focussed on the Bannisters' disappearance. I have gone through them again, and one of them had a son who reported her missing, but he was in his forties in ninety-one, so I don't know if he's still alive or not.'

'Not to worry. There's still a lot of work to do today, so that's something we can look at in briefing.'

'Is it just the one body you've found?'

Dawn gave a sharp nod. 'Because of the late hour when we found it, we decided it was too late to start excavating the area any further, for fear of losing any evidence, so we put a tent over the dig and secured everything ready to start this morning. The forensic team will be starting about eight.' Pausing, she continued, 'Once we get the body removed, we will be extending the search. Given the photographs and newspaper cuttings in the container, I have every reason to believe that there will be further bodies.' She raised a finger. 'And on that note, I have other news.'

Hunter gave her a questioning look.

'Don't look at me like that,' she smirked. 'It was you who made the request.'

'Request?'

'For DNA tests to be done on the samples taken from the Bannisters' house in nineteen-ninety-one. In particular those taken from the floor of the kitchen.'

'Oh, those.'

'Oh, those indeed. Well, you'll be pleased to know it's reaped a reward. Yes, the samples have been corrupted by bleach, but not enough to prevent the team getting DNA from them. And, by cross-referencing with other samples taken from the house, they have found that the traces of DNA from the floor samples belong to none other than David Bannister.'

Hunter's jaw dropped and his eyes widened. 'Wow!' For a few seconds, Hunter was silent as he processed the information. Then, he replied, 'This changes many aspects of the original investigation and it may even change the conclusion. Even if David had killed his wife and daughter, given the amount of blood that was cleaned up from the floor, the SOCO indication was that whoever was attacked there would have been either killed or seriously injured. Certainly in no fit state to do that cleaning job, or carry and transport the bodies away from the house. Someone else had to be involved in their disappearance.'

'I agree with that, Hunter. I've got the Bannister file from the DCI and read through the forensic submission from back in ninety-one. The original analysis was as you've just pointed out. The area of blood that had been cleaned up was significant enough to show that whoever it belonged to would have either needed immediate medical attention or was dead. And as you are aware from reading the report, it was intimated that the blood was that of Tina Bannister.'

Giving a swift nod, Hunter agreed with Dawn's summarisation of facts.

Dawn continued, 'Have you managed to pull together a report of the case?'

Hunter shook his head. 'I made a start on it yesterday. I've updated everything but it just needs typing up.'

'Okay, I want you to crack on with that as a priority. I want you to include the fresh information from the witnesses that are mentioned in the original report from ninety-one, and any new witness you have discovered from your recent enquiries. I want you to map out clearly the gaps you have uncovered and reviewed. Is that understood?'

Hunter nodded again.

'I want it ready for this evening's briefing so we can start first thing tomorrow morning with a fresh investigation into the family's disappearance. Hopefully, when we continue with our search this morning, we will find their bodies and resolve the matter. As you know, David Bannister's car has been removed to the forensic drying room for examination, although I'm not too hopeful about that yielding anything, given its condition.' She sighed. 'I live in hope, though, as they say.'

'I'll work on it straight away, boss.'

Hunter had started to leave, when Dawn continued, 'I want you to deliver that report in person this evening, Hunter. And I want you and Maddie to join the investigation...' Pausing, she added, '...unless you have something more pressing?'

A sudden surge of adrenalin shot through him, and on a euphoric note, Hunter replied, 'No, we've nothing, boss. All we've been working on is the Bannister case. We'd love to be involved.' As he turned, he said, 'What about the DCI?'

'I'll be speaking with St. John-Stevens after briefing, and I'll apprise him of the situation and my decision.'

Hunter couldn't stop himself breaking into a smile as he bounced back along the corridor to the cold case office.

Hunter spent the remainder of the morning typing a fresh summary for the Bannister casefile, adding in all the new material he and Maddie had gleaned over the last fortnight. It now included Roger Mills' recollection of the crime scene, George Evers' information about the man he had seen Tina with at the pub, and the one who'd visited her house weeks before they'd all disappeared, together with the new evidence from former neighbour Denise Harris.

Following the revelation from the forensics lab that the cleaned-up blood from the kitchen of the Bannister home was David's, Hunter was convinced that the latter person seen by the neighbour was now crucial to the investigation and that he was more than likely linked to the car Denise Harris had seen, and he emphasised this hunch in his conclusion. It took him two-and-a-half hours to pull the new report together, and by the time he'd finished it ran to ten pages, four more than the original summary. Printing off the pages and briefly casting his eyes over them to ensure he had captured all the new facts and that it flowed with the original synopsis to make for a legible report, he handed it to Maddie for her to read and check if any adjustments were needed. Leaving her with it, he went down to the locker room, changed into his running gear and made his way out to Manvers Lake for a brisk three-mile run around its perimeter. He felt good as he jogged through the industrial estate, and by the time he had reached the lake, he was in a comfortable stride, his breathing hard but not laboured, his body and mind feeling the best it had been for a fortnight.

In spite of the November chill, Hunter was lathered in sweat by the time he got back, and he took his time in the shower, soaping himself generously while contemplating the report he had put together. He and Maddie had worked so hard on reviewing the case, and he couldn't wait to deliver it at evening briefing. He knew he shouldn't be thinking this, but he hoped St. John-Stevens would be there. He couldn't wait to see the look on his face.

Before making his way back to the office, Hunter grabbed a sandwich and banana from the canteen.

Maddie grabbed his attention the moment he stepped into the office. 'They've found a second body at the dismantlers. This one looks like it's Catherine Dewhurst. Grace rang while you were out. She said the body was right next to the other one. It's definitely female, and the clothing matches the description of Catherine's.'

'They've not found any sign of the Bannisters yet, then?'

Maddie hunched her shoulders. 'Grace was only brief on the phone. It sounded as if she was in a hurry. She just said, "tell Hunter I'll see him in an hour's time."'

'Afternoon, you two,' Grace said, breezing into the cold case office.

Hunter and Maddie lifted their eyes from their work.

'A little bird tells me you're on the team,' Grace said, slouching into a chair and scooting it next to Hunter. She gave him a little dig with her elbow.

'And not a moment too soon. We've been doing your job for you for the last week or so,' Hunter returned sharply.

'Oooh, get you.' Grace made to rise. 'Well, if that's the case, you won't want to hear what I have to say.'

'You are not leaving here, Grace Marshall, until we have a full update.'

Grace laughed, sinking back down in the seat. 'Well, it definitely looks as though the two bodies we've found are that of Alison Chambers and Catherine Dewhurst. The clothing matches with the photographs from the container. Like you said, it certainly looks as if Dylan was following them around for a while before he abducted them. As to cause of death, we should have an indication of that when their post-mortems are done this afternoon.'

'Any sign of any other gravesites there? The Bannisters'?'

Grace shook her head. 'Not yet. Certainly, there are no more next to the two we've found. We've only searched half of the place, though, and that includes looking in all the scrap cars. It's going to be at least another day before we know.' Pausing, looking directly at Hunter, she added, 'Anyway, how are your interviewing skills?'

Hunter looked at Grace, puzzled. 'What do you mean?'

'Well, you've been tossing it off for the past couple of months, what with Sark and this. Thought you might be out of touch.'

Hunter caught Grace winking across at Maddie. 'Cheeky mare,' he responded. 'Any road, why are you asking?'

'You and I have an audience with someone who says he will only talk to you. Dylan Wolfe.'

'Dylan!'

'Mike and Tony have not long done a second interview with him, and he's refusing to say anything other than that he will only talk to you.'

Hunter's lips pursed. 'Why me?'

Grace shrugged her shoulders.

As Hunter entered the interview room with Grace and clapped eyes on Dylan Wolfe, feelings of anger and vulnerability overcame him at the same time, spiralling his memory back to two nights earlier, causing him to catch his breath. The flashback momentarily stopped him in his tracks, but he quickly recovered, making his movement look natural by switching the paperwork he was holding from one hand to the other. He sat down at the table opposite. Grace joined him, and in that moment, silence reigned as Hunter's eyes were drawn to the criss-cross scars mapping Dylan's face that now made him look ugly and evil.

'Take a good look. This is your handiwork,' Dylan said, engaging Hunter's stare and pointing to his face.

Hunter was about to respond, telling him that his injuries had been all his own fault, but quickly stopped himself. That would only create a division between them, and Hunter was here to do a job. He took another deep breath, setting down his paperwork, all the time holding Dylan's gaze. 'I've been told you would like to speak with me,' he said, making himself as comfortable as he could in the secure metal seat and offering up a phoney friendly smile.

His opening seemed to instantly diffuse Dylan's tension, who returned a smile that was more cynical than warm and answered, 'No hard feelings, then?'

'None whatsoever, Dylan. I'm here, aren't I? And so are you.'

'I'd rather be on your side of the table, though,' Dylan gestured.

'Well, we all make our decisions, don't we?' Hunter diverted his eyes to the bunch of papers he had clipped into three bundles — the Bannisters, Alison Chambers and Catherine Dewhurst — wondering which one Dylan would talk about first. 'As I said, I'm told you want to speak with me.'

'Yes, there's something I need to clear up.'

Grace reached across to switch on the recording machine.

Dylan slapped his hands on the table, making them both jump. 'Don't switch that on. I'll only talk off record.'

'We can't do that, Dylan. It's against the rules. Everything has to be recorded or written down,' Grace answered.

Dylan pushed himself back and folded his arms. 'In that case, we're wasting each other's time.'

Hunter leaned forward. 'Dylan, we would be heavily criticised if we went into court and said that you made a confession and we didn't have it recorded. You know that.'

'It's not a confession.'

'Well, what is it, then?'

'I want to make a deal.'

Hunter settled back, breaking into a smile. 'We can't do deals with you. It doesn't work like that. You know what evidence we have against you. Two of my colleagues have already interviewed you on two occasions and told you.'

'I think you'll do a deal when I tell you what I have.'

Hunter looked briefly at Grace. Her face was deadpan. He returned to looking across at Dylan. 'What's it in relation to? Tell us that and we can make a decision on whether it's evidence or not.'

'It's about David Bannister's car.' Dylan's mouth twisted into a cocky grin. 'I think you'll be very interested in what I have to say about it.'

The mere mention of David Bannister had Hunter hooked. 'Okay, Dylan, tell us why you think we'll be interested in making a deal.'

Dylan Wolfe spoke uninterrupted for ten minutes, Hunter and Grace taking in everything he told them without their eyes leaving his face for a moment. As he finished, he eased himself upright. 'Well, is that worth a deal, or not?'

Hunter bundled his paperwork together and picked it up off the table. Glancing at Grace, he returned his gaze to Dylan. 'We'll need to see our boss, Dylan, and speak with her, and we'll also need to make a few enquiries before we get back to you. Only then will you know whether we've got a deal or not.'

The sun was dropping low in the sky when Hunter pulled off the road by Sprotbrough Weir onto a dirt track that led them to an old stone bridge beneath a railway track no longer in use; twenty-five years ago, the track had been used by a local pit to transport coal to the goods yard, but since the closure of the mines, the rails had been ripped up and the tracks were now only used by walkers and ramblers. He slowed the car as he approached the narrow bridge; a concrete bollard at the entrance meant they could travel no further, so he stopped and turned off the engine.

'This is where David Bannister's car was dumped.' Hunter was speaking to Dawn Leggate, who was sitting beside him. In the back were Grace and Maddie.

'Right here?' Dawn responded.

'No. Not exactly here. Dylan told us it was at the other end of the field, through the tunnel. This was once the main thoroughfare through to a hamlet called Levitt Hagg. It's no longer there. It was abandoned in the nineteen-fifties because of the poor housing conditions. Many of the foundations are still there, but they're the only signs of the place,' Hunter answered.

'And you think this is where he brought the Bannisters' bodies?'

Hunter nodded sharply. 'I'm certain. There's an opening at the other end of the field that leads straight to Levitt Hagg. It's just a stone's throw from where David's car was dumped and burned out.'

'And the area was never searched?'

'As far as I'm aware, no. I've spoken with Roger Mills and he says the burnt-out car was reported to the police by whoever found it, but it wasn't traced back to David.'

'And how did Dylan manage to hide it in the container all this time?'

'The local police used to call on Bones to recover abandoned vehicles, and Dylan was working for him back then and so was able to pick it up and hide it.'

'Very convenient.'

'Very,' Hunter agreed. 'And fortunate for us.'

'But we don't know if the Bannisters are actually buried over there?' Dawn pointed through the tunnel to the overgrown wasteland beyond.

'No. But it's my guess they are. The ruins are pretty much overgrown, and there are a lot of dykes and a couple of wells where bodies could be easily hidden. I've spoken with the council planning department and they are going to send me some old maps of the location.'

'And what's the deal for Dylan to give you a statement?'

'We won't oppose a psychiatric assessment or block him going into a psychiatric hospital. He knows that he'll be going down for a whole life term, and he'd rather spend it in a secure hospital than prison.'

'But that's the most probable outcome anyway.'

Hunter gave a wry smile. 'I know, but I never told him that. I said I'd see what I could do.'

'Crafty bugger.' Dawn slapped Hunter across the thigh. 'Well, staying here is not going to get anything done. I've got a search to organise, you three have got some phone calls to make, and we need to pull together the evidence. We'll use your office.'

Back at the office, Dawn Leggate organised a search team with sniffer dogs for the next morning. Hunter, Grace and Maddie took on the new enquiries arising from Dylan Wolfe's interview. Alice Bannister, Roger Mills, George Evers and Denise Harris were all telephoned and asked a series of fresh questions, their responses recorded with a view to getting new statements. Afterwards, following a quick scrum-down, where each of the detectives briefed Dawn on the new information they had been given, she directed a plan of action and then left the three of them to prepare their interview strategy while she returned to MIT for evening briefing. Before leaving, Dawn told them to meet her at Levitt Hagg at 10 a.m. the next morning and to come prepared for a long day.

CHAPTER SIXTEEN

At the following morning briefing in MIT, Hunter fed in the report he had done on the disappearances of Alison Chambers and Catherine Dewhurst, pointing to each of their photographs on the updated incident board as he made reference to them. DCI St. John-Stevens took briefing. Dawn had arranged to meet with the search team at Levitt Hagg, leaving Hunter with specific instructions not to mention anything about the search for the Bannister family and although he kept to the script, he felt as if he was operating underhand. From time to time, as his eyes left his notes and drifted into the audience, he couldn't help but catch a glimpse of St. John-Stevens' face. The look he returned didn't disguise his unhappiness with Hunter's presence, and Hunter wanted to send a smirk his way but resisted the urge as he finished his presentation.

Hunter waited for questions, but the DCI stepped up to the podium, quickly jumping in, begrudgingly thanking him for his input and ushering him back to his seat. St. John Stevens then brought them up to date with the removal of Alison Chambers' and Catherine Dewhurst's bodies to the morgue, where post-mortems were being carried out that morning, and informed the team that the extended search of the vehicle dismantlers yard was continuing in the hope of finding evidence related to the Bannister family. At this announcement, Hunter dipped his head. Under normal circumstances, he would have mentioned the search at Levitt Hagg, but following Dawn's instructions, he said nothing, letting the DCI wind up briefing by issuing the day's list of tasks. Not surprisingly, he left out Hunter and Maddie, and usually Hunter would have been miffed, but not today. This morning, he, Maddie and Grace had an appointment with Detective Superintendent Leggate at 10 a.m.

To avoid drawing attention to themselves by leaving a parked police vehicle near the old tunnel and footpath to Levitt Hagg, Hunter, Maddie and Grace took the longer route to the ruins, through Sprotbrough, leaving their fleet car near The Boat Inn and making their way on foot along the canal side to the old moorings of the abandoned hamlet.

During their journey the wind had picked up, and though it wasn't cold by any means, it was strong, and buffeted a line of trees that fronted the remnants of a set of cottages, whipping up trails of dead leaves. Hunter scrunched through them as he looked for an entrance to the hamlet, a flashback of his childhood exploding inside his head, and he wanted to kick out and scatter the leaves around like he used to.

The gap they found was through the doorway of a shell of a cottage, and stepping carefully over stone debris, they emerged into an overgrown back yard. Hunter heard before he saw Dawn Leggate. She was with a uniform inspector, engaged in conversation, holding between them a large plan of the area, the inspector pointing into the swaying trees where Hunter caught his first glimpse of the search team. The three detectives sidled up, bidding them 'good morning,' as they approached. Dawn and the inspector turned their heads.

Dawn said, 'How did briefing go?'

'Good,' Hunter answered.

'Was any mention made of the Bannisters?'

'Only that the search was being extended down at the vehicle dismantlers.'

'Good, and I'd like to keep it that way. For today, at least.'

'How's this search going?' Hunter asked.

Dawn darted a nod at the inspector. 'Steph here has mapped out an area she wants to try first. This place has two wells and is surrounded by an old dyke. It was probably dug to prevent flooding when it was originally built, but it's long since got clogged up and overgrown, and as Steph has pointed out, if the Bannisters were dumped or buried here, because of the state of the buildings, this is the most likely place to hide them, so we're starting here. We've had a quick look in the wells and there's a bit of water in them, so we can't see the bottom, but we're holding off sending anyone down them until we've searched the dyke first. We've not long started on that, and there's a lot of overgrown vegetation to clear before a thorough search can be done.'

For over two hours Hunter meandered around the old hamlet, visiting some of the ruins, where he caught only the briefest of signs — bits of broken furniture — that the place had ever been lived in. He didn't even know this place existed, or anything about it, until his Google search a few days ago. Resting beside the River Don, this must have been a marvellous place to live in the summer. It was a shame it had been abandoned following the closure of the old limestone quarry a hundred yards along the bank. If any of these cottages were still habitable today, they would cost a fortune to buy.

He was just feeling the pangs of hunger and was about to make his way back to the group to suggest getting something to eat when a shout went up. Hunter whipped his head in the direction of the call and saw an officer with his hand raised. Dawn, the inspector, Grace and Maddie had already set off towards the search team.

When Hunter got there, everyone was looking down into the overgrown gully and his eyes fell on one of the officers who was on bended knees, reaching into the entrance of a manmade stone bridge that had obviously been built to get across the dyke.

'There's something here. It looks like a blanket or something similar,' the uniform officer was calling back, reaching further in. A few seconds later, he scuttled back out on his knees and looking up, he said, 'There's a body. I can just make out a skull.'

A forensics team was there within the hour, and an hour after that the forensic supervisor told Dawn that they had found two adults' skeletons wrapped in blankets beneath the bridge. There was no sign of a child, he told them, but they had also found a household carving knife and a green onyx ashtray. Hunter recalled the latter item being mentioned during one of his conversations with his former tutor and colleague Roger Mills, and he mentioned that to Dawn.

'It looks like we've found the Bannisters,' she responded. 'Though we're not going to know that for definite until the post-mortems have been conducted, and maybe not even then. In the meantime, we seal off this area, get the bodies recovered and get the knife and ashtray fast-tracked for analysis.'

It was 9 p.m. before Hunter got home. Dawn had told Grace, Maddie and himself to go straight home and that she would contact them all later with instructions. It reminded Hunter of his undercover days when a sensitive operation was running. The two skeletons had been recovered, sealed inside body bags with the blankets they had been found wrapped in, and transported to the Medico Legal Mortuary in Sheffield, where Dawn had arranged for post-mortems to be carried out tomorrow. Despite a thorough search beneath the old stone bridge, they had not found any remains of a child and that had left them all puzzled as to whether it was the Bannisters they had found or not, and so Dawn had arranged for a fresh search to begin at first light the next day in the surrounding location.

As Hunter tucked into a pizza, his whole body was fizzing with adrenaline. He would definitely need a couple of glasses of whisky to bring himself down before he went to bed.

He poured himself a generous measure of Glenfiddich, and a glass of wine for Beth — she wanted to talk about his day — and made his way through to the lounge. He had just settled down when he felt his mobile ping in his pocket and he pulled it out. It was a message from Dawn. He read, *You were right about the prints. Meet me at force headquarters, 8 a.m. sharp.*

Following a meeting with the ACC Crime Commander and Dawn, Hunter drove back to the MIT facility with snippets of their discussion and deliberations flashing through his mind, sending his thoughts into overdrive. He had never been privy to anything like it in his career. As he parked up and climbed out of the car, Dawn said to him, 'Are you okay with this?'

Hunter looked at her and nodded.

'Okay, let's do it.'

The pair of them made their way up the stairs, Hunter rehearsing his lines inside his head as he went. As they passed the MIT Office, Dawn poked her head through the door and asked after the DCI. She was told he was in his office and she made her way along the corridor, with Hunter in tow. Hunter's stomach fluttered.

Dawn didn't knock before she entered. The DCI was at his desk, going over some paperwork. He looked up as they stepped in. He gazed at Dawn first and then over her shoulder at Hunter. Hunter saw him pale and his mouth set tight. *He's guessed!*

'Dominic St. John-Stevens,' Dawn addressed him formally.

It was the first time Hunter had heard the DCI's full name.

'I'll be brief and to the point, and it gives me no pleasure to say this, but I am arresting you on suspicion of the murder of Tina Bannister and David Bannister.' As she cautioned him, his face went white as a sheet.

In the Custody Suite, Hunter walked into the interview room feeling both nervous and confident. Nervous, because he had never been involved in the arrest of a senior officer before, but confident that he had his interview thoroughly learned, and if he got tongue-tied at any stage, the interview notes in his hand would get him back to the point. And he had Dawn Leggate at his side — one rank above St. John-Stevens — should he get stroppy about rank privilege.

The DCI was in his shirt sleeves, tie taken away from him by the custody officer as a matter of protocol, his Federation solicitor sitting beside him. He no longer looked the arrogant man Hunter had been confronted with over the past three weeks. In fact, as Hunter sat down, he thought St. John-Stevens looked broken and felt a little sorry for him. But it was only for a second. Then he recalled how the DCI had treated him. How he had tried to ruin his career. How he'd gone to the press to publicly humiliate him. And what he'd done back in 1991. The nervousness was already dissipating as Hunter thought about his opening sequence of questions.

Dawn opened up proceedings with no informalities. She was brief and to the point, reminding him of why he had been arrested and informing him that the interview was being video recorded.

As she finished, St. John-Stevens said, 'You're making a big mistake, you know. You've got this completely wrong. Dylan Wolfe killed the Bannisters and hid their car in the yard. We have the proof. You know that.' Pointing at Hunter but keeping his eyes firmly fixed on Dawn, he continued, 'Detective Sergeant Kerr said that himself. This is nothing but a witch hunt by him. He's getting back at me for posting him in Cold Case. Can't you see?'

Straight-faced, Dawn said, 'We shall see,' and then diverted her gaze to Hunter, inviting him to continue.

'Dominic,' Hunter opened. 'Is it all right if I call you Dominic?'

St. John-Stevens delivered a thunderous look. 'No, it is fucking not. I am a DCI and I want you to call me sir.'

Hunter knew his opening would rattle him. It had worked. He continued, 'I'd prefer not to call you sir while you are under arrest, but I'll call you Mr St. John-Stevens, if that's any help?' Hunter watched the DCI ball his hands into fists. He wanted to smile but kept a straight face. 'Mr St. John-Stevens, I first want to ask you if you knew David and Tina Bannister.'

The DCI threw a quick glance at his solicitor, who gave him a go-ahead look and nod. St. John-Stevens returned his glare to Hunter and answered, 'I knew Tina but not David.'

Hunter anticipated that answer because of his research. He asked, 'And how did you know Tina Bannister?'

'I took a statement from her once.'

'Is that the statement she made in May nineteen-ninety-one, following a fight in the pub where she worked at as a barmaid?'

The DCI sat back. 'You've done your homework.'

Hunter returned a wry smile. 'Thank you.' After a short pause, he added, 'And I believe you arrested a man for that assault and he was prosecuted at Doncaster Magistrates two months later?'

'Yes.'

'Was that your one and only meeting with Tina Bannister?'

'Yes. The man pleaded guilty so she didn't need to go to court.'

'So, you did not meet with Tina Bannister on any occasion other than when you took that statement from her? Is that what you're saying?'

'That's correct.'

'Are you sure about that?'

'Course I'm sure. The only time I met Tina Bannister was when I took that statement from her.'

'Have you ever been to her home?'

There was a brief pause, following which St. John-Stevens replied, 'Course I have. You know that from the case-file. I went there when she and her husband and daughter were reported missing by David's mother, Alice Bannister.'

'Did you go there alone?'

'No. I went there with DC Keith Saker. I was doing my CID aide back in nineteen-ninety-one and he was the senior detective.'

'Did you ever go there before the family were reported missing?'

'No. What are you trying to suggest?'

'I'm not suggesting anything. It was just a straight question. Did you go to the Bannister house at any time prior to the family going missing? That is the question.'

'And I've answered it, then. No, I did not.'

'Thank you, Mr St. John-Stevens.' Hunter looked at his paperwork, pretending to look for his next line of questioning, though he already knew what he was going to say. Giving the appearance he had just found it, he said brightly, 'What car were you driving when you went to the Bannister home?'

For a moment, he appeared flustered. Then, he answered, 'CID car.'

'Yes, but what make?'

The DCI shook his head. 'I don't know. I don't remember. It was nineteen years ago.'

'Let me help you out. I've made enquiries and back in nineteen-ninety-one, the CID at Barnwell had a Ford Fiesta and a Peugeot three-o-seven.'

'It would more than likely be the Peugeot. The Fiesta was the newer car, if I remember, and used mainly by the DS.'

'What colour was the Peugeot?'

St. John-Stevens seemed to think about the question for a moment before answering, 'Maroon, I believe.'

Hunter nodded. 'It was maroon. Your memory is good.'

'Look, where is this taking us? You've asked me how I knew Tina and I've told you.'

Hunter held up his hand. 'Please just bear with me, Mr St. John-Stevens.' Hunter looked at his paperwork again. After a few seconds, he lifted his head. 'Did you kill Tina Bannister, Mr St. John-Stevens?'

'What! Look, this needs to stop right now. You know who killed the Bannisters. Dylan Wolfe. You've been bleating on about him for days. David Bannister's car was hidden in that container down in the yard where he used to work. He put Rasa Katiliene's body in it after he killed her. The man's a known killer.' He looked at Dawn again. 'I've said this once and I'm saying it again. This is nothing but a witch hunt by Detective Sergeant Kerr, and I want to request you put a halt to this so I can make a formal complaint against him.'

Dawn sucked in a deep breath, and pasting on a fake smile she replied, 'I hear that and make note. I will ensure that someone will take your complaint after this interview. In the meantime, Detective Chief Inspector, if I didn't think there was something substantial to interview you about, I would immediately stop this. But at the moment, I don't intend to.' Dawn glanced at Hunter. 'Would you like to continue with your questioning, Detective Sergeant Kerr?'

Hunter said, 'I'll repeat my last question. Did you kill David and Tina and Amy Bannister?'

'No, I did not. This is nonsense.'

'Are you responsible for their disappearance?'

'No, I am not.'

'You've already told me that you and Keith Saker visited the Bannister home following the report by David Bannister's mum, Alice, of them going missing. I also know, from speaking with a colleague who was present, what enquiries you made at the scene, but what were you doing the day before Alice reported them missing?'

For several seconds, St. John-Stevens was silent. Then, he responded, 'Without my pocket book for reference, I have no idea.'

'Well, let me ask you if you went to the Bannister home on the day before they were all reported missing.' Hunter held the DCI's gaze. He saw him gulp. *Got him!*

'My answer is no. I only went to the Bannister house after they were reported missing.'

'What if I were to tell you I have a witness who saw you go to the Bannister home at midday the day before the family were reported missing? And you were also seen there in the evening in the CID car which was parked in the alleyway next to the house?'

'I would say I was never there.'

'I also asked you earlier if you had ever met Tina Bannister other than when you took her statement regarding the assault she witnessed, and you said you hadn't. Is that correct?'

'Yes. Now can we stop this charade?'

Hunter's mouth tightened as he took a few seconds' breathing space. He returned with, 'Well, that is interesting, because yesterday afternoon I revisited a witness called George Evers, a former work colleague of David Bannister's, who Keith Saker spoke to back in nineteen-ninety-one and took a statement from, in which he described seeing Tina speaking with a man in the Travellers pub in a more than friendly manner. When I showed him a photograph the Force holds of you, back when you were a young detective, he immediately recognised you as that man Tina was with.'

'He … he…' St. John-Stevens spluttered, before finally getting out, 'he must have seen me when I took the statement from Tina. That's the only time he would have seen me.'

'I assure you it wasn't when you took the statement from her. It was at least seven weeks after that date. George only reported seeing Tina with this man after the Bannisters were reported missing. And it's my firm belief that you sent Keith Saker to follow up that enquiry with George Evers, instead of going yourself, because you knew he would have recognised you. And I also believe that is the reason George Evers' statement didn't appear in the case-file.'

'This is nonsense. You're really clutching at straws here, Detective Sergeant.' St. John-Stevens leaned back in his chair, and folding his arms, he continued, 'All right, then. How do you explain David Bannister's car being hidden away in the container at the vehicle dismantlers yard by Dylan Wolfe? The man you have been telling everyone is responsible for the

Bannisters' disappearance. That car is evidence to prove he's responsible.'

'I have to confess, that was my initial response when I found that. And I have to say it was pretty condemning evidence, especially with Rasa Katiliene's body being found in its boot. But then yesterday, all that changed. As you know, Dylan Wolfe asked to speak with me, and he and I had a very interesting conversation about that car. Shall I let you in on what he told me?'

The DCI pushed himself forward, unfurling his arms and resting his elbows on the table. 'I am very interested to know what he said.'

'Dylan told me that back in nineteen-ninety-one, two days after the Bannisters' disappearance, whilst working at Bones' dismantlers he was told to take the low-loader and collect a burned-out car that had been found on a lane beneath a disused railway track near Sprotbrough, and when he got there he was met by a detective who told him the car had more than likely been stolen and dumped there. Dylan never thought anything about that until several days later, when the information came back from Swansea — after he had checked the engine number — that it belonged to David Bannister, someone he knew because he only lived a quarter of a mile away. He thought he should report this to the police, and did so, speaking with the detective who was with the car when he picked it up. That detective thanked him for the information and told him he would follow it up. That was never done. I have spoken with Roger Mills regarding this, and he was told the car didn't belong to David Bannister and that it was one that had been stolen and dumped. Dylan, expecting someone to come down to the yard to examine it, stored the car away in the container. As you know, Dylan was later caught by me for the rapes and murder he committed, and so the car remained where it was until a few days ago, when I found it.' Pausing briefly, Hunter said, 'The detective Dylan Wolfe met at Sprotbrough and later spoke to on the phone was you. Why did you cover that up, Mr St. John-Stevens?'

St. John-Stevens did not respond; instead, he stared hard at Hunter.

Hunter held his hate-filled stare. 'Would you kindly answer, please?'

Pulling away his gaze, he answered, 'No comment.'

'Following that information from Dylan, you may or may not know, but we began a search of the location around the area where David Bannister's car was found because I learned there was a derelict set of old cottages near there, and yesterday afternoon we found the remains of a male and female body hidden in a culvert beneath a footbridge close to those cottages. Whilst we haven't formally identified those bodies yet, the clothing they're wearing appears to be a match for the clothing described as being worn by David and Tina Bannister on the day they disappeared. Those bodies were wrapped in bedsheets, and we have also found wrapped up with them a green onyx ashtray that has been identified by Alice Bannister as being identical to one owned by David and Tina. We have found traces of blood on that ashtray and fingerprints. A set of those fingerprints have been identified as yours. What do you have to say about that, Mr St. John-Stevens?'

The DCI visibly paled and his shoulders dropped. He opened his mouth several times, but words never came out. After the best part of ten seconds, he said defeatedly, 'I never meant to kill them.'

CHAPTER SEVENTEEN

The next day, shortly after lunchtime, Hunter pulled up outside Alice Bannister's home, and turning off the engine remained there for several minutes, eyeing the front door, running through in his head again how he was going to present the story he had gleaned from yesterday's interview. He especially wondered how Alice was going to react when he had to explain how it had been one of their own who had committed the murders. She had always believed that David would not harm his wife and daughter and take his own life, and he would be able to console her with that in spite of the bad news.

The other thing troubling his thoughts was her reaction when he got to the part about her granddaughter, Amy. St. John-Stevens' revelation had come as a shock to him, so how on earth was Alice going to take it? As he sat there, the DCI's confession washed around in his thoughts. After he had finally broken him down, the admission of what had happened back in July 1991 came thick and fast. St. John-Stevens quickly admitted he had entered into a relationship with Tina shortly after taking a statement from her as a witness, and had taken to visiting her at her home at least once a week when David had been at work.

Next, as Hunter had guessed, was the news that Tina had got pregnant with his child. It had been St. John-Stevens who had told Tina to have it aborted, and when she had told him what Dr Bhatia had said, that was when the tension had started between them. Initially, Tina had said she would have the baby and tell David it was his, but then she had told him she wanted him to pay her some money to keep quiet. The first sum she'd mentioned was £1,000, but within a week that had escalated to £5,000, and on the day he had visited her — the day before the family's disappearance — she had demanded £10,000 for her silence. There had been an argument, during which he had grabbed her by the throat, and she had fought back. That's when he had picked up the ashtray and hit her. He had cut the side of her head and she had started screaming, running into the kitchen to try and flee. He had followed, hitting her twice on the head, and she had gone down. A third blow had killed her.

As he sat astride her, thinking what to do, David had come home unexpectedly and caught him, and although St. John-Stevens had tried to bluff his way out of this, telling David that he was a police officer and that he had just received a 999 call that Tina had been attacked and that he had found her like this, David believed none of it. That's when St. John-Stevens had picked up a knife off the side and stabbed him repeatedly. It was after this admission that the revelation about Amy had come. He had started to wrap up David and Tina's bodies, thinking what to do next, when he had heard her cries from upstairs and he had found her in her cot, waking from a nap. He'd fed her, covered her back up and then left to go back to work.

That evening he had returned, fed Amy again, cleaned up the kitchen with bleach bought from the supermarket and then bundled the bodies into the back of David's car and transported them to Levitt Hagg, an area he knew from his fishing days during his teenage years. He had returned back to the Bannisters' home, picked up Amy, bundled her up in bedding and then driven to Lincolnshire General Hospital, where he had left her in the back of an empty ambulance that had just dropped off a patient. He'd then driven back to where he had dumped David's car to set it on fire.

Amy was alive. Grace and Maddie had been given the task of tracing her, and sure enough they had found her. She was now called Helena Ridings. She had been adopted by a couple in 1992 and was living near Newark. The news had messed with Hunter's head, so what effect it would have on Alice when he told her she had a twenty-one-year-old granddaughter waiting to meet her was anyone's guess. Taking a deep breath, he removed the ignition keys, stepped out of the car and walked towards Alice Bannister's front door.

A NOTE TO THE READER

Dear Reader,

Cold cases have always fascinated me. As a detective I had never worked on one, all my cases being current ones, and the first one I came across was during a visit to the basement at Barnsley police station when I was seeking some archived missing persons reports. Whilst searching out the files I came across an old investigation from the 1970's which featured a series of sexual attacks upon women, the offender earning himself the nickname The Barnsley Rapist. I could not resist flicking through the incident reports and crime scene photos that made up the interesting bulk of the file, so much so, that whenever I had cause to go down there again I would sneak a further peek through the case file, learning more with each visit. This was during the early 90's and the offender still hadn't been caught, although his attacks had stopped. I mention this particular case because years later, after I had retired and began writing the Hunter Kerr books, I wanted to draw attention to cold case work in one of my storylines and made contact with South Yorkshire Police's newly formed Cold Case Unit to query their methods and gain knowledge on some of the cases they were working on. When visiting the unit it was a pleasant surprise to see that it consisted of detectives I had worked with in the past and catching up with them was a delight. In the time I spent there I got such a fascinating insight into their investigations, learning that their two most successful cases to date was capturing the Rotherham Shoe Rapist, who carried out attacks on women during the 1980's, taking their shoes as trophies, and surprise of all surprises The Barnsley Rapist. I came back armed with so much information to not only develop the book I was working on at the time – *Secrets of the Dead* – but additional material that I knew I could use for a future book. This is that book.

With regards Hunter, over the series I have placed him in situations where he has occasionally decided to bend the rules to either gain the upper hand or bring the culprit to justice, and throughout his escapades he has been able to call on his CID mentor and experienced detective Barry Newstead for help and support. (Barry was an old-style detective whose policing methods came from the 60's and 70's and they have rubbed off on Hunter) Followers of the HK series will know that Barry was tragically killed in *Shadow of the Beast* leaving Hunter without his reliable shoulder to lean on. In this book I wanted to experiment with how Hunter could cope without Barry and I have to say it has been thoroughly enjoyable developing his newly found determination when faced with the character of DCI St.John-Stevens. It takes him into new and interesting territory for the future.

I hope you have enjoyed this book. One of the ways you can let me know is by placing a review on **Amazon** or **Goodreads**. And, if you want to contact me, or want me to appear and give a talk about my writing journey at one of the groups you belong to, then please feel free to do so through **my website**. It has recently been updated and there are some interesting blogs about writing and Hunter Kerr.

Thank you for reading.

Michael Fowler

www.mjfowler.co.uk

Sapere Books is an exciting new publisher of brilliant fiction and popular history.

To find out more about our latest releases and our monthly bargain books visit our website:
saperebooks.com

Printed in Great Britain
by Amazon